VIRTUAL REALITY BITES

AVA WIXX

WICKED Press WIXX

Virtual Reality Bites

Virtual Reality Bites © 2022 Ava Wixx

First Edition: April 2022
Published in the United States of America by
Wicked Wixx Press.
The Wicked Wixx Logo is a trademark of
Wicked Wixx Press.

Cover Art, Ava Wixx Logo, Wicked Wixx Logo, & Interior Book
Graphics by Lindsay Tiry of LT Arts
Edited by Melissa Ringsted of There For You Editing

Print ISBN: 978-1-955950-03-9
Kindle ISBN: 978-1-955950-04-6
EPUB ISBN: 978-1-955950-05-3

For more information visit: avawixx.com

For all of you romance novel junkies.
If you know, you know.

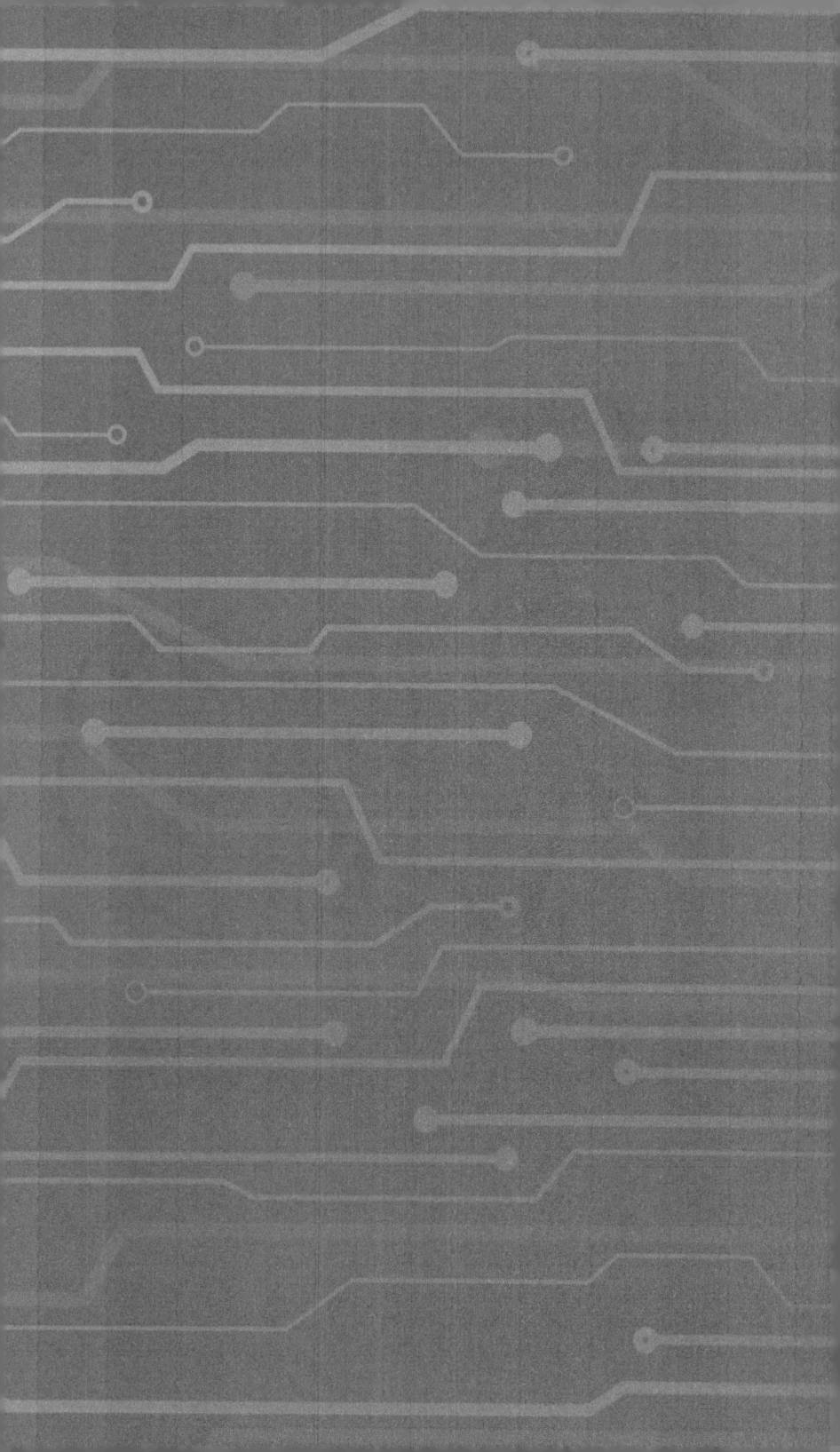

Chapter 1

"**A**lana." *Zane's deep baritone penetrated her concentration, and she whirled as the spell she'd been working slipped from her grasp.*

She blinked, the shock of his presence freezing her in place. "I thought ... I thought you were lost to me."

I stopped typing. Something wasn't right about the scene. Gnawing on my bottom lip, I considered it, my gaze flitting over each word repeatedly. After a few moments of abso-friggin-lutely nothing even close to clarity, I decided to make a note to fix it later.

Now, where was I? Oh, yes ...

Zane closed the distance between them, sweeping her into his arms.

"Are you sure?" Alana swayed within his embrace, her chin trembling.

I paused again. *Do I like the name Alana? Or Zane for that matter? Ugh. Okay.* I made a note to possibly change those details as well.

Moving along.

Zane swore under his breath as his grip on her tightened. "How can you ask me that? I've never been surer about anything in my life. You and me, us ... together forever. Nothing else matters. Nothing."

My fingers stilled once more, hovering over the keyboard.

Nothing else matters? Yeah, right. I barely contained my snort as I glanced around the coffee shop over the top of my laptop.

There was a time when I would have delighted in my surroundings, living in a world of my own making, seeing, well ...

Billions of tiny connections, like brightly colored strings dancing through the air, weaving in and out and around each other, forming links between people designed by the fates themselves. I used to imagine one string or another tugging me steadily toward this guy or that one, kismet surrounding the circumstances of our meeting.

Intellectually, I'd known that I would never walk into a coffee shop, inexplicably pulled there to find the man of my dreams, our gazes colliding across the room, our string taut between us. If not love at first sight, then infatuation, a burning need to get to know each other, mind, body, and soul.

But I'd friggin' wanted it. More than anything else in

the world. Yeah, I knew it wasn't necessarily modern thinking or whatever, to put the desire for a romantic relationship above all else, but I didn't care. Because, sure, I had friends and family who loved me, but a hole existed in my heart, a craving for that ultimate connection—the other half of my soul. To be entwined in understanding and intimacy, to be—

Fuuuuck. Here I go again. I'd learned my lesson. More than once. First with Jason, ex-husband number one. And then with Jared—

My vision wavered, my surroundings distorting for an instant, leaving a dull headache to bloom across my temples as the anomaly passed. I blinked several times, my mind circling back to the thoughts left dangling in my brain.

Yep, I'd learned my lesson. With both ex-husbands, Jason, and then Jared. My ridiculous notions of destiny and fate had left me nearly broke, jaded, and with a massive case of writer's block. What good was a romance author who no longer believed in what she was selling? Sure, witches, vampires, werewolves, fae, and some of the more fantastical creatures who lurked between the pages of my novels weren't exactly realistic, but the sentiments that formed them were. True love was my brand ... or at least it had been. Now my ideas seemed like fevered dreams of an adolescent. *Billions of tiny connections? Bitch, please.*

Slamming my laptop shut, I growled under my breath.

"Careful. You wouldn't want to hurt the poor thing."

"What?" I glanced to the right, staring at the guy sitting at the small table next to mine, venti coffee cup, muffin, and iPad displayed in front of him.

He grinned, brown eyes twinkling as he motioned in my general direction. "I was merely pointing out that you should be careful about the misplaced animosity you were directing at your MacBook."

Pursing my lips, I gave the guy a quick once over. Dark, disheveled hair, bronze-toned skin, good teeth, strong jawline, smart dresser … all of his superficial trappings adding up to make him quite attractive. In the past, I might have thought this our meet-cute, the moment when me, a love-obsessed romance author, finally met her soulmate and was made to believe again just when she was about to give up entirely. There certainly was potential … but nope. I simply couldn't muster one single give-a-damn. I was done with all the bullshit.

Rolling my eyes, I stood abruptly, my chair scraping loudly across the floor. "Not happening."

The guy's smile wilted around the edges. "I mean, yeah, sure, I just wanted to—"

"We both know what you just wanted to do. And I'm saving us both the time and heartache by saying not happening."

He grumbled something unintelligible as I stalked away from him. I rolled my eyes again as I beelined it to the front door of the Starbucks. Luckily, my coffee chain of choice existed in legion, a shop on almost every block in every major city in the country, so not coming back to this one for a while wouldn't be a big deal.

A wall of heat smashed into me as I stepped outside, the sun blinding. Sliding my dark shades on, I scurried to my car, setting the AC on full blast as soon as I managed to clamber inside. Closing my eyes, I rested my forehead on the steering wheel, the cloth wrap on it protecting me from getting burnt. I hated summers in the south. Raleigh, North Carolina to be specific. But Raleigh's proximity to both the beach and the mountains almost made up for the sweltering months. Plus, my friends and family were nearby, so at least my misery had plenty of company.

My phone blared to life in my bag, and I dragged it to my ear, groaning demonstratively. "What do you want, brat?"

"Is that any way to greet your favorite brother?"

"You're my only brother and still not my favorite. What does that tell you?"

Adam chuckled. "Whatever, dork."

"If I'm a dork then—"

"Can you two not do the whole sibling banter thing right now?" Adam's wife chimed in, letting me know I was on speakerphone. "Shouldn't the two of you have outgrown that by now?"

"Spoken like a true only child. Just wait until your girls get older."

Tina sighed dramatically. "They're going to be best friends."

Adam and I both laughed.

"Maybe, but only after they nearly kill each other during their teen years."

"Okay, so yeah, I called for a reason," Adam spoke up. "I wanted to remind you that my twenty-year high school reunion is this weekend."

"Yes, yes, I know. I do possess this marvelous wonder called a calendar. Maybe you've heard of it?"

"Cal-en-dar?" Adam drawled out. "Nope. Never heard of it."

"That wouldn't surprise me at all," I retorted.

"Okay, Adam has to help me do … well, a whole bunch of stuff before this weekend, so I'm hanging up for him. I'm extremely nervous leaving my babies alone with someone for the first time, even if it is you. We need to make sure everything is ready." There was a crinkling sound and a pop. "Ah, I don't know if I can do it. No, no, no, it'll be fine. Thank you so much for sitting for us, Zoe, we really appreciate it. And let me know if you want any specific food at the house before I go grocery shopping this afternoon."

A part of me wondered if Tina would in fact be able to leave her twins for the reunion. I knew if it were up to her, she'd skip the event. However, I didn't voice my doubts and ignored the ramblings of a neurotic first-time mom. "If you could pick up some ice cream, that would be great."

"Chocolate, chocolate chip?"

"You know it."

"Planning on eating your feelings?" Adam asked, hitting a bit too close to home.

"Shut up," I snapped. "I will eat what I want without judgment."

"Okay, bye, Zoe!" Tina cut us off, the call abruptly coming to an end.

Twenty years. Twenty friggin' years since my baby brother graduated from high school. I felt ancient. Granted, I was only two years older than him, but I was also in my forties, while he lingered in his thirties. I'd crossed the imaginary line in the sand of aging. I was officially over the hill, while Adam technically was still considered young-ish.

I slumped back in my seat, staring at my car's roof. Forty years old. I expected my life to be completely different by now. Instead of being happily married to my soulmate with a successful career, I was ... pathetic. Utterly pathetic. Adam's life was enviable in almost every way imaginable, and he hadn't even wanted all the things I not-so-secretly coveted. I couldn't count how many times he informed me that romance wasn't his jam and that he would be a happy bachelor until the day he died. Now, I swear I could see hearts forming in his eyes every time he looked at Tina. And she clearly felt the same for him. Together, they'd built a life filled with all the things I—

No. Stop. You're happy for him ... them. It's just that—Nope. Don't go there.

God, I hope Tina buys a shitload of ice cream.

"WHERE THE HELL IS *MY* WESTLEY?" I mumbled around a mouthful of ice cream. Tears streamed down my cheeks, and I choked on the combination of chocolatey goodness and snot. I was well aware of my current hot mess status. Thankfully I was alone, the twins peacefully slumbering away in their room while I entertained myself until Adam and Tina got home.

I reached for a tissue with one hand while shoving another heaping spoonful of Chocolate Therapy into my mouth with the other. *No one can ever say I'm not a pro at multitasking.*

"*Princess Bride*, huh? I never thought of it as a tear-jerker before."

Screaming, I hurled my half-full Ben & Jerry's pint in the direction the unfamiliar masculine voice had emanated from. It hit the wall, splattering ice cream all over the intruder, just as I leapt over the back of the couch, brandishing the spoon in one hand and the remote in the other.

"Whoa, whoa, whoa, Zoe, put the remote down." He cocked his head. "And spoon? What were you planning to do with that?"

It took my brain a moment to process the fact that the intruder knew my name. "Gouge out your eyes ... of course." Shuffling back a step, I let my gaze skitter over him, something I couldn't quite put my finger on sparking recognition. Dark hair, even darker eyes set in an angular face with full, pouty lips, a scar bisecting his left eyebrow.

I blinked. *That scar ... No, it can't be.* "Xander? Xander Tashiro?"

He grinned, showing off a set of perfect white teeth. "Don't tell me you didn't recognize me."

"I mean, I wouldn't have almost popped your eyes out of their sockets with a spoon if I had."

Xander motioned to the distance between us with a flourish. "I wouldn't say *almost* with most people, but ..." He grimaced, tapping the scar in his eyebrow for effect. "You aren't most people."

It was my turn to grimace. "How many times do I have to tell you that I didn't mean to hit you? I was aiming for Adam. I can't help it if your big head was in the way."

"Three stitches. I had to get three stitches." His eyes glinted with mirth. "I was traumatized."

"Yeah, whatever."

Despite our topic of conversation, I stared unabashedly at Xander. The man standing in front of me, covered in chocolate ice cream, was drop-dead gorgeous. Something else my brain had been slow to process but was more than happy to acknowledge now that I wasn't terrified for my life. And I was quite familiar with Xander Tashiro, simply not in his current post-glow-up form. I was sure it defied the laws of genetics, or physics, or all laws in science combined in some manner that he'd somehow gotten more attractive. Short, spiky hair had transformed into a stylish cut that left it slightly longer on top, his thick, wavy hair cascading haphazardly across his forehead. His cute, and yet kind of roundish face had matured to be cover-of-a-magazine worthy with razor-sharp cheekbones and … and those lips! They once had seemed too big for him proportionally, but now were works of art. In fact, everything about him had morphed from a Crayola drawing to a masterpiece. *No. Stop. This is Xander Tashiro. Your younger brother's best friend. No ogling allowed. Unless you want to up your pathetic level. Plus, don't forget how annoying he always was, and clearly still is.*

Yep, Xander Tashiro was Adam's best friend and had been all through school. The last time I'd personally seen him, though, was before I left for college. Sure, I still heard his name mentioned over the years, and maybe recognized his face from some of my brother's pictures, but I hadn't put the two together. Nope, I had been completely unaware that Adam was harboring details of the massive changes in Xander's appearance. A part of me expected him to somehow have remained the same, just have aged a bit. Maybe if Adam and Tina hadn't eloped then I would have had some kind of clue. But—

But what? None of it matters.

Adam stumbled in behind Xander, taking in the chocolate explosion and my awkward standoff with his friend. "What's going on?"

Xander chuckled, the sound doing things to my insides I simply refused to acknowledge. "I startled Zoe, and apparently she was planning to distract me with a chocolate bomb before gouging my eyes out with a spoon, then probably beat me to death with the remote."

Adam scowled at me. "Why are you being an asshole to Xan?"

After marching past the two of them into the kitchen, I deposited my subpar weapons on the counter and grabbed some cleaning supplies. "He startled me."

Tina chose that moment to appear, obviously having been upstairs checking on the twins. "And the moral of the story is, don't startle Zoe." She swiped the pack of wet wipes from me. "Don't worry, I'll clean up the mess. We should have texted to let you know we were on the way home with a guest in tow."

Adam propelled his clearly intoxicated self to the couch, flopping down with a loud *oomph*. "Hey, Tina, do we have anything good to eat?"

She rolled her eyes at him in my direction, snatching up the remote I'd abandoned. "We have some miscellaneous leftovers."

"How about pizza? We have any pizza?"

Their conversation fell into the background as my focus zeroed in on Xander, who had made his way into the kitchen, his proximity flustering me a bit. He must have sprung up a good foot since the last time I'd seen him as well, and it wasn't a lanky tall either. I could see his lithe muscles clearly defined in his undershirt, now that he'd removed his chocolate-soiled button down. But it wasn't merely his physical changes that were leaving me off-kilter, it was his energy, or aura, that undefinable something that made a person special. It was as if his presence had ballooned past the space of his body and had kept expanding until Xander commanded his own gravitational pull. One that I was currently fighting not to get yanked into.

I cleared my throat, attempting to concentrate on the dishes I was putting away. "You don't seem drunk like my brother."

His lips curled up as he glanced over his shoulder just as Adam pulled Tina onto the couch, his boisterous laugh filling the room. "He drank my share of the alcohol at the reunion. Pretty sure he downed Tina's, too."

Pausing to study Xander, I quirked an eyebrow. "I expected a sober Tina because she hardly ever drinks, even before the twins, but the Xander I knew would have been Adam's partner-in-crime." It was odd talking to the boy I used to know since he was clearly a man now. He was familiar, and yet somehow a stranger. I only knew who he used to be and not who he'd become.

He leaned forward, resting his forearms on the island countertop. "Things change." His gaze slid over me, one side of his mouth lifting. "But not everything."

Instantly defensive—and not sure why—I stood ramrod straight, hands automatically going to my hips. "And what's that supposed to mean, Alexander Dai Tashiro?"

He staggered back dramatically, clutching at his chest. "The full name attack? Low blow, Zoe. You know that activates some kind of Pavlovian reaction in pretty much everyone who had, well, parents."

"Don't care."

All humor drained from his face, and his jaw muscles jumped slightly as he grimaced again. "Why are you being so touchy? You know I didn't mean anything by what I said."

I sighed, staring down at the small bowl in my hands. "Sorry, I've been out of sorts lately." Understatement of the year. More like complete and utter emotional wreck with almost no hope for rebounding to normal.

His voice broke low as he rushed to respond, "I heard about … well, your divorce, there's no easy way to say it. And I know you've been struggling to get your next novel written, but I—"

I threw my hands up in the air. "Isn't that just great? Adam blabbed to you about everything." My skin heated with embarrassment. Xander and I had always kind of flirted, more him with me since I couldn't get past the two-year age gap and the fact that he was my little brother's best friend, but I still didn't want him to pity my life decisions. Especially now when I was having a mid-life crisis.

"He's worried about you. Despite how he does, or I guess, doesn't show it, he loves you."

Before I could respond, Xander pushed a business card across the counter at me.

"What's that?" I stared at it like it was a snake that might jump up to bite me at any moment.

"Fantasy Life, Inc. Have you heard of it?"

"The company that specializes in virtual reality technology?" I'd read an article about them a few months ago, but all I retained was a vague sense of what they did.

He nodded. "It's mine. Fantasy Life, Inc. is my company, and I have a business proposition for you. It's why I came back with Adam tonight. I told him I wanted to talk to you about it."

Was that why he decided not to get completely sloshed with Adam? Because he was coming here to talk to me? Clutching at granite, I swayed slightly, the abrupt change of subject and bizarre info drop jarring. "A business proposition?"

"Just stop by the address on the back of the card anytime this week and ask for me. I'll explain everything then." He shoved his hands into his pockets. "I would have preferred to do it tonight, but things haven't quite panned out the way I hoped." With that, he shuffled into the living room to say his good-byes to the two giggling idiots on the couch.

My fingers danced over the stark white card with black lettering, my eyes unfocused on the text, confusion filling me to the brim. The only reason Xander would make any kind of business proposition to a romance author in relation to Fantasy Life, Inc. was definitely out of a misguided sense of pity. He'd admitted to knowing about my set of rather unfortunate life events thanks to my big-mouthed brother.

Well, things just took a turn for the weird. I hadn't even had time to process Xander's sudden appearance and glow-up reveal, let alone the rest. But of course, I already knew I would go to Fantasy Life, Inc. to hear him out, if only to get some answers for my insatiable curiosity. *Because seriously ... what could I possibly do for his company?*

Chapter 2

A kaleidoscope of colors exploded behind my eyes as they struggled to form any kind of image. It was like my retinas had been scorched by staring directly into the sun. And then there was the ringing in my ears I couldn't dislodge no matter how hard I shook my head.

Strong, steady hands threaded with mine, squeezing gently. The small gesture was comforting and slowed the erratic beating of my heart. Between one breath and the next things abruptly normalized.

I blinked Xander's face into focus. He smiled. "There you are. It takes a minute to adjust."

"Adjust to what?" I squeaked, my head swiveling wildly around to take in my environment. I was in a small, nondescript room, empty except for the overstuffed, brown leather chair I was reclining in. "How ... what—"

"Let me explain."

"Let you explain what? I don't know where I am or how I got here." I squinted, unable to locate any doors or windows. *That can't be right.*

"This is the orientation stage of the Fantasy Life program."

Jumping to my feet, I threw my arms in the air, waving them frantically. "What are you talking about?"

"Zoe, calm down so I can explain."

I sucked in ragged breaths, the room beginning to spin. "I can't. I don't know what's going on." If I didn't find a door fast, I was in danger of leaving a Zoe-sized cutout in the wall. "I need to get out of here."

Xander caught me as I staggered forward, his fingers digging into my shoulders. "You know me, Zoe. You've known me a long time, and you know I would never let anything bad happen to you."

I clutched at his shirt, my anxiety not caring where it got comfort from. "Except for that time you and Adam switched out my hair dye."

He chuckled, the sound rumbling under my ear as I leaned farther into his embrace. "That's not the same thing."

"My hair was bright orange until I could get it fixed professionally. And even after that, there was an undertone until it grew out."

"Zoe," he chastised. "Are we really going to rehash this now? We were kids. And Adam swore it wouldn't be permanent. I thought it would be just a bit of fun."

"I can't help that it popped into my head when you said

you'd never let anything bad happen to me. That was next level traumatizing to a teenage girl."

He sighed heavily. "Fair enough. But you know what I meant."

Random thoughts continued to ricochet around in my brain, most of them centering around Xander and our shared past. At least it gave me something to concentrate on beyond the impending feelings of doom bubbling up from my gut.

"Zoe, listen to me. You're safe. You agreed to this. You signed a contract."

Shoving away from him, my mouth fell open. "Whaaaat?" I understood the words, but not their meaning or concept. *I agreed to what exactly? And sign a contract? I don't even know where I am let alone remember any kind of contract.*

"No. This isn't right." I shook my head rapidly, dizziness threatening to overtake me again. "The last thing I remember is thinking about coming to your company to find out what I could possibly offer you as a romance author."

"And you did. We talked for hours. Literally. You definitely made me work for your signature on that contract. I had to explain that me wanting to use you for the testing of this part of the program wasn't born out of pity. I even had to quote parts from your blog post about how romance novels are an important part of feminism and how I support your views on the matter. Finally, we saw eye-to-eye." Xander spread his arms wide. "Hence the Fantasy Life orientation program."

"But I don't remember anything!" He read my blog post about the tie-in of feminism and romance novels? And he agreed with my points about the shaming of the genre ... him, Xander? *Nope. Not buying it.*

"As per—" He sighed heavily, rolled his eyes, and leaned forward to say, "Totopuppapubbis."

My mouth snapped shut, and I ground my teeth together. "Adam told you about that."

Xander ran his hand through his already tousled hair. "*You* told me your ridiculous safe word. You said you'd probably freak out once you were in here and it would be the only way to calm you down. I hoped you'd be wrong, but here we are."

I considered the situation. Totopuppapubbis was what I'd chosen as a child for the family password to use in case of an emergency. It had become a joke over the years, and still, it lingered in the back of my mind as a special kind of secret. One that I would most definitely use in a situation like this.

I crossed my arms over my chest. "Explain then. You have five minutes before I start down panic attack road again and make an exit ala Mr. Kool Aid."

Grinning, Xander snapped his fingers, and a mirror appeared directly in front of me. I let out a startled yelp. "As you can see, we're already in the Fantasy Life virtual reality setup, otherwise known as Orientation."

My mouth fell open for the second time in the last

few minutes. "None of this is real?" I gazed at my reflection, my wide, green eyes running from the top of my long, blonde hair with freshly dyed blue streaks, down my familiar curvy body, all the way to my sneaker-covered toes. Reaching up, I pinched my bicep. *Ouch.*

My mind was reeling. I couldn't tell the difference between virtual reality and the real thing. I'd always associated VR with a big, goofy headpiece, eyewear, and other miscellaneous bulky equipment. Something that could potentially be cool for a video game, but fool me into thinking it was actually happening? Not so much.

"How is any of this possible?" I swallowed around the lump in my throat. "Holy shit, the Matrix could actually happen."

"You're not the first who went there. Just please don't start freaking out again. This is meant to be fun. Not some kind of facsimile of a bad acid trip."

"Fun." I shuffled closer to the mirror, inspecting myself as I twisted back and forth, even peeking briefly down my shirt. My D cups were encased in a blue sports bra, which I at least hadn't had to wrangle myself into. So bonus, I supposed. I also appeared to be about my normal slightly taller than average height. Everything seemed to be in its proper place. Even the parts I wished weren't, like that stubborn tummy pooch hiding my six-pack abs. "Right. Okay."

Xander sidled up beside me, our gazes clashing in our shared reflection. "So, there are a few rules you need to be aware of. The Fantasy Life program is kind of like a video game in the sense—"

"This mirror is stupid. I feel like I've been forced into one of those romance novel clichés where the character's description is revealed when he or she looks in the mirror. The only part missing is—"

Screaming, I scrambled to cover my suddenly naked body as I stood dripping water onto a bathmat like I'd just gotten out of the shower that now was reflected behind me. "What the hell is going on?" I danced from foot to foot as if I could keep my private bits blurry by not remaining still. In theory, it could work, but I was pretty sure I'd have to do my little embarrassed jig a lot faster.

Xander cupped the back of his neck, his eyes darting everywhere but on me. "I was getting to this part. To simplify it for you, this is like the setup part of a video game where you get to pick your main outfit for your avatar, gear up, and—"

"I don't play video games! I'm not you and Adam! Just tell me how to not be naked right now, Xander!" It might have been virtual reality, but I didn't want to be standing around sans clothes regardless. It simply felt too real, which meant the accompanying mortification was as well.

"Picture yourself in clothes."

Squeezing my eyes shut, I imagined my favorite comfy jeans and a soft, navy-blue T-shirt.

"Are you doing it?"

"Yes." I glanced down the length of my still very naked body. "Why isn't it working, Xander? Are you … you're punking me, aren't you? This is like that time you walked in on me when I was getting out of the shower when I was seventeen." Anger surged through my veins, heating my blood, scorching away all traces of embarrassment. Balling my fists at my sides, I marched toward Xander. "This is not funny. At all. Asshole. And I swear on all that is holy that if you don't—"

"It's not my fault!" Xander stumbled back a few steps. "You have full control of this!"

"Then why am I still naked? Huh?"

"I-I don't … hold on a second." He pixelized briefly before vanishing.

I spun in a circle. "You've got to be fucking kidding me." I stood there naked and alone, not exactly sure if the alone part was an improvement. "I should have at least gotten a towel," I grumbled. "Not even romance heroines drip dry straight out of the shower. There's no way I did this to myself." I wrung out my hair, the simple act miraculously evaporating all moisture from my tresses. *Huh.*

Xander reappeared, clothes draped over his arm. "Here. Put these on."

After snatching them from him, I tugged on the very same jeans and T-shirt I'd been imagining. I scowled. "So far this virtual reality thing bites." At least for me. Xander probably was getting a ton of amusement from my humiliation. Of course, he'd been the only one to see me make a fool out of myself. Unless there was some way to record the debacle.

"Apparently your brain prefers to do things the old-fashioned way."

"What's that supposed to mean?"

"It means we're going to have to do things differently with you. But it's good. Don't worry. This is precisely why we need to test the program before making it widely available to the public. We need to see how all types of people react and how we can adjust to serve those needs as well as the needs—"

"I don't care. Tell me what I agreed to." Exasperation had replaced my anger and skepticism. If I was there to do a job I would do it and quickly.

"You're going to run through different romance tropes for the program."

"And how will I do that exactly? We're going in circles, Xander. Just spit it out already so I can get going on whatever this is."

He nodded slowly, staring at me like I was an insect under a microscope. "My research team has a list of pre-approved popular romance tropes that you will enter into as if you are the main character. You will tell us what works and what doesn't. That's it. Our goal is to have all sorts of Fantasy Life options in the future. Some for escapism, some for working through trauma, some for adrenaline junkies to get their fix without the danger ... the possibilities are endless. You are merely helping us with an area you're considered an expert in."

"I'm going to roleplay in romance tropes?" Now it was making sense why I would agree to this. I could help

Xander while hopefully getting my author mojo back. It had the potential to be win-win if the whole naked thing wasn't an indicator of things to come.

"Roleplay? Yeah, that's one way to look at it."

"How else would I look at it?" And how far was this program going to take things? Because although I enjoyed reading and writing about sex, I wasn't sure I could throw myself into something that felt as real as Fantasy Life did. Then again, it had been a while since—

Ew. What am I thinking? You are not having virtual reality sex. That's just weird. Aaaalthough—

No.

Xander winked. "You'll see."

"See what?" Did I miss something while I'd been off musing about virtual reality sex?

Grabbing my shoulders, Xander spun me to face a red, wooden door that hadn't been there a moment ago. "Executive decision," he declared with a dazzling grin.

The door swung open, and Xander shoved me through. "You can thank me later."

"Xander! What the hell?" I stumbled forward into pitch black.

Chapter 3

"**X**ander? Hello? Where am I?" I was in the kind of absolute darkness that didn't offer even the tiniest speck of light. I widened my eyes as far as they would go, as if that would help, and yet somehow it made me feel slightly better. I spun in a small circle, arms stretched out in front of me.

"Please tell me something, anything is loading." That had to be the answer. It was simply taking a few minutes to load the next part of the program. Unless … well, unless my brain was wonkier than Xander had expected, and I was trapped inside some kind of virtual reality black hole. *Oh, God, please don't let that be what this is.*

Taking in a few not-so-calming breaths, my thoughts began to swirl around the reality of the virtual adventure I was about to embark on. I would be beta testing romance scenarios for the masses. Of course, I was sure there would be many more tests after I was through, but it was kind of flattering that Xander had come to me as his romance expert. Maybe I wasn't such a failure after all.

The goal of all my books, of my career really, was to help people find a bit of escapism while helping to beat back the patriarchy one sexually empowered reader at a time. It might not be world-altering or as noble as saving the rain forests, but if I could help people take a much-needed break from the stresses of their lives and open their eyes to a new way of thinking, then I was helping. In the end, all I wanted to do was help people in my own way. To offer them hope and my brand of romantic optimism. And also—

I sighed. That there was one of my biggest problems, the crux of my writer's block. I was trying to create the same type of characters and stories as I always had, and I couldn't anymore. I was older, and if not wiser, definitely jaded. I wasn't the same person as I'd once been. Therefore, I had to evolve my writing to match who I'd become, but I didn't know how to do that exactly, or who I was for that matter.

Oh, stop being so dramatic. Sure, I'm a bit of a hot mess lately, but this is going to help me turn it all around. I can take this amazing opportunity that just fell into my lap and use it to my advantage. I'll check for any issues, or plot holes if you will, in the scenarios as they're laid out for me, and hopefully find my lost inspiration in the process. It can potentially all work out wonderfully if I can get out of my own way.

Blades of bright green grass sprung up under my feet, bringing with them an explosion of color and sensation as a magnificent landscape unfurled before my eyes. Within seconds I stood in a lush, rolling countryside, an overcast sky topping it off. Glancing down the line of my body, I noted that my clothing had changed to something resembling what I would expect in a historical romance—a long, simple dress, greyish blue in color, possibly made of wool? I let my fingers run over the material of the bodice as my gaze darted around my new surroundings. Once again, I was dazzled by the realism of it all. I literally couldn't tell the difference between real life and the scene in front of me. *How is any of this possible?*

"Xander?" I called. "Do I get any kind of directions or do I just go ..." The rest of my sentence was swallowed as a man on a horse galloped up a nearby hill, heading straight for me. He wasn't close enough that I could make out his expression yet, but I could see that he had long, dark hair that swept away from his face ... and he was massive. Like Conan the Barbarian massive.

I gulped, my first instinct to run. As the horse's hooves thundered closer, I could no longer sublimate my flight response, despite knowing I was in a fantasy world. Spinning on my heels, I took off at a dead sprint in the opposite direction. I made it only about a few yards when my feet tangled in my annoyingly cumbersome skirt, and I fell to my hands and knees.

"Shit," I muttered, glancing frantically over my shoulder at my pursuer.

"Clara, lass, why are you runnin' from me?" The man's deep voice, dipped in a delightful Scottish brogue, washed over me as he pulled the horse to a halt, bewilderment playing across his chiseled features.

"Do I know you?" *Hmmm ... interesting. I also sound Scottish.*

The man's full lips turned down into a scowl as he dismounted and made his way to me. Before I could utter another word, he'd lifted me to my feet, resting his warm hands on my shoulders. "Are you all right, Clara? Did you hit your head?"

Nice touch. He sounded Scottish but not ridiculously so. It wasn't historically accurate, but who needs perfection when it comes to fantasy? Besides, I hated when other authors wrote too much of an accent into their books, making it almost as difficult to decipher on the page as it would be out loud. Of course, I often got criticized for doing the opposite. To each their own, I supposed ... *Although, I probably should mention to Xander that it might be a good idea to let the client choose that particular detail. It isn't one size fits all when it comes to fantasies. Or, maybe it already is a choice and this is just mine? Yeah, it would have been really helpful if I had more information going into this. Thanks a lot, Xander.*

"Clara? Tell me what's goin' on with you, lass. You have me worried."

I wasn't exactly sure how to play this one. "Umm ... maybe I hit my head? I can't be sure."

The man blinked a few times as if processing my response. "What do you mean by you can't be sure? Do you not remember?"

I nibbled on my bottom lip. "No?" Now that I was no longer being motivated by fear, all I could do was stare at the perfection of man-candy being offered up to me. Where had the image for him come from? My mind? Algorithms? *Bah. Guess it doesn't matter. He's here, and he's beautiful.*

Scooping me up in his arms, the man hopped back onto his horse with no effort, as if I weighed less than nothing. "I told you not to go wanderin' off by yourself. Now you've gone and hit yer head, knocking Lord knows what out of it. What am I goona do with you, Clara? You're the most stubborn woman I've ever laid eyes on."

"What's your name?"

"Och, I have a full day of training, but I can see yer goona be needin' a doctor immediately." He swept some of my hair off my forehead, gazing down at me tenderly as he cradled me closer. "Don't worry, Clara, I'll take care of you."

Butterflies divebombed my stomach. "Okay," I managed on a breathy sigh, much to my horror. *Oh, get a hold of yourself. This guy doesn't actually exist. He's made up of pixels and ... other techy stuff. Whatever.*

With a click of his probably perfect tongue, we set off at a trot, the ride jarring despite the steady rhythm of the horse's hooves hitting against the ground. I clenched my teeth. It figured in my fantasy I'd end up getting a headache. I rubbed at my temples.

Or is this something else? Something more ominous? Like the VR technology is frying my brain, and while I'm ogling the

Scottish beefcake I'm dying in the real world. Great. I am quite possibly an unreliable narrator in this situation. Gah! I hate unreliable narrators. It's why I write in third person for crying out loud!

"Xander!" I hissed. "Please tell me I'm not dying. I could do with a little bit of reassurance right about now." Or any kind of perspective, really.

The Scotsman frowned down at me. "Lachlan. Not Xander. How hard did you hit your head, lass?"

I stared up, at Lachlan apparently, blankly. *Hmmm ... good name, if not a bit cliché for the genre. It seems as if I can't crack open a Scottish Historical lately without finding a Lachlan inside. Ugh. Stop nitpicking, Zoe. Enjoy this. Go with the flow and let yourself get swept away. Just make mental notes of the glaringly obvious stuff that might need fixing. Most people aren't going to care what the guy's name is once they get a look at him. Fantasy. Repeat ... fantasy. Fantasy. Fantasies are supposed to be fun. So have fun, Zoe. Have fun.*

"Lachlan?" Batting my eyelashes, I stared into his mesmerizing azure eyes.

"Yes, Clara. What do you need?"

"Will you stay with me? When the doctor comes ... and after. I'd feel so much better with you by my side."

He nodded resolutely. "Consider it done. You know I care for you deeply. Have since we were bairns."

Humming under my breath, I continued to stare at Lachlan. It simply couldn't be helped. It wouldn't be the first time I'd developed a thing for a fictional character, although it would be the first time I'd interacted with one outside of my head.

"Sooo … we've known each other since we were child — bairns then?"

"Amnesia of some sort then. It must be. It's no wonder she ran," he mumbled to himself before responding to me. "Yes, I'm your brother's best friend. Do you remember him?"

I stiffened. *What in the crap? Brother's best friend?* "No, I don't remember anything. I didn't even know my own name."

"Your brother is Adam."

Seriously? I can't even escape my brother in here? "Is he my older or younger brother?"

"Younger by two years."

Of course. I sighed. "And who are you to me then? Friend of mine as well or—"

"You're like a sister to me, Clara."

Sister? I contained a snort. *Please.* He certainly hadn't been giving me sisterly vibes before. At least I officially knew the general trope I was in now. The whole forbidden fruit slash friends to lovers thing. Accept I didn't want to play along. It was my job to test the romance scenarios in the Fantasy Life program and test I would.

Besides, I wouldn't be the only one who would decide to draw outside the lines once inside the program. If it could only follow a limited script and not adjust it would have limitations. Ones that would need to be disclosed before spending money on something that could potentially be a disappointment. What I was about to do was exactly what I was there for.

Leaning up in his arms, I cupped the side of Lachlan's stubbled jaw. "I don't think you have sisterly feelings toward me. I think you—"

"Clara!" Lachlan jerked away from me as if I'd slapped him. "I know you hit yer head, but you need to control yourself. Please. Once you get your memories back, I'm sure you'll be truly embarrassed."

"Oh, come on, Lachlan. You can't tell me you've never thought about kissing me. About doing more than that, in fact. Much more."

Our ride came to an abrupt halt. "And what would you know about kissing? And these other things? Has someone been showin' you?" Anger darkened his visage. "Has someone put his hands on you, Clara?" His fingers dug into my back painfully. "Tell me."

"How old am I, Lachlan?"

"Twenty."

I decided to overlook the fact that my subconscious had felt the need to cut my age in half for this trope … because, let's face it, historical romances had different rules since they took place in times before feminism existed in its modern forms. But my brain was on warning despite all of that. There was no place for my age-related insecurities in any kind of fantasy. It was one thing to feel old sometimes, especially since four decades isn't anything to sneeze at, but it was quite another to let myself indulge in the toxic behavior that only the young can find love. People of all ages need and deserve any kind of love they desire.

Unless my subconscious isn't the culprit with the age thing at all. I'll add it to my list of possible changes to discuss with Xander about this trope.

I cleared my throat. "Would you be jealous if I told you that someone had indeed been putting his hands all over me?"

While I waited for his answer, I leaned into him, inhaling deeply. He smelled like leather and man with a hint of some undefinable note I couldn't quite put my finger on. I wondered once again how all of this was so incredibly realistic. Was the program somehow tapping into my sensory memories and using those to create full immersion? But how? How was any of it possible? Shaking my head, I decided to save those kinds of questions for Xander if I made it out in one piece. For the moment, I would do my job and enjoy it along the way. *Or die trying. Please, Lord, don't let me die trying.*

"Well? Would you be jealous or not if some man has been putting his hands all over me?"

Repeating the question spurred a reaction, finally. Lachlan's nostrils flared, and his jaw muscles twitched. "I'll kill whoever it is who would dare steal any scrap of innocence from you. I'll swear this here and now. Not only have they disrespected you, but they disrespected your brother ... and our entire clan."

"I'll take that as a check in the jealously column." I

couldn't help but laugh at anyone thinking I was innocent. I hadn't slept with a lot of men, but I was very open about sex, and well educated on the matter, even about subjects I hadn't personally experienced. I wasn't an author who overlooked research. Plus, frankly, I enjoyed sex. Therefore, I'd never been shy about reading about it even in my teens. My curiosity on the matter had been piqued early in life.

Lachlan's expression abruptly smoothed out, relief washing over him. "I'm sure this is all a product of your head injury. Mayhap you think yourself someone else. Someone with looser morals."

I ground my teeth together. It felt like he was somehow slut-shaming me, and I'd had about enough of that in real life, there would be none of it in my fantasy. "Excuse you? Looser morals? There is absolutely nothing wrong with a woman having the desire to sexually express herself."

Panic pulsed within Lachlan's gaze, and with a kick, we set off at a gallop. If he hadn't been gripping me as tightly as he was, I was positive I would have gone sailing off the back of the horse into the mud. *Good thing I can't get physically hurt here. I hope.*

"Lachlan! Slow down! What are you doing?" Instead of slowing, he picked up the pace, the landscape blurring by impossibly fast. "If you don't slow down, I'm going to be sick! I mean it, Lachlan! I'm going to puke all over you!"

As if he couldn't hear a single word I said, we continued

to race across the countryside. Unfortunately, as promised, my stomach decided to upchuck whatever it thought it had eaten. Surely, I wasn't simultaneously throwing up in the real world? Then again, it would serve Xander right if he had to clean up my puke since he failed to update me on the parameters of the Fantasy Life program once I was inside and my memory had gone a bit wonky.

Groaning, I wiped at my mouth with my sleeve. "Oh, God, it smells like the real thing, too. Why can't it smell like flowers or something? Another friggin' fail, Xander. Another friggin' fail."

"Och, she's babblin' complete nonsense now," Lachlan muttered, the words somehow discernable over the wind whipping around us.

"Umm, hello? I just upchucked all over us. Can we please slow down before I do it again?"

He continued to ignore me.

"Oh, come on. This is not what I signed up for."

Lachlan's big hand swept down to cradle the side of my head. "Doona you worry, Clara. We're almost there. I'm sure you'll be fine in the end. You have to be."

Closing my eyes, I gritted my teeth. "I'm so over this."

Male voices called out in the distance in alarm. Lachlan's hand left me for a moment, probably to signal to the men the urgency he felt we were under.

Finally, we slowed, but before I could collect myself and get my bearings, Lachlan was off the horse and running with me in his arms. For someone concerned that

I had a head injury he certainly wasn't being careful with me.

I decided to squeeze my eyes shut again and wait for my nausea-inducing journey to come to an end. A commotion broke out around us, loud voices whipped into a frenzy reaching my ears, but the meaning of the words were meaningless. I couldn't help but wonder if that was on purpose to heighten the turmoil of the situation or if I was simply overwhelmed and having some sort of meltdown. There was a possibility I was overstimulated by the program, my brain seeking some sort of reprieve. Or at least I guessed it could be a possibility. What did I know? Literally ... what did I know since Xander had failed to re-introduce me to the information I apparently learned before entering Fantasy Life.

My thoughts wandered, and I drifted into a restful state, not sure if I was falling asleep, or the VR equivalent. I decided to just go with it.

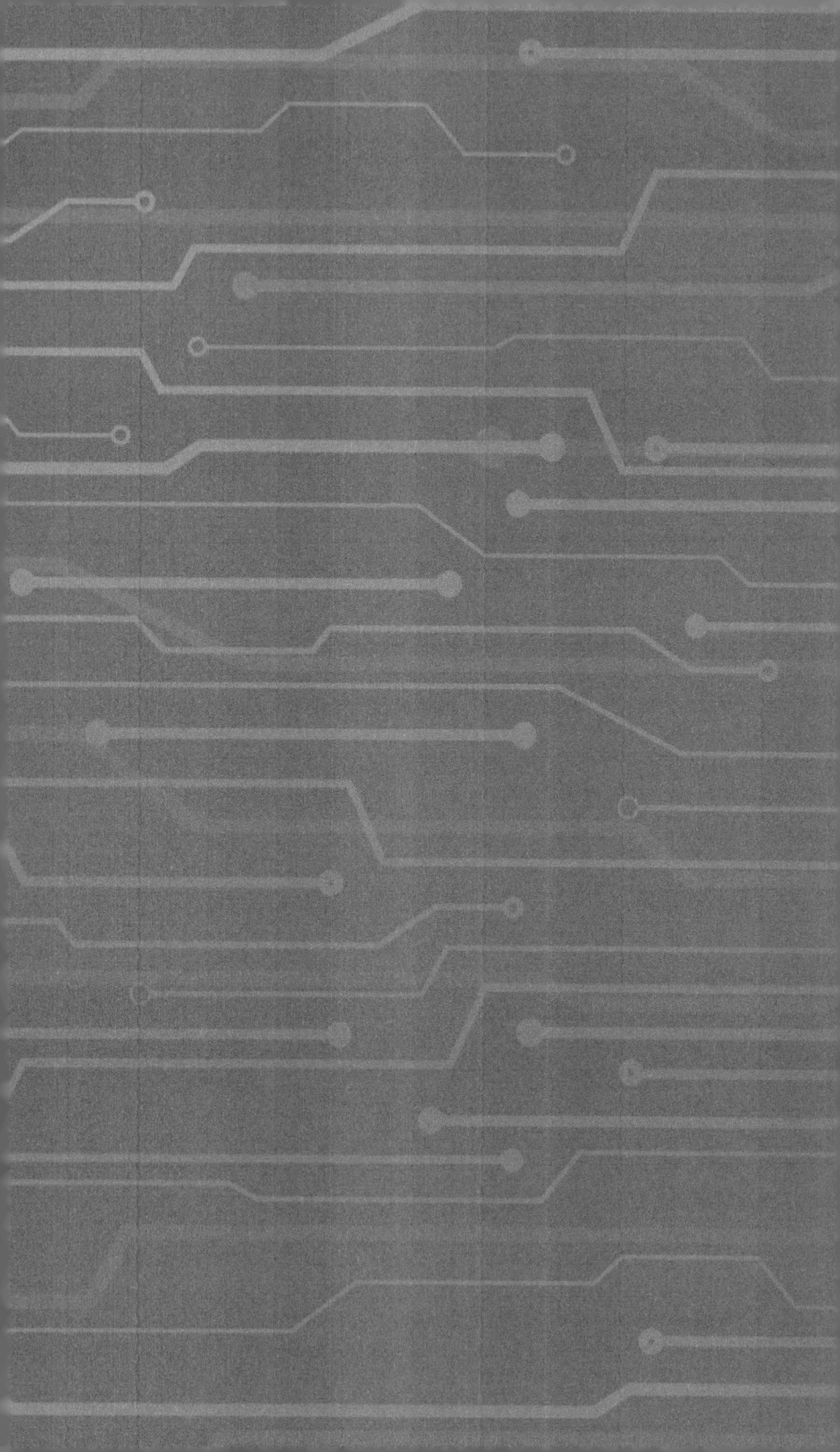

Chapter 4

"**C**lara."

Lachlan's deep voice seeped into my consciousness, stirring me from wherever I'd mentally gone. Peeking from under my lashes, I took in the stern set of his jaw combined with the worry flitting through his gaze.

"You're awake. Doona pretend you're not."

Sighing dramatically, I opened my eyes fully. "I was hoping I'd get a free pass on this trope since I'm clearly not enjoying it, and maybe wake up in another world. Guess that's not the case."

I scanned my surroundings. We were in a small, stone room, lavishly decorated for the period I supposed. Brightly colored tapestries covered the walls and small window, with a roaring blaze in the fireplace. Several candles were set about the room as well, giving more illumination than I thought was realistic, kind of like movie-style lighting. But again, I wasn't going to pick at those kinds of minor inaccuracies. I was laid out in a large canopy bed, nestled under a mountain of blankets. Lachlan was perched beside me, an elderly man with a full head of white hair hovering just past his shoulder.

"Thomas said he couldn't find any physical signs of injury. How are you feeling now?"

"Thomas?" I wiggled under the blankets, unsure if I was clothed or not. I was certainly not liking the idea of a male I didn't know examining me while I was unconscious and possibly naked. Yeah, none of it was real, but that kind of paranoia follows women into whatever world they end up in, especially this woman.

"I'm not feeling good about getting examined while I was out cold." My fingers found an edge of sleeve bunched at my wrist, and relief washed over me. Most likely, I hadn't actually been examined. At least not in the traditional sense since it was VR. Plus, how naked would I need to be to have my head examined? Surely, Xander and his team hadn't created pervert characters. I let that prospect comfort me.

Lachlan scowled. "This is the kind of nonsense I was telling you about," he muttered to Thomas before redirecting his attention back to me. "Thomas has known us since before we were born. You can and have trusted him with your life many times over. And what were you babblin' about free passes and other worlds?"

"Xander," I hissed. "Xander. Can I please move on to

the next trope? Maybe I can circle back to this one once I give you the extensive notes I already have."

"That name again. Xander." Lachlan jumped to his feet, the muscles in his arms constricting. "Could she mean Alexander from clan McDonnel?"

Thomas shuffled forward, speaking in a hushed tone to Lachlan, "It is quite possible that her issues are not related to a head injury directly. I have seen this type of thing before when—" His gaze darted to mine briefly. "When a maiden was taken against her will. A violation such as that can traumatize more than the body."

Silence fell over the room. *This is why historical romances aren't for everyone.* I was utterly flabbergasted. I'd entered a romance trope hoping to have some fun, but instead, I'd somehow ended up with the characters thinking I got raped. This was not the choose-your-own-adventure I would choose any day of the weak.

"Umm, no. Nobody took me against my will. There was no raping or pillaging or any such nonsense."

Lachlan's cheeks flushed as rage swept over him. "Are you tryin' ta tell me you willingly laid with a man outside of the marital bed?"

Waving his arms frantically, Thomas stepped in front of Lachlan. "It is also common for the victim of such a crime to attempt to make peace with the act by claiming it be their choice."

"No! That is definitely not what's happening here." Wrestling my arms free of the blankets, I yanked at my hair, which had somehow tangled around my face.

"Thomas," Lachlan growled low, "thank you for your help. As always with matters such as this, I will appreciate your discretion. But I would like to be alone with Clara so I can get to the bottom of this."

"Yes, yes, very well. You know where to find me if any other … issues arise." Thomas spared me one last glance laced with pity before he hurried from the room, firmly shutting the door behind him.

Lachlan stalked closer to the bed, his gaze thunderous. "Well, which is it, Clara? Did you willingly lay with a man outside of the marital bed or were you taken against your will?"

I narrowed my eyes at him. "I just told you I wasn't raped."

All anger melted away from Lachlan, suddenly replaced with anguish. "Why, Clara? Why would you do such a thing?" He dropped to his knees, face in his hands, a broken cry escaping from him.

I didn't know if I should laugh or take the situation seriously. "My body my choice?" I managed to squeak out the answer in the form of a question, not exactly sure why I said it.

"You'll be ruined now. No man will—" He stilled, whipping his head up, visage fierce. "I know what I have to do."

"You do?"

"I will marry you."

"What? No, you can't—"

In a flash he was back by my side, clasping my hands

within his. "Let me do this for you, Clara. But not just for you, for Adam, and for all our clan. If what you've done gets out, it— No, it won't get out. Surely, I canna stop the rumors from the abruptness of this, but over time, none will remember nor care."

Marriage. Can't even escape it in a fantasy. Ugh. "And what if I don't want to marry you? After all, you told me not that long ago that you thought of me as a sister. People usually don't go around marrying their siblings."

"Don't be difficult in this, Clara. As you well know we aren't blood-related, despite how I feel about you. But it is also how I feel about you that compels me to do this. I refuse to let you be ruined."

"Just because I'm not a virgin doesn't mean I'm ruined. I mean, really, think about it. What does it say about a man who thinks that by inserting a part of his anatomy into a woman that she's the one ruined? Hmmm? Seriously, I …" Sighing, I gave up, knowing I was wasting my breath. I was neck-deep in a historical romance trope where modern sensibilities didn't apply. But damn it, you can take the modern feminist out of reality, but you can't take the modern feminist sensibilities out of her.

"Clara," Lachlan gritted out between clenched teeth. "What are you tryin' ta do, kill me? My heart—" He dramatically clutched at his chest. "I swear it's goona stop beating the next time you say something like that."

I sniggered. The whole situation was beyond ridiculous.

"And you laugh at my pain."

"You know, since you've basically proposed, and I'm no longer a virgin ... how about joining me here in bed?" I wiggled my eyebrows suggestively. Apparently, I'd changed my mind about having sex within the Fantasy Life program. And why shouldn't I experience the full package, in more ways than one?

Lachlan froze, shock leaving his eyes comically wide. If he was human and not a bunch of pixels and programming, I would have been worried he was having an aneurism or a stroke of some kind.

I waved my hands around in front of his face. "Hello in there. What's your answer? Care to join me in bed? Naked, in case you didn't catch my meaning."

"Are ye pregnant? Is that what this is about? I already proposed. We can have a hasty wedding if you're worried about a bairn—"

"Just forget it." I couldn't seem to break the program off track. If I wanted to have sex with Lachlan, which suddenly I very much wanted to, then I was going to have to play along within the parameters of the time period the trope was set in.

"It is about a bairn then."

"Yes, mmm hmmm, that's right. So, if you want to make an honest woman out of me then we're going to have to get married as soon as possible and get to the tupping so there aren't any questions."

Lachlan flushed, his azure gaze going wild. Abruptly, he spun on his heels and marched to the door. "I will speak with Adam and your father. Don't ye worry your little head about any of this. I'll make sure you're safe, Clara." He made a hasty retreat without a backward glance, locking me in my quarters before he left.

"Oh, come on!" I hit the pile of blankets in frustration. "He seriously just locked me in here. What does he think is going to happen? That I might go throw myself at some other man before he can marry me?"

A small blue bird pushed its way into the room through a crack between the tapestry and window. It dove straight at me, screeching like a hawk instead of a songbird.

Screaming, I flung the blankets over my head. I could feel its tiny little legs moving above me. "Oh, my God, did it just peck at the blankets? Help! Xander! Help! There's a rogue killer bird in this program! It's a glitch or something! Help!"

A familiar laugh wafted through the wool and cotton. "You should have seen your face. You're in a fake world and a tiny, little bird terrified you." He choked back another laugh. "Try to take out an intruder with a pint of ice cream, spoon, and remote control, but hide under the covers from a bird."

I flipped the blankets back expecting to see Xander standing there, but instead the bird side-eyed me while bobbing up and down. "What the hell?" I glanced around the room once more before settling my gaze back on the bird. "Xander? Are you in there? Is your voice coming from the bird?"

It chuckled. "Yep. It's me, Xander, in the feathers."

"What … what the hell are you doing showing up as a bird?" I crossed my arms over my chest. "You scared the crap out of me going all angry bird. And I've been calling for you since I got here. I don't know what I'm supposed to be doing."

If a bird could smile, this one most certainly did. Or maybe I simply sensed Xander's amusement somehow. "What you're supposed to do is test out the romance tropes in the Fantasy Life program, and you're off to a great start, already testing its limits." Bird Xander's head shook back and forth. "But poor Lachlan, you almost fried his circuits there for a minute. This is the first time someone has pushed his boundaries."

I blinked, taking in his words. "What do you mean I almost fried his circuits? Why are talking about him like he's a real person or like a robot or something? He's just a part of the program, right?"

"Weeeeell, not exactly. He's a bit more sophisticated than that."

"What do you mean *not exactly?*"

Bird Xander launched himself into the air, circling the room once, before landing back on the bed. "Lachlan isn't like a character in a video game programmed to react to the players. He's AI."

"AI? You're talking about artificial intelligence? Like Johnny 5 is alive … or Lachlan is?" My heart thundered against my eardrums.

"I can't believe you referenced that old eighties' movie. I didn't even think you liked it."

"I didn't, that's not the point. Are you going to sit there," I waved my hands about, "or perch there, and tell me that Lachlan is alive and has feelings?"

"It's more complicated than that. But in a sense, yes."

"Oh my God!"

"But he doesn't know he's in a VR program. He believes his life is real."

"Oh my God!" I repeated, at a loss for anything else. My mind was reeling. Then it hit me. "You're matrixing him!"

"Don't be ridiculous."

"Oh my God, you are!"

"Would you please stop saying *oh my God*? I am not—"

"Lachlan believes I'm Clara, and he also believes—"

Bird Xander chuckled. "Yep, he believes you went off and slept with some random guy in another clan."

"No, no, no, no, no. This is not what I signed up for, Xander. Knowing that I'm hurting the poor guy, AI or not, sucks all the fun out of this for me. I thought he was a bunch of pixels and programming. This … this is not what I signed up for!"

"It's exactly what you signed up for."

"You're telling me that you disclosed the bit about the AI to me? Because it doesn't sound like something I'd agree to. The rest was believable, but now …" I quirked an eyebrow and crossed my arms over my chest. "You keep reminding me how well I know you, Xander. And I do. I most definitely do."

Bird Xander flapped his wings. "All right. You got me. I

might have omitted the AI part. But it doesn't make much of a difference."

"Why would you do that?"

"Because I wanted your help, and I knew you might have some issues with the rest."

"You lied to me."

"I omitted."

"A lie of omission, but a lie all the same. I want out, Xander. Now. This has to be some kind of breach of contract." Plus, it was starting to get to me that I still hadn't remembered going to his office. Shouldn't those memories have popped back into place already? He said I needed some time to adjust, but how much were we talking?

"You can't quit, Zoe."

I rolled my eyes. "I can and I am. Now get me the hell out of here."

Bird Xander did a weird little jig before taking flight. He circled the room several times and then grabbed onto the tapestry by the window. Very much out of my reach, I noted. "If you quit before playing out the scenario with Lachlan it'll be worse for him."

"Bullshit. What happens when I leave at the end of the … plot? Or whatever you call the full scenario of each trope. Either way, I'll be gone. You're just trying to con me into doing what you want."

"No. He's programmed to complete the scenario and then he will go into a stasis until he is activated again. While in the stasis he will do the AI equivalent of dreaming. Kind of like reliving his time with you until someone else comes along."

"That doesn't even make sense. How does he believe he's alive if he goes into this stasis? And how does he think each person that comes into play with him is Clara? How does—"

"Those kinds of loopholes were worked into his initial programming and the rest is complicated." He made a weird sound in the back of his throat. "Just believe me when I tell you that you must stay in this until the end, or you will hurt him a lot more than you are now."

Tugging on my hair, I groaned. "I don't know if I can believe you, Xander. I'm starting to feel like you're fucking with me. Like old times, you know? Is Adam out there with you laughing his ass off about this? That seems more believable than what you've been telling me."

Bird Xander stared at me. "We're not kids anymore. I wouldn't do that. And Adam has nothing to do with this."

"Allow me to express my skepticism." Sure, Xander had always seemed to simply be along for the ride with all the pranks aimed at me, but he'd participated. And who was to say that Adam hadn't cooked up the plan when he found out Xander needed someone to beta test this particular part of Fantasy Life? My brother could be an asshole, but he wasn't stupid. I hated to admit it, but there was more than one occasion in my life where he'd tricked me.

"What if … well, what if …" I scrambled for a solution, grasping at half-baked ideas. "You could bring in someone else to serve as the main character and I could simply observe." It wouldn't fix the entire problem, but at least it could assuage my guilt from directly interacting with the AIs myself.

"Multiple people can't be in the same virtual reality session," Xander snapped.

"Umm …" I pointed at myself, then Xander, then back again. "One, two. I count two right now, and that's technically multiple people."

Xander's eyes widened, a glint of panic flashing. He knew he was caught in a lie. But quick as lightning he relaxed, his expression shifting to one of indifference. "I'm different. I can go places no one else can." His dimple crept out as he gave me a slow grin. "Come on, Zoe. It can still be fun if you let it."

Fine. Maybe it wasn't a lie. I was still suspicious, but as the creator and owner of the company, it was highly plausible that he did have the ability to go places within Fantasy Life others couldn't. "It's kind of creepy. Lachlan thinks I'm Clara. And he thinks badly of me, which I don't like, and goes against my feminist sensibilities that I care. Basically, I hate myself for caring about what he thinks about my sexual choices."

Bird Xander hopped about as if he was about to speak, but I wasn't done with my little rant.

"Besides, I didn't pick this historical romance trope. And I especially never would have if someone would have informed me about the AI thing. I don't want to be slut-shamed in my fantasy, Xander. Some women might enjoy this kind of thing, and to each their own when it comes to kink, but I'm not one of them. I've had enough slut-shaming in real life and I'm not about to put up with it when I don't have to. Plus, can we talk about the morality of this whole thing. Lachlan is alive—alive as any of us as far as I can tell—and you're playing God with him. Like literally playing God. Doesn't any creature with self-awareness on that level deserve some kind of free-will or at least—"

A knock sounded on the door just as it swung open. "Who are you talking to?" Lachlan demanded.

Glancing over to where Bird Xander had been, I wasn't surprised to find him gone. *Just wait until I get out of here. I'm going to wring his neck, I swear.* "Myself." Suddenly it was difficult to meet his gaze knowing that real intelligence, artificial or not, resided behind his baby blues.

"Yourself?" Lachlan stalked around the room, peeking in every nook and cranny as if I could shrink a man and hide him somewhere.

His actions were enough to make my blood boil, but at the same time, I had to acknowledge the time period. Lachlan believed it was normal to act the fool in that manner. In fact, it was expected of him to act like such a neanderthal. I was pretty sure men were impossible to change, no matter their species or biological material.

"Yes, myself," I retorted, my jaw aching from how tightly my teeth were clenched. *Hmmm ... wonder if I'm grinding my teeth in real life right now, or my brain is making me feel the pain because it thinks I should.* Again, my mind reeled in an attempt to understand how any of this was possible. *Ugh. Best not to question that now. Focus on doing this job because Xander isn't going to let me out since he's an asshat. Ask questions later. Because there will be tons of questions later. And probably some violence.*

Satisfied that I wasn't harboring a man in my room, Lachlan relaxed, though he still regarded me with wariness. "I spoke with your brother." He ran his hands through his hair, shifting from foot to foot. "I hated lying to him. I hate that he thinks me a scoundrel who seduced his only sister. But it served its purpose. We will be married tomorrow."

"Tomorrow!" I screeched.

"Aye, tomorrow. You best prepare yourself." Without another word, Lachlan fled the room as if his hair was on fire, locking the door once more behind him.

"Xander!" I hissed. "Get your feathered butt back here so we can finish our conversation!" *And I can convince you to get me the hell out of here.*

But he didn't come, and neither did anyone else for that matter.

At some point, I finally dozed off, or maybe I went into my own kind of stasis. Either way, at least I got a bit of a reprieve before the insanity would surely begin anew.

Chapter 5

Yawning, I sat up in bed, nothing seemingly changed since I'd mentally checked out. And I do mean nothing. The fire continued to burn in the fireplace, and the light outside was steady, showing no signs of night or a new day. The most disconcerting part was that I didn't seem to have any bodily needs. I wasn't hungry or thirsty, nor did I have the urge to go to the bathroom. As someone who had one of the smallest bladders in existence, that little detail was a nice touch. I refused to let myself consider the possibilities of what that could translate to in the real world, like catheter and IV, etc. I would simply enjoy the tiny bits of escapism in any form while I could get them. Because once out of Fantasy Life, I would not be a returning tester or customer. I refused to play God with AI the way Xander did.

Speaking of the devil. "Xander!" I hit the bed in frustration. "Xander!"

When I was in the orientation part of the program, I was led to believe I would have more control over things than I actually did. Hence the debacle with being naked. Unless that situation had forced an overcorrection to accommodate my wacky brain. Of course, how would I know since Xander was playing things close to his vest. It was the not knowing that was getting to me the most.

The door swung open, the heavy wood thumping against the stone wall. I let out a startled gasp as Lachlan strode in, his face a mask of determination. Behind him was another man, tall, with red hair and beard, mostly unremarkable, especially next to the perfection that was Lachlan.

Rising from bed, fresh despite not having changed or showered—something I could definitely get used to—I crossed my arms over my chest. "I suppose today is shotgun wedding day."

Sighing heavily, Lachlan addressed his companion, "See what I speak of, Adam? Nonsense spews from her mouth."

Ah. This man was supposed to be my brother. He nodded in agreement as he turned his gaze toward me. "I wish to have a moment alone with my sister before the wedding."

My face twisted in annoyance. The voice coming from my supposed brother was none other than Xander's. "Yes, I also wish to have a little chat with my dear brother."

"Try not to kill each other," Lachlan muttered. "I'll be

right outside o' the room where I can stall yer mother and the lasses when they arrive." He reluctantly made his way into the hallway, sparing us a worried glance before pulling the door shut behind him.

"You asshat!" I stalked across the room, my face and neck heating. "I told you I wanted out of here, and then you just disappeared."

Despite being in a completely different body, the smirk that curved Xander's mouth was familiar and unwelcome. "And I told you that you needed to stick this one out. Besides, I'll let you pick which trope you do next."

"No, no, no, no, no." I poked him in his burly chest. "I'm not getting married to Lachlan when I know he thinks this is real."

"I thought you were all about seducing him. That's the way it seemed when you quite literally asked him to get into bed with you naked." He raised his eyebrows, his green eyes boring into mine.

"How did you know that? Were you spying on me?"

"Of course I was spying on you. This is a beta test. I need to monitor things."

I lurched away from him, anger coursing through every molecule in my body. It was a wonder I didn't explode into pixels. "Then you really were ignoring me when I was calling for you. You are such an asshat!"

"I believe you already called me that."

"And it won't be the last time." Why in the world did I agree to do this for him again? I should have known that despite his extraordinary physical glow-up, and weird bigger-than-life presence, underneath it all Xander was still the same immature kid who used to torment me alongside my brother.

"Zoe, calm down. We went over this. If you—"

I cut my arm through the air, huffing out a string of obscenities before I could find coherent words. "I don't give a shit about your completely unbelievable explanation, Xander. I can't participate in this. It's morally wrong."

"But you—"

"Plus, I do not like the fact that you're keeping tabs on my every move in here. I mean, would you have watched me have sex with Lachlan?"

His nostrils flared. "No, of course I wouldn't watch that part."

"But how would you know when to look away, so to speak?"

He ran his fingers through his shoulder-length red hair in the same manner I'd seen him do with his own hair more times than I could count. "By monitoring your cerebral responses. I would know what was transpiring without having to witness it."

Somewhat mollified that he hadn't been planning on going total voyeur on me, I relaxed a bit. "Okay, even still, I don't want to be here anymore because of my moral objections to us playing God to the AIs."

"Come on, Zoe, be reasonable. They're already created. If they're not doing this, then what do you suppose we do with them? Would you be satisfied if they're ... for lack of a better term, deleted?"

I gasped. "That's emotional blackmail, Xander. You're basically saying if I don't continue on then you're going to delete Lachlan."

"I said no such thing."

"I read between the lines which wasn't difficult to do in this situation."

"Zoe, please." Xander dropped to his knees, clasping his hands in front of him. "I'm begging. I'm literally on my knees begging you to do this."

Tilting my head, I studied him for a moment. *Why does he seem so different in here? It can't be just the Scotsman costume he's hiding in. It wouldn't change his personality. Plus, he seemed a bit off in the orientation part of the program as well.* Shoving the thoughts aside, I chalked it up to us both being in avatars, even when we looked like ourselves. I supposed the *je ne sais quoi* of humanity was difficult to shove into VR, despite the rest, which explained a lot. Probably.

I poked Xander's forehead with my index finger. "Technically, you're not doing any begging since you're not even in your real body. Which is probably the only reason you're able to do it." It was oddly freakier having Xander's voice come from a different man's body than it had been coming from a bird.

Ignoring my commentary, Xander bent over farther, pressing his cheek into the floor while gazing up at me with a pleading eye. "Please, Zoe. You're not just helping my company with this project, but you're helping yourself. You need to get your writer's mojo back. Exact quote if I remember correctly."

Scowling, I glared down at him. Again, I couldn't help but circle back to the fact that this was some very unlike Xander behavior. It had to be because he was in an avatar-type situation, it just had to be. Because the Xander I knew would die before begging anyone for anything. He was proud to a fault. Or maybe me staying in Fantasy Life for the time being was actually important to him and his company. Either was plausible, I supposed, although I couldn't override my mistrust of Xander in the current situation.

"Yeah, well, I don't remember anything from our meeting where I signed the contract. Which I find suspicious. In fact, I'm beginning to find this whole thing suspect. You're up to something Xander, I'm just not sure what yet."

He had the audacity to chuckle. "Always so paranoid."

Hunching over, I poked at his exposed cheek. "Don't you dare try to gaslight me with this. Something weird is going on with my memories and I don't like it."

Awkwardly rising to his feet, he stared at me a few moments before responding. "The only weird thing going on is how obstinate you're being for someone who willingly entered into this."

"Then why don't I remember?"

He shrugged. "We ran a scan, there's nothing wrong

with you, your brain, or the program. The memories are there, you simply aren't accessing them."

Rubbing my temples, I sighed. It was a relief to know there was nothing physically wrong. Although the rest didn't bode well for my mental state, but that wasn't news.

"What? Did you think you were damaged or dying or something?" Xander had the nerve to chuckle again. "And I repeat, always so paranoid."

I didn't know what to do. I wouldn't admit it to anyone other than myself, but part of the reason I wanted out of Fantasy Life was because I was lowkey terrified that my brain was getting fried. Yes, I truly felt some moral ick factor about Lachlan being AI, but it wasn't my number one motivation. And if I was to believe what Xander said, without people visiting the programs, Lachlan had no purpose. In the tech world, things like Lachlan that didn't serve a purpose got destroyed or deleted. Then again, I wasn't sure I could trust what Xander was attempting to sell me.

"I do need to get my writer's mojo back," I grumbled, hating myself a bit for even thinking, let alone saying it. Throwing my hands in the air, I let loose an exasperated scream. "I hate this, and I'm pretty sure I hate you now as well, Xander."

His eyes widened slightly. "What? You didn't hate me before? After all, I did help Adam change out your hair dye." He raised his hand to his mouth, cupping it to the side. "I heard there was an orange undertone even after you went to get it professionally fixed."

Throwing my head back, I laughed. It had been some time since someone had dragged such a quick and sudden burst of amusement from me. I welcomed it despite how things were going in Fantasy Life so far. One had to find joy, no matter how small, wherever one could.

"Don't you think Lachlan is attractive?"

Well, that's an abrupt subject change. Sobering, I narrowed my eyes as I studied the ruddy face of the body Xander was inhabiting. I found the current version of him more difficult to read than his real body. Difficult, but not impossible. Apparently, even though I hadn't spent time with Xander in approximately two decades, I'd learned his tells long ago. The way he shifted his weight from foot to foot while not quite meeting my gaze.

"What are you trying to say, Xander?" *And what are you up to now?*

He shrugged, the motion at odds with his larger-than-normal body. "I'm attempting to ascertain whether or not your attraction level to Lachlan has anything to do with your protests."

"You think I'm not attracted to Lachlan?" I snorted demonstratively. "Even a straight man can see that he's perfection."

Xander tapped at his eyebrow and the phantom scar there. "And isn't that what everyone wants? Perfection?"

"Are you calling me shallow?"

His head snapped up. "What? No. Where did you get that from? I just—"

"Look, Xander. I wish I didn't care about appearance at

all, but unfortunately, I can't control who and what I'm attracted to. And attraction is needed in a romantic relationship, plain and simple. That type of love is like a recipe, and it needs all of the right ingredients to work. One of those ingredients for me happens to be attraction. If that makes me shallow, then so be it." I choked back the rest of my tirade, not having the emotional energy for it at the moment. If Xander wanted to look down at me for valuing some level of physical attraction, what did it matter to me? So much more went into attraction than appearance though. The physical aspect was simply step one, kind of like a peacock with its feathers.

Xander stared at me. "Who isn't shallow to some degree?" His lips turned down into a scowl. "I know I am."

"Don't backtrack, Xander."

"Here is not the place for this discussion." He ran his hands through his hair, seeming to steel himself. "If you're attracted to Lachlan then there shouldn't be a problem in … having some fun with him." He gritted out the last part. "You're here to test out the program. All of the program."

Tension hung in the air between us for some unfathomable reason. It seemed to be from more than we were discussing, but for the life of me I couldn't figure out the cause.

Finally, Xander cleared his throat and then said, "I'll be here, playing the role of Adam, your pissed-off brother … because for shame, Zoe. How could you have sex with some man outside of the marital bed? And with a man named Xander, no less." He winked.

I forced a smile. "Yes, having sex with a man named Xander would be completely scandalous."

He cupped the back of his neck and glanced at the door. "I suppose we should get on with this. After all, this is only the first of many tropes you need to test."

"*If* I agree to continue on with this—"

"You did sign a contract."

"*If* I agree to continue on with this, then I want to pick the next trope at the very least."

"Fine."

"And I also—"

"We'll sort out the details when you finish with this scenario."

Dropping my face into my hands, I groaned. "I don't know if I'm cut out for this."

"You're Zoe Woods, and she can do anything she puts her mind to."

I waved him off. "No need for that kind of false flattery. I said I'd help you with this, even if I can't remember saying it." I gave him a withering glare, causing his massive faux body to shrink away slightly. "And I do need to get my writer's mojo back. If this doesn't help, then I don't know what will."

Xander hooked his arm through the air, grinning maniacally. "That's the spirit."

A loud knock reverberated on the door. "Is everything all right in there?" Lachlan called. "I thought I heard a scream."

"We're both alive and well," I responded with saccharine sweetness. "For now."

Xander smirked.

"Well," I fluttered my hands impatiently, "let's get this show on the road. I don't want to be stuck in this trope forever."

Chapter 6

Romance novels aren't all about sex. Sure, sex is one component of an intimate relationship, therefore the romance novel. Personally, I enjoy some steamy scenes in both what I read and what I write, but the genre as a whole has been relegated to the classification of porn by misogynistic asshats. Not that there's anything wrong with porn. It's just its own beast. And because of that misconception, people seem to think you can't have a romance book without sex, which is absolutely absurd.

Romance novels are about personal empowerment through choice. Which is what true feminism is about— the ability to decide for yourself what you want out of life. Basically, there are no wrong choices in romance. And of course, although the romance genre is dominated by women, it doesn't stop with them, it encompasses anyone who wants to be included. Any gender, any race, and any sexual orientation, there's a space for you. Choose whatever sets your heart and possibly your loins on fire.

Which was the problem at the moment. Sex with Lachlan was supposed to be a potential fun bonus, not the primary goal of my first foray into VR world. Despite being in virtual reality, some kind of intimacy or bond needed to be forged before that happened to make things work properly, at least for me. And yet somehow, I'd lost my choice in the Fantasy Life scenario currently unfolding before me. I wasn't sure if it was irony since romance was supposed to be about choice or my own personal hell paved by good intentions. Either way ... I was not a happy camper.

Clad in a royal blue gown with a blue and green plaid sash, I stood beside Lachlan who wore a kilt in the same plaid colors. Crowded into the small church around us were people I was supposed to know, friends and family to Clara. Xander, still wearing his Scottish Adam body, winked at me when I glanced in his direction. I bit back a growl.

Suddenly Lachlan's lips were on mine in a gentle yet firm kiss. Dazed, I did nothing to reciprocate. *Holy shit. I'm married ... again.* I knew it wasn't real. None of it was, but I couldn't help but feel odd going through the motions of something I'd put so much stock into once upon a time. Now, just like with so many other things, I was jaded and bitter when it came to the entire subject of matrimony.

When Lachlan pulled away, he snagged my hand within his, raising it into the air. The small crowd cheered, even as the man who thought he was my father frowned at Lachlan. Xander clapped him on the back and whispered something to him, drawing a laugh from the older man.

"It's time to celebrate!" Xander yelled, eliciting more cheers from the crowd.

My so-called mother stepped up beside me, smiling warmly at the two of us. "Lachlan, my dear, would you mind giving me a moment of time with my daughter before you whisk her off?"

"O' course."

My mother linked her arm with mine and led me to the corner of the church. "You seem a wee bit out of it, my dear. Before I thought it was nerves ..." She paused, searching my face for answers. "Are you still? Nervous? I thought under the circumstances you wouldn't be about your wedding night at least."

Everyone except Xander and Lachlan had studiously remained mum about the strange circumstances surrounding my and Lachlan's sudden betrothal and hasty wedding. I was hopeful that it would stay that way, but apparently, my faux mother was broaching the subject in a roundabout way. "This all happened so fast. I don't know what to think." Which was the truth, kind of.

She dropped her voice to barely a whisper. "Or did you and Lachlan not ... go all the way?"

I could feel my cheeks flame. It wasn't embarrassment exactly. Or maybe it was. Again, I found myself not knowing how to react with my modern sensibilities in a bygone era of sorts. "What did Adam say? About all of this?"

Lachlan told me he'd take care of everything, and he made it seem as if he portrayed himself as the scoundrel who stole my innocence, but it was best to be sure before I said something to make things more awkward for myself.

Oh, stop. These people may be AI and therefore be alive in a sense, but they're programmed to be a part of this. You acting weird isn't doing anyone, least of all your writer's mojo, any favors. Alas, I couldn't manage to go back to my pre-AI-knowledge carefree attitude. For better or for worse, being AI translated to being alive, and alive meant I cared what they thought. *Ugh. Why am I like this?*

My mother cleared her throat. "Don't think that all of us were ignorant to the way Lachlan always looked at you. Your father and I were not surprised when we heard the news."

Changing my mind, I decided I didn't need or want to hear whatever lies Lachlan had spun. "It's fine. I'm just a bit dazed by all of this. It all seems so surreal." If she only knew the half of it. With that thought, my mood pivoted, and I had to bite back a laugh.

"You know you can come to me with anything. You may belong to Lachlan now, but you will forever be my daughter."

I wanted to shout for everyone to hear that I belonged to no one but myself, even if it was a fictional possession and a faux marriage. Instead, I patted her on the back of her hand, forcing a brittle smile. "Thank you."

"It's my turn to have a quick word with Clara before the celebration." I whirled to find Xander, aka my brother, hovering a few feet behind us.

My mother, or I guess our mother in this storyline, smiled warmly at him. "Don't take too long. I'm afraid the groom is already growing impatient."

As soon as she was out of earshot, Xander closed the distance between us. "What's it like to be married for the third time?"

I scrunched up my nose. "Ha, ha. I'm not amused."

"Maybe that's your problem right now. You need to let go and enjoy this."

"It feels like you just told me in the middle of an anxiety attack to simply calm down. Not helpful." I shook my head. "Nope, not helpful in the tiniest degree."

"We're about to go to a party, so that should be fun."

"I can't even drink my worries away, so how much fun will it actually be?"

Xander grinned. "You can get drunk. And the bonus is no hangover."

Utterly flabbergasted, I couldn't do much more than blink at him for several seconds. "How does any of this work? Seriously, I don't understand how any of this is possible."

Xander reached out with one of his character's burly hands, booping my nose gently. "Don't you worry about it. Not your department."

I sighed heavily, following up with a dramatic eye roll.

"Whatever. I will be getting some answers when I get out of here."

He turned to go, apparently satisfied with his check-in.

I smacked at his arm. "Hey! Wait! I have one question you can answer for me right now and I want to ask it before I forget."

Raising his eyebrows, he tilted his head with curiosity. "Go ahead. As if you were waiting for my permission to ask anyhow."

"The accents and word choices everyone is using here. When I first met Lachlan, his brogue was stronger, maybe, and also his word choices were not as modern. Now everyone sounds, I don't know, normal. For me, totally not a problem, but what's going on with that?"

Xander shrugged. "What's the saying 'not my circus, not my monkeys? In this case, it is your circus, and they are your monkeys, in the way that it's your brain and they defer to your preferences when it comes to that kind of thing."

"So you adjusted the settings because of the naked incident to give me less control over certain things, but I still have control over the less problematic things?"

"In a nutshell, yes."

"But then why did it change? I mean, in the beginning—"

"Stop worrying about it. You're not going to be in this trope for very much longer, and I have a feeling the one you're going to pick next won't have a language issue."

I snorted. "You got that right." I enjoyed reading a

historical romance every now and again, but write one? Nope, never. It was entirely too much research for this author. Unless I did an alternative history of some sort. Now that was an idea. Hmmm ...

"Zoe," Xander hissed. "You need to stop standing there and staring off into nothing."

"Oh. Oops. Sorry." I gathered the skirts of my dress and rushed back to Lachlan, who immediately wound his warm arm around my waist, tugging me into his side.

For someone who'd claimed to only think of me as a sister just a short time ago, he didn't seem to have a problem switching gears now that we were married. And what was it my faux mother had said about the way he always looked at me?

Angling my head up to meet his intense gaze, a shiver ran down my spine. *Maybe I really am shallow.* Despite being AI, Lachlan still wasn't flesh and blood. He didn't look at me like I was his sister because he'd been programmed not to, plain and simple. He was alive, but not human.

"Come on, lass," Lachlan murmured into my ear, his voice a soft caress sweeping into stoke a heat within me, much to my chagrin. "We have some celebrating to do."

"And then our private wedding night celebration, right?"

His fingers dug into my side as his entire body tensed. "About that. There's something I've been meanin' to talk to you about."

"If it has anything to do with not consummating our

marriage then I don't want to hear it." Or did I? I couldn't seem to make up my own damn mind about what I wanted out of my VR experience. Maybe I was to blame for Lachlan's uncertainness as well for that reason.

Studiously ignoring me, Lachlan guided me along beside him as we made our way to our post-wedding celebration. No one seemed to be calling it a reception, and I wasn't sure where that term stacked up historically, and honestly, I didn't care.

The rest of the evening blurred past me, filled with smiling faces and lots of alcohol. Again, I found myself uncertain as to why my perception of time in this trope was skewed to kind of skip over certain parts and to slow down for others. If I had to guess it would be that it was like skimming over parts in a book I found uninteresting. Maybe the focus of things was also controlled by me without my knowledge.

Why do I still have no recollection of my time in Xander's office before entering the Fantasy Life program? It would be extremely helpful if I could remember any instructions or tidbits of information I may have gotten in that meeting.

"Good luck." Xander's voice still coming from Adam's visage reached my ears just as Lachlan hoisted me up into his arms, offering our guests a hearty good-bye. Lots of hooting and hollering followed us, echoing off the stone walls as Lachlan carried me to what was to be our new shared room.

Everything went dark for a single moment, no more than a heartbeat's worth of time, and then—

"What the hell?" Lachlan was sprawled out beside me, face down, and completely naked. His perfectly sculpted ass held me in thrall for a few seconds, possibly hours, before I shook myself out of my lustful stupor.

Lifting the sheets from my body, I gasped when I found myself in the same state of undress. "What the hell?" I muttered again.

I glanced from my naked body back to Lachlan's again. Had my first virtual reality sexcapade blown my mind ... literally? The last thing that happened before my blackout was us entering our shared chamber for our wedding night and then bam ... nothing.

"Good luck." Xander's voice ricocheted around in my mind.

Good luck, not have fun ... and the tone, something had been off about it. Something that raised my suspicions the more it bounced around in my thoughts.

"Oh my God!" Suddenly it dawned on me, the horror of the situation too great to accept. "No, no, no, no, no. He did not— Oh my God, he did not seriously put me in a fade to grey romance trope." But the truth of it was lying right next to me in slumber.

"Xander," I hissed. "You have some explaining to do. And you better get in here right now so you can start doing it." He'd made it seem like I had a choice in the sex or no sex in Fantasy Life debate. What had just gone down was not my choice by any means.

Balling my fists up, I hit the bed several times in frustration, Lachlan not stirring in the least. Because of course not. I might get a peek at something I shouldn't since I was living in a PG-13 world at the moment.

A large, brown rat emerged from under the door, sitting up on its haunches to regard me warily, even as its eyes glinted with mischief. "What's wrong, Zoe? You seem upset."

I ground my teeth together. "Now I have proof positive you're fucking with me."

"I thought we went over this already."

Crossing my arms over my chest, I glared at the rat, deciding his choice of avatar was spot on after what he'd done to me. "Clearly you lied."

"Is it because you didn't get to have sex with Lachlan? I thought you were morally opposed to treating the AIs like—"

"You made it seem like I could do whatever I wanted in this world. So if I wanted to have sex with Lachlan on my wedding night, then I should still be riding him like I'm a cowgirl and he's a stallion I need to break."

Rat Xander tugged at his ears as his nose twitched in agitation. "Well, that's one way to put it."

With brisk movements, I managed to wrap the sheet around me and totter out of bed. "Now you listen here, Xander." I lurched toward his little rat body, making a grab for him.

He scurried just out of my reach, whiskers twitching. "Zoe, come on. I didn't do it on purpose. Yes, it's a setting option within Fantasy Life. After all, not everyone has the same kink level, but I didn't do this to you."

"Then why did you wish me good luck in that sarcastic way? You knew this was going to happen, and you were taunting me when I didn't even know it at the time."

"Obviously your subconscious was not fully on board with the whole sex with Lachlan thing."

"Mmm hmmm ... I call bullshit."

Rat Xander raised his little paws in the air in an attempt to cute me into compliance. It was a move he'd used many times on me over the years in human form. He'd deploy his dimple, and boom, suddenly I was seeing things his way. "Zoe, I thought just throwing you into this trope would be a great way to get you started, but I might have missed my mark a bit."

I quirked an eyebrow, choking back a laugh. "You think?"

"Lachlan has a lovely memory of his wedding night with the woman, Clara, he's been coveting for years. I suppose we could move on at this point."

Throwing my head back to gaze at the ceiling, I shouted, "Thank the heavens." I glanced over at Lachlan to see if I'd disturbed him. He didn't so much as move a muscle.

"Don't worry about him." Xander rose onto his hind legs. "He won't wake up. He'll stay there until the next Clara comes along."

"And then what? He starts this whole crazy thing over again?"

Rat Xander stared at me, his nose twitching. "Yep, pretty much."

My gaze roamed the sculpted backside of Lachlan, coming to rest on his glorious ass once more. "It hardly seems fair to the AI. Any of this."

"We've been over this part before as well. They were created for this."

"But they have consciousnesses. Who are we to say what makes something alive, truly? Is it a heartbeat or intelligence? And does one make the other less important? The inclusion of AI in Fantasy Life gives me pause. Like, what if someone that comes in here is abusive? And what if what I did could be considered emotional abuse? What if—"

"You're overthinking this." Rat Xander ran his paws over his whiskers. "Although, you do make an excellent point about abuse. I don't want people to come into any scenario thinking they can do whatever they want." He nodded once curtly. "I'll go over the issue with my people and come up with some protocol for that."

"I have other notes and suggestions."

"I'm sure you do. But we can deal with those later when you're done with testing all the tropes on the list."

I rolled my eyes. "Like I'm going to remember it all at the end. I should be able to give you the information after every trope."

"We'll pull the notes from the program."

"And how exactly are you going to do that?" I squeaked. "Because that implies probing into my brain somehow." Again, I wondered how any of this was possible, my ability to understand it, or not understand it as was the case, causing panic to flutter in my chest.

"Don't worry about it."

Clutching at the sheet, I glared at Rat Xander, tempted to dropkick him. "I don't like not knowing how things work. Call it fear of the unknown, call it neurotic, I don't really care. I like answers, and you're not giving them to me. Like how is all of this so real? Even the smells. Where are the smells and sensations coming from? Would the sex have felt real? I can't tell the difference between this world and reality. What if I get lost in here? Or—" I gasped. "Oh my God. Am I just another AI? Is that why I don't remember parts of the office visit and such? Because my memories are—"

"Calm down!" Rat Xander pixelized, reappearing the next second as human Xander. "Zoe, please." He strode across the room, hesitating for a moment before engulfing me in his arms. "The only reason you're not enjoying this is because you won't let yourself."

I harumphed, hating that I reveled in the comfort of his embrace. I sniffed at his shirt, the familiar scent of his soap, laundry detergent, and that undefinable part that only belonged to Xander washing over me. "How do you smell like you?"

"Like me? What do I smell like exactly?"

Shoving at him, I shuffled back, clutching at the sheet tighter. "Umm … well, like you, I don't know. I've spent enough time around you over the years that I don't think about it, I just know." I did not want to describe to him how his scent was both mouthwatering and comforting at the same time. His ego didn't need a boost of any kind.

Xander's face became a mask of uncertainty. "Do you like it?"

"What? I-I don't know. You're the one who has all the answers. Not me. You can go check my brain waves or whatever and gauge my reactions." I rubbed at my temples. "But my point is, I know it's your scent. I just do. So how is that possible?"

"Your brain is providing the memory. You smell what you expect. Sooo … yeah, I'd be careful with that." He winked at me, disarming me with his humor.

"Noted." I giggled, hating myself a bit for the reaction. *Why do I keep letting him convince me to do things his way and to forget about my reservations? This is Xander, the same punk kid I grew up with.*

"You ready?"

"To get out of here?" I nodded vigorously. "Hellz yeah, I am."

Bowing, he waved his hand with a flourish as he peeked up at me from under his dark eyelashes. My stomach dipped, which I chose to ignore. "The next trope awaits you, my lady." An ornate blue door appeared directly in front of me.

I pursed my lips. "You said I got to pick the next trope and I didn't utter a word about what I wanted."

Xander's lips curled up into a smirk as he straightened. "You didn't have to. I know you, Zoe, and I know what you want."

"I swear to God, Xander, if the next one ends up a repeat of this debacle, then we're going to have a problem. The kind that might just give you a matching scar in your other eyebrow."

He frowned. "Stop with the violent threats. You're supposed to be a mature adult."

"It needed to be said." Yeah, I was acting immature, but it was difficult not to under the circumstances. I would try to do better. Or not, depending on what lay ahead of me.

"Just go through the door and you'll find a trope more your speed. I promise."

Dubious, I forced myself to reach for the handle. "Fine. Might as well." Turning the doorknob, I flung the door open and stepped through. *I'm going to regret this, I know it.*

Chapter 7

Blue grass, a lavender sky, and foliage every color in the rainbow. Nope, there was nothing familiar about the new world I'd stepped into. Trees had faces, and a nearby patch of flowers appeared particularly murderous. As in, they had blades for petals and glowing red eyes.

As for myself, my body felt and looked the same from what I could tell. My hair remained blonde with blue streaks and was curled, flowing freely over my shoulders. The sheet I'd been wrapped in was replaced by soft jeans, a faded blue T-shirt, and beat-up tennis shoes. Clearly, I was in a trope where I was the human in a foreign land since I hadn't grown a tail or anything else odd. Much to my delight, I was guessing I was currently in Fantasy Life's version of a fae world.

A part of me was bitter that Xander had been right, interacting with fae in a fantasy romance trope would definitely be my jam. I would have preferred to be one of the natives though, because how cool would it be to play at being a fae queen with elemental powers? But I would wait to judge until something of interest happened. At any rate, I was sure to enjoy the fantasy aspect better than the historical I'd just come from. Besides, maybe the same conditions that helped provide things such as scent from my memories would limit what I could change about my appearance. Again, I didn't have that particular information, but I made a mental note to ask Xander about it later. Speaking of...

"Xander!" I yelled, spinning in a small circle. "I know you didn't suddenly decide to stop monitoring me so closely. How about a bit more instruction with this one? Because," I waved my hands in the direction of the murder flowers, "there seem to be some hostile natives."

Could I feel true pain in Fantasy Life? I did have a pretty realistic puke session already which pointed at yes. That was minor in comparison to the big question though. Could I die like in a video game? What would those things mean for me in reality? Would a wound in VR translate to a wound on my actual body? The mind is a powerful thing indeed, but I didn't know how powerful in this case.

"Xander! Are we seriously going to do this again?"

"What are you doing here, human?" a raspy, baritone voice demanded.

Whipping my head around, I witnessed a tall male clad

in all leather emerging from the woods, his full hood casting his face in shadows.

My gaze zeroed in on the exposed skin of his right hand as it came to rest on the hilt of his sword, the silver tinge to his flesh unmistakable. I swallowed hard, and my heart set off at a gallop.

This is it! This is as close to a real live fae as I'm ever going to get! It was almost embarrassing how excited I was. Almost. After all, this character, whoever he was, would be AI just like Lachlan. Sort of alive, but not exactly. It wasn't an actual fae. Although, I wasn't sure I gave two shits anymore. *Because ... seriously ... hot fae about to be revealed.*

"I spoke to you, human. If you do not wish for me to slit your throat from ear to ear—"

Without a second thought, I let loose a high-pitched squeal, and then rushed him. He took a few unsteady steps back as I approached, obviously startled by my reaction when he'd been in the middle of a brutal death threat. I wasn't to be deterred. Flinging my arms around him, I lifted myself up and wrapped my legs around his middle.

"If you're listening, Xander, which I know you're here somewhere, I better not get a fade to grey situation again."

Yep, I'd gone full fae fangirl. All my lady parts declaring their approval. Apparently, playing God with AI, and the rest of my pesky moral issues went out the window when faced with a male fae warrior, and I hadn't even seen his face yet. I sniggered to myself. Like his face would even matter to me at this point. *Huh. Guess I can be shallow.* Not that I cared about that part at the moment either. *Call me whatever you want, I will be getting freaky with this fae.*

"G-Get off m-me, human," the fae sputtered, his hood falling back.

I heaved a sigh of satisfaction. Everything about him was complete and utter perfection. From his long, black hair to his ice-blue eyes, and everything in between. I couldn't have designed a better specimen of a fae warrior myself. Squealing again, I tightened my grip on him. "You are the best thing to ever happen to me."

"The human has lost its mind." Xander's familiar voice filtered into my ears, causing me to scrunch up my nose. He obviously decided playing a character in this trope as well was a good idea. I didn't need him anymore, though, since I had my fae warrior to fawn over.

"Don't just stand there, get it off of me."

"Not sure I should. You seem to be keeping it calm."

The fae warrior tugged at my hair in an effort to dislodge me. I let loose a moan. I was pretty sure I was going to spontaneously combust from how turned on I was. In any other circumstance, I would have been humiliated to let Xander witness me in such a state, but again ... fae warrior.

"I think it wants to have sex with me." The fae warrior's tone was a mix of disgust and curiosity.

Lifting my head, our noses touching as I stared into his wide eyes, I nodded vigorously. "Yes, please. I would very much like to have sex with you. We should go do that immediately. Or right here. I won't be particular about the where, just as long as it happens."

"Thirsty much?" Xander grumbled.

"Is that its problem? It's delirious from dehydration?" the fae warrior asked, his brows drawn together as he studied me.

"I'm thirsty for you." I grinned, probably appearing a bit demented.

I didn't care how ridiculous I was being. This fae warrior from my dreams was created for me. And damn straight I wasn't going to let things like morals and questions get in the way like I had with Lachlan. It was kind of like when I nitpicked every small detail when reading a book I wasn't into. But give me a book that sucks me fully into the world and I'm willing to overlook a lot. *And I'm about to overlook everything for this fae, no questions asked.*

"I think we should bring her along, Caz. She'll at least make our journey interesting."

"Absolutely not. Her insanity could be contagious. Is that what's happening here?" Caz pawed at me again as if I was a piece of lint he wished to brush off.

It only made me cling to him tighter. If any of it was actually real, I would have already dropped dead from the rejection, but I knew this trope and he was supposed to hate me and my human ways … at first. Then he would be drawn to me like he'd never been drawn to anyone before, and I would die from happiness instead of mortification. Or a shit load of orgasms. Whichever came first.

"Insanity isn't contagious, and she wields no magic."

"Then explain to me what's going on, Mattius?" Caz demanded.

Xander chuckled. "What's going on? I don't understand what you mean."

"I find myself not wishing to kill this pathetic human. I don't like her, but I also don't wish to see her dead. Something unnatural is afoot."

"There's nothing unnatural about what's going to happen between us." I was aware I sounded somewhat like a douche guy at a bar throwing out desperate one-liners. But again, I didn't care ... fae warrior.

Xander grunted. "Do what you wish with her, Caz. Bring her. Or not. But either way, we must continue on soon."

Craning my neck to get a good look at Xander in his Mattius persona, I froze, nearly choking on my own saliva. *Dear Lord, have mercy on me and don't let me spontaneously burst into flames.* Unlike when he'd donned the Scottish Adam skinsuit, he kept his general appearance, while transforming into a fae warrior himself. His long, black hair was braided to keep it off his finely tipped, pointed ears. Also encased in leather from head-to-toe like Caz, his lithe muscles were showcased to perfection.

Ugh. Perfection. I'm certainly using that word a ton in this trope. But eh. This isn't about choosing the right language in my head to describe what I see but rather about enjoying the experience. Plus, who will know?

Xander's dark eyes glittered. "Like what you see?"

"Wh-What?" I spluttered.

He had every right to play dress-up if that's what he desired, but I drew the line at him attempting to flirt with me while dressed like such a tasty morsel. Especially since my entire body clenched as it screamed at me to climb him like a tree as well. *Two fae warriors for the price of one. Oh, no, no, no, no, no. I did not just think that with Xander being one of the two.*

Deciding he was messing with me by way of making me feel uncomfortable, I smirked right back at him, determined to not let him win. "Well," I purred, "maybe a little threesome is what this situation needs."

Xander scowled. "You're right, Caz. The human has lost its mind." His jaw muscles rippled as he ground his teeth together. "Still think we should bring her along though. Like I said, it'll keep things interesting."

Caz finally managed to dislodge me, and I landed on my ass, arms and legs akimbo.

"You can manage her then." He sniffed, dusting off his immaculate leather as if I sullied it with my human cooties. He then strode off, head held high.

Xander crouched down next to me, his expression pinched. "I told you this trope would be more your style."

Reaching up, I sifted my fingers through his silky locks, tugging lightly when they snagged on one of his braids. "You might want to think about making this your real-world look because I must say ..." I started out wanting to lighten the mood with a few teasing remarks, but suddenly the air between us was thick with undefinable emotions as our gazes clashed.

He swallowed hard, his Adam's apple dancing up and down in his throat. "You have a thing for fae, huh? I mean, I knew it in theory, but to see it in action is something else."

"I think the seeing it in action is the whole point. Fae don't exist, so I never thought I'd have a close encounter of the romance trope kind with one."

"Huh." His gaze pulled away from mine to dance over my features, making me squirm a bit. "Did you ever consider the possibility that this is why your relationships haven't worked out in the past?"

My stomach twisted into a knot, and heat suffused my cheeks. "What are you trying to say, Xander?"

He shrugged. "I don't know. Maybe real men aren't good enough for you because your expectations are set too high."

My nostrils flared as I sucked in an unsteady breath. "Oh, no, you didn't. You did not just imply that because I'm a romance author and into romance in general, I set unrealistic standards for the men in my life."

"I didn't exactly imply. But what I mean is that I simply think—"

"Stop thinking, Xander. I'm serious." Jumping to my feet, I glared down at him. "That's some misogynist shit right there. Sure, most couples in romance novels are exceptionally attractive, because it's fantasy, and why not? But that's not the point, and it's not why people flock to them in droves. Let me ask you this: Is it wrong to ask to be desired fully and completely? Is it wrong to ask to be treated with respect? Is it wrong to want to feel as if my man loves me above all else, like I'm the most important thing in his world? I just want to feel wanted, loved, and to be treated like the queen all women deserve to be treated like. And yeah, it's about exploring our sexuality, too. But spoiler alert, we always get ours in the end in romance. It's about being the focus of love and desire, being cherished. I want Caz because I know he's going to be all about me sexually, therefore making me feel exceptionally special, and he's wrapped up in a pretty package to boot."

I paused to suck in a breath before continuing, worried I was rambling and losing sight of my original point. Bringing up Caz and shining a spotlight on my shallowness wasn't going to help anything, and I wasn't sure why I'd done it. "It's a bit more complicated than that, but yeah, if a man thinks those expectations are too high, then the fault lies with him."

Xander raised his eyebrows. "Ah, but you throwing yourself at Caz has to do with only one thing. You don't care about his personality."

Damn it. I knew I shot myself in the foot when I brought him into this. "He's not real and he doesn't have a real personality. He's only here for the sexual exploration part I mentioned. Sex with fae. My fetishes are fine, whatever they are. Don't fetish shame me or anyone else." *Okay, I have lost control of this now, and I'm just spouting nonsense.*

I pinched the bridge of my nose, averting my gaze as I scrambled to regain my metaphorical footing. "Besides, why is it okay to use sex to sell everything except love? The romance genre is a business, too." *There. That should help my argument. I think. I'm not sure if we're talking about book tropes or my love life anymore. Both? Neither? Why do I keep letting Xander fluster me to the point where my brain shuts down?*

Xander ignored my response. "Also, romance includes more than just straight couples, therefore playing the sexist card is—"

"It doesn't matter the sex or orientation. Anyone who reads romance wants those things from their partner. And if their partner thinks it's too much, then it's misogynistic values and the damn patriarchy ingrained it into everything we—"

Standing, he raised his hands to ward me off. "Okay, I get it. You need to calm down."

"And then you go and say that. Yes, Xander, I can simply calm down now because you told me to. Let me give you a word of advice … if you want a sure-fire way to anger a woman, to have her fly off the handle, tell her to calm down."

He sighed dramatically, and combined with his put-upon expression, he effectively expelled any attraction I had for him, even dressed as a drop-dead gorgeous fae. *See, not that shallow after all.*

"I don't want to fight with you, Zoe." His dark eyes bored into mine, and I was ensnared once again.

Then again, my shallowness status is yet to be determined because damn he is hot.

I crossed my arms over my chest, ignoring the warmth blooming low in my belly. "Then don't."

"I'm not." He crossed his arms to mirror my stance. "You're the one being defensive. If I'm wrong, then I'm wrong. No need to—"

"I knew you didn't agree with my views about the romance genre and feminism." I was letting him get to me; letting his comments trigger self-doubt in myself. I'd gone as far as to question my motives and call myself shallow for having sexual desire. We were literally in a fantasy world. I was supposed to be shallow under the circumstances. Plus, he wasn't wrong about me being touchy on the subject at hand. After dealing with criticism from haters for so long, I was quick to jump into attack mode. It was self-preservation for someone like me who used to be a doormat. Also, Xander wasn't a hater, he was merely an idiot. And an asshat. An insanely hot, idiot asshat.

Confusion knitted his brows together. "I don't even know what you're talking about anymore. You can't possibly—"

"What is taking so long?" Caz strode our way, his gaze swinging between the two of us. "What could you possibly have to talk about with this human?"

"Nothing," I snapped. "We have nothing to talk about because Mattius is an idiot asshat. And," I slashed my hand through the air, "the human has a name … it's Zoe. Use it."

Plastering a lecherous grin on my face, I swaggered closer to him. "Preferably when you're naked and you can't contain it from all the pleasure I give you."

"Don't objectify him," Xander grated.

I rolled my eyes. The whole purpose for Caz's existence was to be objectified, and I refused to let myself be shamed for desiring him. So, unless Xander wanted to pull me out of Fantasy Life he was going to have to shut the hell up.

Curiosity played across Caz's features, which he quickly hid behind a mask of disdain. "Do not speak of such acts involving me with a human. It's—"

"Going to happen. You might as well accept it." With a flip of my hair, I pushed past him, heading in the direction he'd just come from.

"I don't think it's wise to bring an insane human with us. It could endanger our lives," Caz stated loudly, obviously wanting me to hear.

"Oh, yes, it's definitely unwise," Xander replied. "But let's do it anyhow."

"I will not bed her," Caz hissed.

"Huh. I don't remember saying anything about that." I could hear the bemusement in Xander's voice.

"I want to make sure you're clear on the matter."

"Oh, I'm clear."

I chuckled under my breath. Poor Caz, he had no clue about his programming. He was already feeling the pull, much like every romance hero in the history of romance heroes. The biggest difference being the fact that he wasn't made of only paper and ink. He was alive. Sort of.

My heart fluttered in my chest, pushing doubt through my system. *If he's alive, shouldn't he get a choice? Just because you're attracted to him doesn't mean you have the right to take what you want from him. It wouldn't be like I would force myself on him, and the only reason I'm being so demonstrative is because I know he will eventually want me back. But does that make it okay?*

I didn't have the answers to my questions. Quite possibly nobody else did either. Yet, as a woman, I couldn't help feeling empathetic toward his plight. There was a time when we'd had no civil rights to speak of, and no way to vote to change that either. Women's lives were largely decided by the men in their lives, the lucky ones having males who cared and loved them. Choices, no matter their social and financial status, were limited. In a sense, wasn't that what Xander was doing to his AI?

Or maybe I was overthinking all of it, and making a mountain out of a molehill? *Ugh.* Being a trailblazer with these types of things meant not yet having all the information needed to make important decisions. I would have to discuss a lot with Xander when I got out of Fantasy Life. All I knew was that I had to do my best to stand staunchly against anything morally icky, even if I had to be the fun police.

"The human is going the wrong way," Caz said, his deep voice monotone.

"Hey, human!" Xander called, playing along. "Maybe

you should try following us since we know where we're going!"

Doing an about-face, I shuffled after the two fae warriors, hating how I was probably about to ruin my fun ... again.

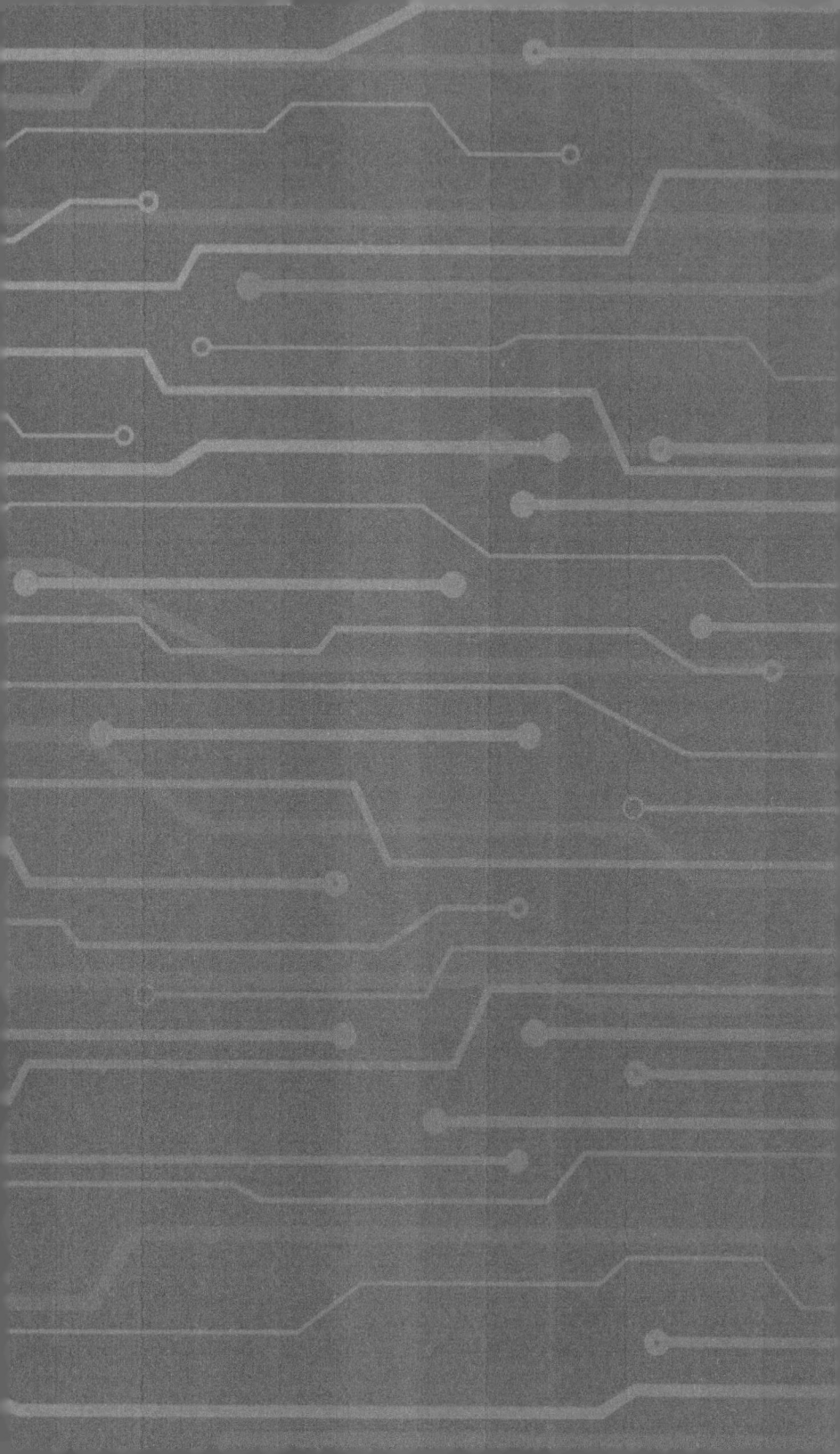

Chapter 8

A blue-tinged fire blazed in the dark, the three of us huddled around it. We walked for what seemed like miles, another bonus of VR being that I was only slightly tired. I was still in awe about not needing to eat, drink, or use that bathroom, although I continued to be dubious about what that meant for my body in the real world.

Caz stood abruptly. "I must gather some supplies for our journey tomorrow."

"But it's dark out there," I said automatically.

"Fae have talents beyond human comprehension. However, I will not waste my time explaining why the dark won't be a problem for me."

"Yeah, okay," I muttered.

Caz stared at me for a few moments as if he expected more of a protest. When I didn't offer him any other commentary, he glided into the woods silently.

"Not even an innuendo about his talents? I'm disappointed in you, Zoe."

Cupping my face, I propped my elbows up on my knees. "I don't think I'm the best one to be testing out these romance tropes for you, or any part of Fantasy Life for that matter." I followed up with a long, dramatic sigh.

I stared into the fire, letting the flames dance and twist to form images I couldn't quite decipher.

"Zoe—" Xander started, but I cut him off.

"I don't know anything anymore."

"About Fantasy Life?"

"Yes, but not just that. Everything. I don't know anything anymore."

Xander scooted closer to me, his gaze riveted by the fire as well. "What are you talking about? You're Zoe Woods. I've never known anyone to be so completely sure of who they are."

"Maybe that used to be true, but not anymore. The person I once was … I'm not her anymore. And I don't know how to become her again. Or if I even want to."

"Perhaps you simply forgot how to be her, and you just need to be reminded."

I grunted in response. In theory, what he said made sense, but it was more than just being reminded of who I was. I was desperately seeking some undefinable thing. Or I was just desperate. The fact that I threw myself at Caz, fae warrior or not, well … it bothered me. Not because I'd done it. No, that wasn't the issue. It felt like it had to do with Xander somehow. Which was ridiculous since he was nothing more than my little brother's punk-ass friend. And yet the truth was in my actions. It was as if I was attempting to prove something to Xander, although what I wasn't sure. And then I—

Stop. Xander doesn't matter. His opinions, his presence, nothing about him matters. At least not to you in any way beyond what any human being matters.

"Are you still mad at me for what I said before?" Xander's voice broke the silence, startling me from my self-reflection session. "Because I've been thinking about how I could explain myself ..."

He cleared his throat. "I didn't mean to blame you for your failed marriages, I honestly don't know what happened with them. Adam didn't go into specifics. It's just ..."

He clicked his tongue. "I don't understand how any heterosexual male who had the chance to be with you would be the one to walk away. It doesn't make sense to me that they wouldn't do everything in their power to give you everything you want. Therefore, the only explanation I could come up with was you having unrealistic expectations."

Silence settled between us again, my heart doing a tap dance against my eardrums. I swallowed several times around the lump in my throat, failing to dislodge it. To have someone like Xander—someone who'd seen me at my worst—say that I deserved the kind of love I wanted, craved ... It churned up emotions I had no definitions for. Emotions that needed to be buried deep and locked away.

"Say something, Zoe. Please."

"Maybe the real world isn't enough for me." I nibbled my lower lip as I considered my next words. "I've built my life around fantasy. Not just what I read or what I write, but how I imagine things should be. The things I want out of life ... it's possible I want more than the world has to offer. Maybe I do expect too much in my relationships. Like I said, I don't know anything anymore though."

"The things you said before, the list of what you want in a relationship, none of those are unreasonable. They should be expected. Don't let my asinine comments get to you."

I snorted. "As if they could." I would never admit to him that they had indeed gotten to me. It might make him think he had some kind of influence or power over me, which he most definitely didn't. The whole thing was a fluke because of how low I was emotionally. Practically anyone off the street could have gotten to me in my current state. No need to give Xander the wrong idea.

"Right. What was I thinking?" He rose quickly, and shuffled off into the forest, leaving me alone.

"What was that about?" I grumbled. I was the one having an existential crisis, not him.

Caz appeared directly in front of me, blocking my view of the fire. Gasping, I fell backwards. Before my head hit the ground, Caz was crouched beside me, lifting me up.

"Careful, human. If you are to die it will be by my blade. Not because of your clumsiness."

I glared at him. My interaction with Xander had put me in an even darker mood since Caz was annoying me now as well. "That was hardly clumsiness. You startled me."

"Whatever you say, human."

"Where are we going anyways? Neither you nor Xa— Mattius said."

Caz waved his hand, stoking the fire with his magic. "It does not matter. To you."

I opened my mouth to deliver a snarky reply but suddenly lacked the motivation. Instead, I turned my focus back on the flames as they swirled higher into the night.

A dark dot undulated within the churning blue, growing larger with each passing moment. Leaning forward, I swiveled my head back and forth as I studied it. *Could it be a glitch of some sort?*

"What do you find so interesting in the fire, human?"

"My name is Zoe," I muttered.

"Human," Caz said, doubling down on stupid. "I asked you a question, which I expect an answer to."

Hmm ... at least in this trope the language choices are a bit better. Caz sounds how I would expect him to sound. Although I haven't been paying close enough attention to whether or not he's been consistent. It goes back to me probably being too nit-picky in the Scottish historical trope.

The black dot doubled in size. "What is it? A glitch?"

Caz followed my gaze with his. "What is what, human?

I see nothing but fire before us. Is it the color? I know you may not have seen blue flames before, but—"

I pointed. "No, that black, blobby thing. You don't see it?"

The dot grew again, causing dread to spike through my system. I knew it was illogical, especially because none of what I was seeing was real, but it's impossible to rationalize with irrational fears. It simply doesn't work.

"Zoe, what's wrong?" Xander dashed from the nearest line of trees, his face etched with worry.

"You're calling the human by its name?" Caz sneered. "I thought better of you than to adopt a pet so easily."

Ignoring Caz, Xander knelt beside me, peering into the fire much like Caz just had. "What do you see?"

My heart pulsed within my temples, pain spiking through my skull. "Something's wrong. I just …" My hands fluttered, unsure of what to do. "I don't feel right."

Xander grabbed me by the shoulders, forcing my gaze on him. "You're fine. Whatever you're experiencing is all in your mind."

I expelled a shuddery breath. "Yeah, and so are panic attacks technically." I wasn't about to regal him with how many times I'd sent myself to the hospital because I was convinced I was dying, the whole ordeal turning out to be nothing more than a panic attack. I didn't even want to think about what would happen if I had a panic attack inside of Fantasy Life. I might die from stroking out or something. *Oh, God!*

"Okay, okay. You need to calm down. Your pulse is

too fast." My eyes widened, and he grimaced. "That wasn't meant to scare you. Nothing bad will happen, aside from you might make yourself pass out. You're not dying, Zoe."

"Dying?" I squeaked. "I didn't ask if I was dying. But now I think I might be."

Bright light exploded, washing out everything. Then a flash of Jared, ex-husband number two, standing on the front porch of my house. *"What are you doing?"* My scream echoed, dizziness assaulting me.

"Zoe! Please! Focus! Stay with me!"

I blinked Xander's fae façade back into view, panting hard. "What? I mean …" Glancing over his head, I exhaled some of the tension when I realized the black void was gone. "A glitch? Is that what it was?"

"What does she mean by glitch?" Caz interjected himself into our conversation. "And why does she seem to think you have all the answers, Mattias?" He scowled down at us, confusion and suspicion warring. "Have you met this particular human before?"

His focus remaining on me, Xander stood. "Not this one. But I've seen a human have a panic attack before."

"When?" Caz barked. "When could you have possibly seen a human have a panic attack before?"

"You don't know everything about me, Caz. I have a right to secrets. Just as you do."

Caz's nostrils flared, anger rolling off him in palpable waves. "I will speak to you in private. Away from the human."

Xander glanced at me, and I gave him a brittle smile. "Go ahead. Whatever that was seems to have passed."

"He does not need your permission, human," Caz growled, this voice low and guttural.

"Whatever."

Caz opened his mouth to respond, his body trembling with anger, but Xander grabbed him by the arm, tugging him back toward the line of trees at the edge of the clearing.

"No," Caz grunted. "The human needs to learn some respect."

"Let's speak first, and then if you don't like what I have to say we can discuss punishing her." Xander shot me a wink.

My throat dried up. *Punishment? From the sexy fae warrior? Yes, please.* Certainly, that was why Xander gave me the wink, right? He was letting me know he was going to get the plot of this trope back on course. Then again, he'd mislead me with Lachlan, letting me get my expectations up, merely to have them crushed in the end.

Thinking about having some spicy time with Caz brought me right back to the beginning of my moral dilemma. *Great.* And what would Xander be doing if I decided to go ahead with all the amazing fae sex? Would he monitor it like I was a science experiment, or would I get a bit of privacy, at least for the actual act?

Xander and Caz eased back closer to the fire, Xander warily observing both of us. I held my breath in anticipation of the verdict.

Caz's ice eyes locked with mine. "Mattius has informed me of the debt he owes your family line. Therefore, I will not punish you for your disrespect. This time."

"Debt?"

Xander nodded in encouragement.

"Oooh, right. The saving of his life and stuff."

Biting back a laugh, Xander turned away. I shot the back of his head a death glare. He reached up a hand and rubbed it through his hair as if he could feel my annoyance boring into him.

Caz positioned himself on my left, openly appraising me. "How old are you ... Zoe?"

Whatever bullshit story Xander had sold Caz had done the trick. It made me wonder if every person to enter Fantasy Life was going to need a guide or if it was because we were still in the testing phase. I couldn't see Xander doing it himself, and it depended on a lot of other factors, such as—

"I asked you a question."

"What?"

Caz huffed out a long breath and crossed his arms over his chest. "I asked how old you are?"

"Oh, I'm forty."

"Isn't that old for a human?"

Really with the age thing again? Closing my eyes, I counted to ten in an effort to calm myself. In trope number one I'd questioned whether I'd subconsciously cut my character's age in half since I knew I had internalized issues about the subject I still needed to work on. This time, I had proof positive that the age-shaming was not on me.

Xander was going to get some notes when we were done, some serious notes with lots of exclamation points, because people enjoyed romance for escapism and to feel good about themselves, not to be reminded of how shitty the real world is where sexism and ageism were alive and thriving.

"Although," Caz continued before I could read him the riot act, "you don't look old at all. In fact," he inched closer to me, his gaze riveted to my features, "you are quite attractive for a human, no matter your age."

"Mmm hmm." Pursing my lips, I turned my attention to Xander. "I think I need to have a little chat with our dear friend Mattius."

Surprise slackened Caz's mouth. Guess he wasn't programmed to expect any kind of rejection or slight from a human when he paid them a compliment.

Xander grimaced, something he was doing an awful lot around me lately. I expected him to have a bit more control over his expressions in VR, but what did I know? Which again, for the hundredth time, was precisely the point.

"I don't think—"

I pointed an angry finger at Xander, silencing him. "We need to talk." I stalked over to the line of trees, a popular place for discussions apparently, and waited as Xander shuffled over, his head bowed, hand on the back of his neck.

As soon as he was close enough, I poked him in the chest. "I know I said it before, and I know I agreed and signed a contract and all of that bullshit, and I know I'm meant to be testing all of this so if I have problems with certain things that's the point of me being here so I can help you make things better, but ..."

I heaved a huge sigh. "First I was slut-shamed, and now I get to hear about me being old and looking good for my age? Who the hell did you have working on these programs? I mean, were they all white males born in the fifties?" I shook my head. "Maybe there's no point in going any further with these tests right now. I could always come back after you make things better. Start fresh with—"

Xander grabbed my hand, flinging it away from his chest. "I know the programs have some content issues, but the person we originally had overseeing the kind of thing you're talking about didn't finish the job. It's another reason why you're here. And who do you think you're talking to? Once you leave, you're not coming back. Don't lie to me."

"Don't you dare give me that face, Xander," I hissed. His expression was a mixture of hurt and anger. Like I was letting him down personally, betraying him in some way. My gut twisted, nausea roiling.

His gaze darted to his feet, and his long hair fell forward, serving as a curtain between us. "When did you start giving up so easily? The Zoe I know isn't a quitter."

The tips of my ears heated. He was right, I didn't used

to throw in the towel so early in the game. I'd been determined once. Where had that all gone? I sighed. "Do you ever think about the fact that it feels like we try on all these different characters as a kid, to see what sticks, and then one day when we're an adult we're expected to pick one personality. What if we picked the wrong one? Or what if none of us know who we really are? Doesn't it seem like it's all an act sometimes, Xander? And I'm too exhausted to play the part anymore."

He lifted his head, his eyes sparking with some unknown emotion. "I get that you're exhausted. We've all been there. And I've seen you have more than one existential crisis over the years, especially when you were a teenager. But, Zoe," he reached out, his hand stopping short of touching my cheek, "it's going to be okay. You'll figure it all out just like you always do."

My lower lip trembled, and my eyes burned. I hated being vulnerable in front of anyone, let alone Xander. Sure, he was being nice to me now because he wasn't a 'kick someone when they're down' type of person, but if, and when, I wasn't falling apart, this would all come back to bite me on the ass. I could hear it now *"Oh, hey, Zoe, remember that time you started babbling about everything being an act and you don't even know who you are? Yeah, me too. It kind of reminded me of that time you came home high when I was staying over with Adam, and you were super paranoid and freaked out. Ha, ha. And you told me you thought I was pretty. Yep, that was hilarious."*

"This whole thing is ridiculous. Fantasy Life, these

tropes, nothing makes sense. And not much is happening either. If this was a novel I'd be bored out of my mind by now."

Xander tapped at the scar in his eyebrow. "Is that what it is? You're bored? I thought going on an adventure with two fae warriors would be—"

"Adventure?" I scoffed. "What adventure? Since I've gotten here, I threw myself at a thus far unreceptive fae, and walked for a bit in the woods." I snapped my fingers. "And, oh yeah, also sat by a fire some, and got reminded that I'm old as fuck now … for a human. Good times, Xander. Really good times."

"This is the beginning of the adventure. Things need to ramp up."

I nibbled on the inside of my cheek, trying not to scowl yet again. "If that's the case it needs to ramp up fast."

"I can't do anything about getting the sex part to ramp up any faster because that's dependent on you and Caz." When I glared, Xander raised his arms in defense. "You're the one who doesn't want to play God with the AI, which means you have to work within the parameters of the program."

"That was the case anyways."

He waggled his eyebrows, and a small smile twisted his lips. "Maybe or maybe not. Guess you'll never know how much I'm able to adjust things on the fly."

"Hey!" I shoved at him. "If you're able to adjust things like that then—"

"Ah-ah-ah. Nope. You can't seem to make up your

mind with some of your stances, so I need to do what I think is best. One of those things is not telling you how much power I have in here while I'm interacting as one of the characters."

Resisting the urge to pout, I crossed my arms over my chest. "Not fair."

He shrugged. "Not much is."

"But what if—"

"I think it's time to get this party started since you're bored." He grinned, his dimple popping out.

My stomach dropped into my feet. *Oh, shit, what have I done now?*

Chapter 9

"**T**hat was quite the long conversation the two of you had." Caz raised his perfectly shaped eyebrows. "What was the topic?"

I hadn't considered what Caz might think of Xander and me while we were off having our little pow-wow a few feet away from him. I took it for granted that I could have such moments without any repercussions. After all, I was taking my lead from none other than Xander.

"Don't worry," Xander dropped his voice so I could barely hear it. "He's programmed to trust my character." Smiling impishly, he waved his hand at Caz. "Boring human nonsense. As you already know, I'm obliged to care for this particular human because of—"

"The debt you owe. As you've already explained." Caz uncoiled himself to his full height. "But I'm not sure I believe any of it." He narrowed his eyes at me, and then slid his skeptical gaze over to Xander. "I'm beginning to think you merely have a soft spot for her because you have always cared for wounded animals and you're making excuses as to why we need to help her."

Xander scowled. "That's not the case at all."

Poking at his foot with mine, I snagged his gaze, shooting him an ocular message, hoping he would understand. *"Thought he was programmed to trust you?"*

He shrugged in response, as if to say, *"He doesn't not trust me as in, he thinks I'm a traitor. He's still working within his program. No worries."*

I snorted. What I couldn't figure out, beyond all the inconsistencies in and around my foray into Fantasy Life, was how the hell I let myself get talked into any of it by Xander. Yes, it would be potentially helpful to me by way of getting my writer's mojo back, but again, it was Xander. He had matured in a lot of ways, but beneath it all lurked the same mischievous nature from his youth. I still wasn't one hundred percent sure he wasn't messing with me. He had two speeds around me when he was a teenager—flirt with Zoe or torture Zoe. Therefore, I couldn't let him continue to run the show. I needed to take back as much control as I could to protect myself.

Shoving around Xander, I hurried to Caz's side, grinning up at him. His brow furrowed when I slid my hand along his arm, enjoying the feel of his muscles bunching under the smooth leather. "I was trying to persuade your dear friend into revealing some tips on how I could seduce you quicker."

"Tips? On how to seduce me? Quicker? And how would Mattius know such information?"

Batting my eyelashes, I rose onto my tiptoes. "He's with you all the time, isn't he? He's one of your closest friends, isn't he? How could he not know such things?"

Muscles rippled along Caz's jaw. "It has been quite a while since I have sought out the company of a woman."

Internally I sighed. Whoever created Caz was on the money with him. The whole outwardly gruff fae warrior with a heart of gold ... yes, please. And of course, that heart would have room for no one, consumed with the need for revenge, duty, or honor, until the heroine came along and slipped past his defenses. In this case, I was the lucky heroine. Which once again brought me full circle back to my moral dilemma. I'd never been as indecisive in my entire life, I swear. It was because I had entered uncharted territory with the AI in Fantasy Life. There were no precedents to help guide me. Well, beyond the limited amount of sci-fi books and shows I'd consumed over the years.

Xander thought nothing of using the AIs like playthings and was encouraging me to do the same. But it wasn't that simple. Xander and his team had created Caz and others like him, therefore even though they knew what the AI was because they'd been born out of programming, there had to be a sense of disconnect. I didn't know the rest of the workers at Fantasy Life, but I knew Xander wasn't a sociopath. He wouldn't tell me to not worry about something if he truly believed I could be causing harm to something with emotional intelligence.

It's all up to me. I must be the one to figure out what's the best way to handle the AI in the romance tropes. At least as far as where I let things go. It came down to one question: To have sex or not have sex in Fantasy Life?

"Did you hear that?" Xander said, drawing me from my inner musings.

Caz shirked out from under my touch, producing a long, thin blade from nowhere. "What is it?"

"Not sure. But the forest is suddenly silent. That is never a good sign." Xander produced a sword of his own.

My heart punched its way into my stomach. The two of them together, dressed in head-to-toe leather, swords at the ready, long hair flowing … *I may just spontaneously combust. I wonder if I can stroke out from overstimulation?*

God, maybe Xander was right. Maybe my expectations for real-world men are too high in certain aspects, like them being fae. And if they weren't before, this is going to be impossible to live up to. I am so screwed. No amount of normal role-playing is ever going to do it for me again. Unless … An image of Xander dressed in his fae costume in my bedroom danced across my brain. *What? No! Bad brain! Very, very bad brain! You can't let yourself think that way about Xander even for a second. He is off-limits for so many reasons. So many. The number one reason being: He is Xander.*

"Stay here," Caz commanded.

By the way he and Xander were acting as a team, I was guessing the order was aimed in my direction. And that was a big nope from me. "I'm not anyone's pet, so I'm not obeying *stay here.*"

Caz scowled at me while speaking to Xander, "I told you she would be trouble."

Xander's eyes glinted as he bit back a smile. "I never said she wouldn't be."

I shuffled forward, pretending to be interested in whatever was going on in the woods. The truth was, I knew Xander had drummed up some kind of peril to heighten the tension in this trope, but when it came down to it, the threat wasn't real. I supposed it could be exhilarating though, sort of like riding a roller coaster. Although technically, the ride could break, and I could be thrown from it. The same could be said for the mental adventure I was involved in. Something could go wrong, and I could end up as a vegetable. Basically, it was a whole bunch of *could happens* with no guarantees one way or another. Not that Xander had expressed the need to be worried, but it wasn't necessary to since I was anxious by nature. It didn't take much for my imagination to drop me into a plethora of worst-case scenarios.

My arms and legs tingled, my heart rattling around in my chest, threatening to break free as I sprinted after Caz and Xander's retreating forms. I was not going to risk bodily harm in VR translating to the same injuries appearing on my body in real life.

Skittering to a stop, I nearly ran into Xander's back. "What is it? What's in there?" Peeking around him, I stared intently into the rainbow-colored forest before us. It would be difficult to spot anything out of the ordinary under the circumstances since to me everything was out of the ordinary in fae world.

"Shhh," Caz hissed, gripping his weapon tighter. "You do not wish to draw attention to yourself."

Normally I would have had a snarky comment ready, but he did have a point. I shuffled a bit closer to Xander, placing my hands against him. He tensed, rolling his shoulder blades. Not caring if I was crowding him, I plastered myself to his back, my anxiety forcing me to seek comfort. Obviously, a part of me, deep down—extremely deep down—felt safer with Xander than with Caz. Which didn't make sense when I considered it. Caz was literally programmed to eventually fall for me and therefore he would keep me safe at all costs. Plus, since he thought the stakes were legit, he'd try harder as opposed to Xander who knew we were essentially playing a game.

Forcing myself away from Xander, I threw myself at Caz's back, wrapping my arms around his waist and pressing my cheek into the warm leather encasing him. Caz grunted in displeasure, and Xander side-eyed me, his lips forming a flat line. I shrugged at him, causing his nostrils to flare.

"I can't fight anything like this." Caz used his free hand to pry me loose, but as soon as my fingers were unlocked, I grabbed onto him again before he could move out of reach. He turned to glare at first me and then Xander.

A menacing screech rode the wind, causing all the hairs on my body to stand on end. With a shudder, I tightened my grip on Caz. It didn't matter if the monster wasn't real, neither were the terrors that kept me awake after watching a horror movie. Fear was fear, and I'd gone from laissez-faire about the whole issue to wanting to have a bit more say in whatever Xander had unleashed on us.

"Xan— Mattius, I changed my mind."

One side of his mouth curled up as he tapped his eyebrow with the scar.

Oh, no! That's never a good sign when he's dealing with me.

"I have no idea what you're talking about. Changed your mind about what?"

The screech had morphed into a chorus of beastly cries, their discordant song vibrating within my skull, causing me to grit my teeth. I fought the urge to let go of Caz to cover my ears. "You know exactly what I'm talking about. I was wrong. I'm not bored. Not bored at all," I gritted out.

The other side of Xander's mouth hitched up, his teeth glinting briefly. "Bored? How could a human be bored here? Yeah, I have no idea what you're talking about."

Using my distraction against me, Caz broke my hold once again and darted forward. Without so much as a backward glance, he sprinted into the woods, his sword held high.

Xander spared me a wink before following suit.

With no other option that I particularly liked, I ran after them, calling out, "I should at least get offered a weapon!"

"I told you to stay!" Caz's arm snagged me as I passed the first row of trees, yanking me against his hard body.

Inhaling a shaky breath, I let myself relax against him, quite enjoying his firm grip keeping me flush against the delicious lines of his body. I wiggled a bit, shameless in my pursuit of Caz once more.

And the pendulum swings ... yes, I'll sex up the hot fae warrior ... no, I will not abandon my morals to sex up the hot fae warrior ... and back and forth I go. Ugh. No wonder romance readers get frustrated with the whole will they or won't they plotline. I'm living it and I'm about to hurl myself off a cliff.

"Remain still." Caz's fingers dug into the soft flesh of my abdomen to stop my wiggling.

I bit my lip to keep from grinning. His body wasn't as opposed to my actions as Caz himself was, as evidenced by the growing hard-on poking into my ass.

"Where's Xa— Mattius?"

Caz dipped his head, his breath fanning across my cheek as he replied, "I would be with him if not for you charging in after us. If he gets himself killed because of you, then I will run you through with my sword."

"Oh, yes, run me through with your sword, please and thank you."

"Did you just ... did you turn my death threat into an innuendo?"

I nodded slowly, all anxiety about the monsters in the woods melted away by lust. "If you're so worried about Mattius, then why are you here with me anyways?"

"Mattius owes you a debt, therefore I owe you a debt."

"I'm not sure that's how debts work, but sure, okay. I have the perfect way for you to pay off his debt." I reached behind me, letting my hands roam along the sides of Caz's hips.

Suddenly, I found myself pressed against the base of the tree, Caz's face millimeters from mine. I sucked in a sharp breath, my entire world narrowing down to his blazing eyes. "You could never handle me, human."

"I thought you were going to call me by my actual name now?" Sticking my lower lip out, I pouted.

Caz's gaze darted to my lips briefly before ensnaring my gaze once more. "Zoe," he purred, "let me repeat, you would never be able to handle me."

Wow. It didn't take long for Caz's hatred for me to morph into lust. *Guess they're two sides of the same coin sometimes.* I wasn't complaining exactly, but some people might prefer more of a slow burn, which in my opinion would be abundantly more realistic. Then again, how realistic can fantasy be? I was beginning to think that the Fantasy Life romance tropes were going to be heavily dependent on man—or woman—candy, with noticeably weak plots. If that was the case, then I wasn't sure why I was the one chosen by Xander to help with the testing. He would have been better off with a sensitivity reader or someone of that ilk. The notes I would offer for changes would be more novel-oriented, and this, all of what I'd experienced so far, wasn't quite romance on the whole, but a chance to have fun with characters from a romance. Or maybe I was flustered because of—

Hold on there, Zoe. Snap out of it. Time to stop overanalyzing this for now. There will be plenty of time for that later. This is when you play with the hot fae warrior in front of you because you'll never get another opportunity like ... ever.

I slid my hand down the front of Caz's pants, cupping his cock. "I think I could handle you just fine." Lifting onto my tiptoes, I skimmed my lips against his. "And if you don't believe me then I think you should take me up on the challenge."

A low growl rumbled in the back of his throat. "If I break you, then what will Mattius say?"

I smirked. "What will he say if I break you instead?"

Okay, not the witty batter I had hoped for in a situation like this, but my lady parts did not care one iota. Nope, Caz could be making random grunting sounds and I'd be on board with getting naked with him. It seemed as if I'd always been too harsh on the heroines in the books I read and criticized. Real life, or even virtual reality as in this case, didn't play out the way a perfectly choreographed novel or screenplay did.

"Are you kidding me with this right now?" Xander's annoyed tone broke through our lust-laden bubble, and Caz spun away from me, leaving me panting and bereft.

"Mattius."

Xander sliced his arms through the air, pieces of goo flying off in all directions. "Someone was bored and wanted more excitement."

Caz quirked an eyebrow. "Are the creatures disposed of?"

Xander's upper lip curled into a snarl, his focus entirely on me even as he answered his supposed friend. "Yes, I killed every last one of them. Which is how it works once they're ... unleashed. And here the two of you are—"

Shoving off the tree, I narrowed my eyes at Xander. "Maybe if I had more control here, I could have conjured a weapon or—"

"If you had any more control than you do, you probably would have been naked this entire time."

I glanced at Caz and shrugged. "Not seeing a problem with that here."

"Ha!" Xander spat. "You would not be fine walking around with no clothes."

"Fine. Not walking around without any clothes the entire time, but—" I shut my mouth, my teeth clicking together audibly. No, I would not like to be sans clothes unless sex was involved. I was not one of those women who had self-confidence in spades. There were parts of me I didn't want showcased in the harsh lighting of daylight. Like the cellulite on the back of my thighs, came to mind first. After all, I was not a girl in my twenties, or even thirties anymore. My body had mileage and some speed bumps.

Caz sidled his way in between us, his head turning back and forth to regard us both with some unreadable emotion flitting across his features. "What are the two of you speaking of?"

"Nothing you need to worry about," Xander offered. "Silly human stuff."

Judging the way Caz's eyes narrowed, and his brow furrowed, he wasn't buying the lies or excuses anymore. "Arguing about her walking around naked hardly seems like silly human stuff. I'm beginning to believe you're hiding something from me."

Xander froze. "You think I'm hiding something from you?"

So much for Caz being programmed to trust Xander's character. "I think he's hiding something from the both of us."

Xander frowned. "What? That doesn't make sense."

"Oh, yes, it does." I tapped my chin while nodding slowly, giving my best contemplative vibe. "Just think about it."

Xander's frown deepened. "Think about what?"

"Hmmm, hmmm …" I widened my eyes at Caz in encouragement, hoping he'd jump to his own conclusion with a little push from me. "It all makes total sense."

When Caz angled his body toward Xander, my face temporarily concealed from his view, I stuck my tongue out at Xander whose mouth fell open in outrage.

"Zoe, I swear I'm going—"

Caz spoke over Xander. "There is a familiarity between the two of you that should not exist under the circumstances in which I understand them."

Shit. I wanted to throw Xander under the bus because

… well, just because he deserved it for too many reasons to list, but Caz seemed to be latched onto us deceiving him together. Not that he was wrong. According to Xander, though, it shouldn't be possible with Caz's programming.

Quirking an eyebrow, I said, "Johnny Five is alive and going off book." And I supposed with that being the case it told me a lot about where my moral line should be when it came to sexing up the natives in Fantasy Life. If Caz was evolving, it raised more questions that I would need answered before I could make a decision. *The pendulum keeps on swinging.*

"Now, now, now." Xander shifted from foot to foot, flustered by what was going down. "Caz, my oldest and dearest friend, I've merely gotten to know Zoe in the brief time she's been with us, unlike you."

"No," Caz growled. "Something isn't right about this. Any of this." Whirling around, he snagged me by the wrist, his gaze wild. "Tell me what it is, human."

Within his eyes, I saw anger, confusion, and panic. It was as if he sensed the answers he was demanding would blow his worldview. A part of him wanted to know, but a larger part of him possibly already did and didn't want to be faced with the truth.

I glanced up at Xander who was making a slashing motion with his hand. Gnawing on the insides of my cheeks, I considered my options. There were only two: lie or tell the truth. Neither was a good option as far as I could tell. I wanted more for the AI, but I also didn't want to blow their circuits by giving them information they couldn't handle. I simply wanted them to have more of a choice in their own lives. But how much of a choice can anyone or anything have when they don't know all the details to make said choice?

"Umm …" Indecision warred as everything around us went silent, the only sound the thumping of my heart in my ears, and the erratic breathing of Caz.

Caz jostled me roughly as if he was attempting to shake the answers from me. "Tell me, please."

I winced. It was the *please*. He could have demanded until the end of time without swaying me one way or the other, but the desperation encapsulated within that one little word wormed its way into my heart and formed a death grip.

"None of this is real."

"Zoe—"

"No, Xander, it has to be this way."

Caz's fingers dug into my flesh painfully. "What isn't real?"

"Zoe, stop." Xander shoved at Caz, freeing me from his hold.

"Xander, I have to."

"Then you leave me no choice." Xander swung me up into his arms like I weighed nothing and took off at a dead sprint.

"What the hell are you doing?" I slapped at his chest. "Like this isn't suspicious or anything."

"As soon as we get far enough away, I'll jump us into

the next trope and then send Caz into stasis. We'll also need to wipe you from his memory because of what you did and there's no telling how that's going to affect him. So good going, Zoe."

"He deserves to know."

"This is what he was created for."

"Put me down right now or I swear I'll bite your ear off." Twisting in his arms, I snapped at his earlobe.

Xander came to an abrupt halt, dropping me unceremoniously on the ground. "Are you trying to sabotage my life's work? My career? Everything? Is that what you're doing?" He leaned closer, his cheeks flushed with anger. "I didn't think you hated me. I mean, sure, we give each other a hard time, but I thought … I don't know, I thought after everything …" The muscles in his jaw rippled as he ground his teeth together.

"What are you talking about? You can't be seriously taking this personally. I just feel bad about the AI and what—"

"Of course I'm taking this personally!" he shouted.

"Then stop!" I shouted back. "For such a smart person you certainly are completely blind sometimes!"

"Ha! Hi, Kettle, I'd like you to meet, Pot."

An invisible force curled around me, lifting me into the air. "Hey!" My arms and legs flailed uselessly as I struggled to get down.

Xander spun in the direction we'd come. "Let me explain."

Caz glided across the ground, one hand extended

toward me, palm up. "I'm done listening to your lies, Mattius. If you even are Mattius. Or perhaps you're under a spell?" He inclined his head. "I will find out soon enough because I'm taking the human with me to get what I need from a seer."

"Xander," I hissed, continuing to flail. "A little help here." Vertigo hit, causing nausea to roil my gut. "Please, I think I'm going to be sick."

"Caz, no!"

Everything went dark.

Chapter 10

Jolting awake, I came to instant awareness, none too happy to discover my whereabouts. Alone in a stereotypical movie-style dungeon, where dark and dank was taken to the next level of disgusting and creepy, I was left in a heap in the corner like discarded trash.

Rubbing my temples, I groaned. Had I suffered a mental overload and blacked out or had Caz done something to me? Was it even possible for him to do something to me? And where was Xander? Could all of this be part of the trope? Or had things gone off the rails and the AI were now running the asylum?

After pulling myself to my feet, I ambled over to the rusted bars, pressing my face into the scant space between the cold metal. "Hello?" I called. "Anyone there?" I scanned everything I could make out in the low light, hoping to find something of use, possibly a means of escape. Much as I expected, I came up empty. Sighing dramatically, I mentally chastised myself. What did I expect, a key hanging conveniently close to my cell?

I considered doing my usual spiel of demanding for Xander to show up, but surely, he knew where I was even if he wasn't directly responsible for it. Instead, I opted to try to get someone else's attention—someone who would be of more use to me under the current circumstances. "Caz! I know you're here somewhere! Caaaaaz!"

Throwing my head back, I let loose a scream that rattled my lungs. I was beyond frustrated with this entire situation. Fantasy Life hadn't gotten off to a great start, and just when things seemed promising, they took another nose-dive.

A gnat buzzed past my ear, and I swatted at it absentmindedly.

"Psst … Zoe, it's me." The voice was tinny and barely audible, but I recognized it immediately.

"Xander." I lifted my hand in offering for the gnat as a landing spot. It scurried along my finger, its tiny legs tickling me. Snorting, I watched as it spun in a small circle before stopping. "I can't decide if you showing up as a gnat, one that I particularly want to squish right now, is appropriate or irony, or something else entirely."

Gnat Xander expelled a soft wheeze, which I think was supposed to pass for a put-upon sigh. Like he was the one having a rough go of things and not me. "Now isn't the time for your sarcasm."

"What I said wasn't technically sarcasm even though it

was delivered in a sarcastic tone. Maybe someone needs a teeny, tiny dictionary."

"Zoe—"

"Oh, no, don't you Zoe me. You don't get to be annoyed right now. I'm the annoyed one. This whole Fantasy Life thing was meant to be fun. Isn't that what you kept telling me?" I flung my arms out, dislodging Gnat Xander. "Dungeons aren't on my list of fun things."

Gnat Xander buzzed around my head, landing on the top of my ear. Despite knowing it was him, I had to fight the urge not to swipe at him. "Yeah, things haven't gone the way I planned with this trope either."

"How did I end up here at all? And most importantly, how are you going to get me out? Because I wanted to play romance, not medieval torture or whatever else Caz may have cooked up for me because he definitely doesn't trust you or your character like you claimed he did."

"Caz having magic, or what passes for magic in this world's programming, may have given him more power than I counted on. This entire fae world has morphed into something beyond what we originally created. It's both exhilarating and terrifying."

Dread glided its icy finger up my spine. "What do you mean by terrifying?"

Gnat Xander's tiny wings buzzed. "I don't want you to freak out, but Caz has more control here than I do."

"Umm ... what?" My voice had gone shrill. "How? What? Am I going to die in here?"

"Don't be ridiculous. Even if you die in here, you should be fine in the real world."

"*Should?*" I squeaked, my knees going wobbly. "For someone who doesn't want to freak me out, you are certainly picking all the choice words to do precisely that."

"I didn't mean it like it sounded."

Spinning my arms in wild circles, I motioned to the dungeon again. "Get me out of here right now, Xander. And I don't mean just this dungeon or this trope, I mean all of it. I'm done. D-O-N-E."

"You're overreacting. Again."

"Am I? Am I really?" Anger surged through my system, my arms and legs tingling. "I'm in a dungeon. A very realistic dungeon that smells about as rank as I imagined one would. And before you say that's because I shaped that aspect with my mind, well, fine, but I never wanted to go back in time. Or go on an adventure like in one of those dystopian action movies I like watching. Do you understand that? Hmmm? I'm the person who thinks about the lack of modern medicine in time travel romances, and I'm the one who thinks about the constant stress going through one of those dystopian situations would be. I don't even like to wake up early. Do you understand that? Do you, Xander? Do you?"

"Ummm ... yes and no."

"Let me make it simpler for you then. I don't want to be here. And I shouldn't have to be."

"Don't worry. I'll get you out."

"Then why are you sneaking around as a damn gnat?

Why didn't you pop in here and open a door out of this stupid trope? Or better yet, why am I not awake in the real world? Why is this conversation even happening? Why, Xander, why?"

"Calm down so I can explain."

"No!" I screeched. "I will not calm down. I will not deal with you persuading me to do one more thing I don't want to do."

"Zoe, please. You need to listen. It's not like before, I swear."

Dropping to my knees, I slapped the ground with open palms. I knew I was having a mini-meltdown, and frankly, I didn't care. I most likely would later, but for the moment I wanted out of Fantasy Life and if I had to throw a toddler-style tantrum, I wasn't above it.

I groaned long and loud. "And to top it off, you've gone and made me become the whiney main character, that if I was actually in a book, everyone, including myself, would hate." Pausing, I further considered, my mouth falling open at my next revelation. "Oh my God. I'm too stupid to live. I have become the too stupid to live heroine in this trope. How did any of this happen?"

If I make it out of this in one piece, I might even reconsider my judgmental stance on certain main characters that I previously wanted to drop-kick in the face. Them and their idiotic love interests who couldn't seem to get anything right until the last five to ten percent of the book.

"Mmmm ..." Xander's little legs moved along my skin. "You can't compare your situation to a romance heroine.

If anything, you're currently closer to a gamer or even a—"

"No. Just no. I'm not arguing semantics with you about any of this, even though I technically just was. I'm moving past that. Starting now. So focus on getting me out of here without any more of your excuses."

"They're not excuses, Zoe. It's the plain truth. I can't help it if you don't like what I have to say."

His words repeated in my head, taking on a déjà vu vibe as they bounced and circled my mind again and again.

"They're not excuses, Zoe. It's the plain truth. I can't help it if you don't like what I have to say. They're not excuses, Zoe. It's the plain truth. I can't help it if you don't like what I have to say."

Spots danced in front of my eyes before the world tilted, and the floor came up to meet me.

A flash of Xander standing in my living room, clothes and hair rumpled, his expression stricken. *"They're not excuses, Zoe. It's the plain truth. I can't help it if you don't like what I have to say."*

"No. Wait. You don't understand. You have it all wrong."

"I think I have it exactly right." He tugged at his hair. *"I thought ... I thought you and me—"* He raised his hands and backed away slowly. *"It doesn't matter what I thought. I was wrong."*

"If you won't listen to me, then all you have to say is a bunch of bullshit excuses. It's not the truth at all. You don't even know what the truth is."

The scene changed to Jared, ex-husband number two, standing on my front porch. *"What are you doing?" My scream shattered the image.*

"Zoe." Xander crouched over me, back in his fae persona. "Focus on me." His hands hovered over me, one near my face, the other over my sternum. It was as if he wanted to touch me desperately but was afraid of what would happen if he did.

Lifting my gaze to his, I stared into the dark pools of emotion, unfathomable things churning deep within. My heart fluttered wildly, and I sucked in a sharp breath. "What did I just see? It was like a memory, I think."

"It can happen when you panic. Don't worry about it. What I need is for you to focus on the here and now."

I cleared my throat before shoving up onto my elbows. "I am."

Xander stayed where he was for a moment, putting us in a space a bit too close for my comfort. "Good, yeah, good." He tugged at a braid in his hair.

"Why did you change back to Mattius?" Not that I was complaining, mind you. I'd take some fae warrior eye candy over a gnat any day. *No. Stop. This is Xander. How many times do you have to remind yourself? Yep. Too stupid to live.*

He pulled himself to his feet, glancing over his shoulder. "I don't know. Being human-sized seemed more appropriate than being a gnat. I'm not sure me buzzing around your head would have been comforting."

I grinned, picturing him crawling around my ear

yelling for me to snap out of it, and me accidentally on purpose squishing him. "I might have been comforted."

Xander tapped his scarred eyebrow. "You were imagining squashing me, weren't you?"

"No, not at all." My grin stretched impossibly wide.

"You were. I can tell."

"You can't tell anything."

"Yes, I can."

"You think you know everything, don't you? Well, you don't."

He snorted. "Please. I never said I know everything, and I certainly don't need to. I merely have to read the expression on your face. One I've seen thousands of times before, and it always spelled trouble for me one way or another." He tapped his scarred eyebrow again. "Even if you were aiming for Adam."

I sighed. "You don't know me as well as you think you do, Xander."

His nostrils flared, anger darkening his countenance. "You're right. I've made that mistake one too many times."

"Okay ..." There was something else he was saying, something lingering underneath his response that I didn't quite grasp—something that made my stomach twist and anxiety slide through my chest.

"Well, well, well, if it isn't Mattius come to rescue his human." Caz stood outside my cell, neither surprised nor flustered to find Xander with me.

"She's not my anything," Xander snapped. "But I do owe her family a debt. A debt that doesn't include throwing her in a dungeon while waiting for you to come to your senses."

Lips drawn back in a snarl, Caz leaned forward. "I don't believe a single word that spews from your traitorous mouth."

"Traitorous mouth? You've got to be kidding me."

"Yep, he totally trusts you." I paused, then hissed out of the side of my mouth, "That was sarcasm, by the way."

Xander spared me a quick glare.

I shrugged.

I didn't know whether to laugh, cry, or wipe up the drool that was surely leaking from the corners of my mouth. Caz and Xander were a sight to behold in all of their leather-wearing fae glory with the testosterone and male posturing saturating the air between them. For a moment, I let myself shamelessly gawk, ignoring the part where Caz was an out-of-control AI, and Xander my younger brother's asshat of a friend.

Oh, yes, how about some shirtless wrestling? Bet that would help sort out your issues. Quite possibly I shouldn't be objectifying them. Although I feel like I'm owed something so simple for being locked up in a dungeon.

"Did you have sex with her?" Caz's question to Xander zapped me out of my lusty reverie.

Xander stared blankly at Caz. "Why would you think that?"

"Speak the truth."

Shuffling forward, I cleared my throat. "Ahem. I thought fae couldn't lie. If that's the case, then why don't you trust Mattius anymore?" Why didn't I think of that simple defense before?

Caz's gaze was cold when he turned it toward me, his disdain a physical touch. "Who told you that? Fae can lie as much and as often as your kind can. Isn't that right, Mattius? Or," he canted his head, "are you lying to her as well? Was it that easy to get her to believe whatever lies that fell from your treacherous mouth when she thought you couldn't lie at all?"

Caz seemed extremely focused on the relationship between me and Xander. Was it possible that since he was programmed to want me that he'd grown jealous of a perceived slight enacted by Xander having encroached on his territory? Could it be that simple?

"Please." I rolled my eyes. "Mattius didn't tell me that. I read it in a book."

"A book?" Caz repeated, his eyebrows lifting slightly. "What kind of book?"

Okay, so why not go with the truth and see what happens? What did I have to lose? I was already locked in a dungeon. "Well, it was a fiction book. Romance actually. And maybe I should say more than one book. But I've come to find that sometimes truth makes its way into fiction, and since so many seemed to agree ..." I shrugged.

Caz's lips twitched. "You're making judgments and decisions about this world based on fiction novels?"

I wasn't about to explain that since we were in a world made up to fit romance tropes that it would make total sense to draw conclusions from books I read, and even ones I created. Instead, I shrugged again, remaining mute.

"Hmmm …" Caz stared at me, our gazes clashing, me refusing to look away. "For some reason, I believe what you say to be true."

Xander threw his hands in the air. "You believe her but not the man you've known almost your entire life?"

Ignoring Xander, Caz took a step closer to the cell. "I will talk to the human alone now." He waved his hand, and my cellmate disappeared.

Startled, I let loose a high-pitched yelp. "What did you do to him?"

With another wave of his hand, the bars between us evaporated. "Why do you care?"

Xander was fine, I knew that intellectually, but somehow being alone with Caz felt a little too real. Especially because he wasn't following any kind of script anymore. He could do whatever he pleased to me, and I hoped it wouldn't involve pain since I wasn't entirely sure how I would register such a thing.

"I care because he's my friend." Maybe. I wasn't exactly sure. He was Adam's friend … his best friend. But what was Xander to me, other than a current pain in my ass?

"Friend? I thought he was mine not very long ago. You'd be wise to rethink that classification." One side of his mouth curled up slightly. "I could be your friend if you want. And let me assure you, I am a much better friend to have than Mattius."

Frozen in place, all I could do was blink repeatedly.

What is happening here? What do I even want to happen? From the first moment I laid eyes on Caz, he'd set my libido on fire, but despite how things had changed, I still had the moral dilemma of him being an AI to consider.

"I-I don't kn-know," I managed to stammer.

"Mmmm …" He closed the scant distance between us, focus intent on my lips. "Maybe I can persuade you."

Oh shit. He's going to kiss me. And daaaamn, this moment is straight out of a romance novel. I mean, the dialogue is a bit stilted but—"

His lips came crashing down on mine, and my mind went blissfully blank.

Chapter 11

Caz's tongue swept into my mouth, tangling languidly with mine at first before a guttural sound escaped the back of his throat and the kiss turned borderline brutal.

Fragments of thoughts swirled through my brain, floating across my consciousness.

He tastes like cinnamon.

He is the world's best kisser.

Too bad he isn't real.

He feels real though.

Really real.

I'm getting lightheaded.

Is he kissing me to death? Oh well, at least I'll die happy.

No, wait. If kissing is this good—

Caz grabbed my hair, tugging just the right amount to mingle pleasure with pain.

Oh, yes, now this kind of pain I can handle.

Every molecule in my entire body was set to combust at any moment. I wanted anything and everything Caz was willing to give me, no matter the cost to my moral code. I'd live with the guilt. It would be worth it. Real, fake, or somewhere in between, it turned out that having a fae direct his attention toward you sexually was just as good as advertised, or I supposed, imagined.

"You're seriously making out with him right now? In the friggin' dungeon?" Xander's slightly exasperated tone wiggled its way into my ears, registering, but not truly processing.

Caz stole his lips from mine, leaving me bereft and flustered. Sliding a possessive hand to rest over the nape of my neck, he regarded Xander, who stood a few feet away. "Back so soon? I expected it to take you longer to escape."

"Zoe." Xander snapped his fingers repeatedly. "Hello?"

"Huh?" I'd written scenes where the MC is lost after a kiss, her brain addled with lust, but I wasn't sure I ever experienced it until Caz. Which was pathetic. Shaking my head, I attempted to duck out from under him, but his long fingers held onto me, just shy of digging into my flesh.

I internally groaned. Again, I considered the possibility that Xander had been right all along. My expectations for real-world men were too high. Caz was designed to do all the right things at just the right moments. He was programmed for success and scripted to a certain degree. Which meant even if he went off book a bit, he still stuck to the basic plotline of the trope. It was crystal clear what had happened. Caz was developing his fake feelings right on schedule but got jealous because of Xander. Being an AI, Caz then simply ... went with it. Which also meant Xander's presence was complicating things and the best solution would be to get rid of him to let the rest of the trope run its course.

Then again ... If I let it run its course, that meant some sexy times were in my future with a certain tall, dark, and handsome fae warrior who might be more of an anti-hero or villain but—

Oh, yeah, that's why I can't seem to resist him. I've always been a sucker for the enemies-to-lovers trope, but add in the villainous love interest aspect, and I am done for.

"Hand over my human," Xander grated, his expression thunderous.

Caz tensed beside me. "Your human? She belongs to me."

When I read it in a book it was sexy as hell. All the "she's mine" and "keep your hands off of her" ... but when everything seemed so realistic, the whole thing shriveled my ovaries.

I slapped at Caz. "This human belongs to herself and herself alone."

He glanced down at me, a smirk twisting his lips. "We'll see about that after I get you naked and underneath me."

My stomach dropped as my pulse picked up speed. Again, if I'd read those words within the pages of a book I

would have swooned, but hearing them directed at me ...
Nope. Just a bit ole' noppity-nope.

"I think ..." I inched closer to Xander. "Um, I'm just going to go now."

Caz wouldn't give up easily, it wasn't in his programming to do so.

Xander's dark eyes lit with mirth, even as he managed to keep his stern expression in place. "Sounds like the human has made her choice."

"No," Caz snapped. "She belongs to me. Not you."

Slinking closer to Xander, I kept my gaze on Caz's hands, surprised he'd let me get as far as I had. "Like I said, I don't belong to anyone but myself. Thanks for the offer though."

Going back to my original stance of wanting to get the hell out of Fantasy Life ASAP, Xander was my only option. I couldn't let a mind-blowing kiss from a fictional character scramble my brain and delay my exit. *I truly am as shallow as Xander claimed. But I can do better. I can always do better. As long as I learn from my mistakes and realize my shortcomings then I can improve. I will improve.*

"It's you, isn't it, Mattius? I thought she was some kind of witch and she worked a spell on us, but it's not her at all." Caz reached for a dagger at his belt. "She's meant to be with me. I can feel the connection even though I hate that I have such a bond with a human, and you are determined to steal her from me." Drawing the dagger, it glinted in the low light ominously. "Who turned you against me? Was it my brother?"

"You'll thank me later when you realize the truth." Xander drew his own blade, dropping into a defensive stance.

"And what would that truth be?"

"That Zoe doesn't belong with you. The bond you feel isn't real."

Had Xander alluded to Caz's AI status? Was he actually going to let the Fantasy Life cat out of the bag? I gasped, unable to help myself. It was like being dropped in the middle of a soap opera. I was part of the drama, and yet it still felt like I was watching it unfold before me on TV.

"I know what I feel." Caz took a step in Xander's direction. "And I know you can't be trusted."

I contemplated letting them fight over me because if I wasn't going to get laid, then at least I could gather some material for my next novel, or for my spank bank. But alas, if I wanted out of the trope and the entire VR world, I needed to leave with Xander before I ended up in another version of the dungeon I was still kind of trapped in.

Diving toward Xander, I reached out with both hands.

His eyes widened in surprise. "Zoe—"

"Stop!" Caz roared.

"Get us out of here!" I screeched, falling just short of making any kind of contact with Xander. *Can't I be slightly athletic even in here?*

Dropping his dagger, Xander scooped me up in his arms. "I don't know if this is going to work with you," he muttered. "But here goes."

The dungeon pixelized, followed by a sensation of falling. A moment later we were in front of a large, free-standing door in the middle of another oddly colored fae forest. Or perhaps it was the same one. Either way, it was exactly what I'd been hoping for … a way out.

Extraditing myself from Xander, I lurched for the door, my heart thrashing against my ribcage. I was almost there, but not quite. I half expected Caz or even Xander to stop me at the very last possible second.

My hand wrapped around the doorknob, and I turned it. Heaving a sigh of relief, I stepped over the threshold, leaving another mess of a trope behind.

Chapter 12

I had a lot to consider. Like the stagnant state of my career, my non-existent love life, and my inability to make up my mind about anything lately, to name a few. Basically, the hot mess I'd become, and how exactly I was going to change my circumstances. I thought I had a decent plan with the whole Fantasy Life virtual reality thing, but as it turned out ... not so much.

Ugh. What to do? What to do?

Primarily, I needed to figure out who the hell I was as a person at this particular point in my life. I knew who I wasn't anymore, which wasn't necessarily a bad thing like I'd originally convinced myself. It was kind of like when I was a kid, and I hated the color pink. When I got older, I realized I didn't hate pink, simply what it represented as far as being gender normative for females. As a female, I'd been expected to choose pink over blue, but blue was my favorite color. Instead of merely asserting my like of blue,

I'd gone too far and rejected pink for no other reason than it was expected of me to like it. By doing that I was letting myself be controlled as well, I simply hadn't seen it. The same thing happens when teenagers all don the uniform of nonconformity. They're becoming exactly what they're rebelling against in a weird way.

Oh. Ugh. I rubbed my temples. *I'm thinking myself in circles and I'm pretty sure my brain is getting fried by Fantasy Life as I run myself around the same mental tracks. Shallow? Not shallow? Who and what kind of person am I? To have sex or not have sex with the AI? It's all ridiculous and I'm having an existential crisis times ten.*

"Zoe."

I continued to stare straight ahead, my face cradled in my hands and my elbows resting on my knees. "Nope. The only thing I want to hear from you is how the next door is taking me out of Fantasy Life."

Sitting down beside me on the ground, Xander heaved a loud, dramatic sigh. I was now convinced he did them for my benefit. A way to let me know I was putting him out without actually uttering the words. "The last trope going sideways wasn't my fault."

I shrugged. "At this point, it doesn't matter whose fault it was. In the end, it went sideways, and I was once again left with something I didn't sign up for."

"I don't know, you seemed pretty delighted to be making out with Caz in the dungeon."

"It was a momentary lapse in judgment."

"I think it lasted more than a moment."

"I wouldn't know, I didn't have a stopwatch to time my make-out session with your AI gone wild."

"I think you would have gone all the way if I hadn't shown up when I did."

Spearing Xander with a death glare, I growled under my breath. "Wasn't that kind of the point? I was there for the trope. The romance trope. Which includes, I don't know, a romance. One that was supposed to involve me and Caz." It was easier to be angry at him now that he'd ditched his fae garb, returning to everyday, boring, human-style in jeans and a T-shirt.

Xander tapped at the scar in his eyebrow, avoiding my gaze, although I was pretty sure he could sense it. "I didn't feel right about the two of you together." His cheeks flushed. "What I mean by that is … that, um, well, Caz wasn't behaving normally. The entire world there wasn't behaving the way it was supposed to, and I didn't want to risk something happening to you."

"And what could have happened to me? I mean, sure, when I thought he was going to torture me that would have been bad, but—" But what? I'd come to the conclusion that it was the best decision to not have sex with the luscious fae warrior and to get out of Fantasy Life ASAP. And yet, what I was saying to Xander made it sound like I had regrets. Did I?

"The next trope will be better."

I jumped to my feet. "No. I've had enough."

"Just give yourself a few minutes to catch your breath, to gather your thoughts, and then we can head into—"

I flicked Xander on his scarred eyebrow.

"Hey!" He slapped at my hand.

"You're not listening. Contract or not. When the AI morphs into something beyond what was designed, it's time to call it quits."

"It was probably just that world. Because of the faux magic. Add in the fact that the fae designed for that trope think they have control over their world and voila, it caused problems."

I crossed my arms over my chest. "Problems that need fixed."

"Yes, but my point is that the other worlds slash tropes that don't involve the complicated stuff like that should be fine."

I quirked an eyebrow. "Should be?"

"Don't you see? Now we *have to* test the other tropes after what happened in fae world with Caz. We owe it to the scientific—"

"I owe nothing to anyone. Send someone else in to test this stuff."

Xander unfurled from the ground, towering over me. "Come on. We are the first ones to ever experience this." He widened his arms. "Any of this. Aren't you curious?"

"What I'm curious about is why you don't want to let me leave Fantasy Life. Also, why you seem to be sabotaging me in these tropes. Oh, and let's not forget about how strange you've been acting." I slammed my mouth shut, not wanting to bring that last one up. It was something I couldn't ignore anymore. Xander was acting

... well, not like the Xander I used to know, at least in regards to me. Not only that, he seemed off somehow, like he wasn't quite himself. I couldn't quite put my finger on it, but it was there, or I should say, not there. I thought it was because we weren't us, instead stuck in avatars meant to be us, but it was something else. I couldn't shake that feeling.

Xander stared down at me, his left eye twitching. "I'm not sabotaging anything. Nor am I acting strangely."

I wasn't going to argue with him. Much. "What about the part about not wanting to let me leave Fantasy Life? No denial about that part?"

He shrugged, his gaze darting over my head. "No. Although I've already explained why."

I rolled my eyes. "Mmm hmm ... yep. You most certainly have given me the whole song and dance about that one." Logically his explanation made sense, and yet there was something off about it just like with him.

He scowled. "What's that supposed to mean?"

"I think you know."

He sighed dramatically for what seemed like the thousandth time. "I'm not a mind reader."

'Round and 'round we went. My brain wasn't the only thing spinning me in circles. Xander was doing a damn good job of it as well. *Time to end the insanity.* Pulling myself to my feet, I narrowed my eyes at Xander. "Why are we still sitting here? Do you seriously think if you give me enough downtime between tropes that I'll change my mind and want to stay?"

"Yes, actually I do." Xander inched closer, gazing down his nose at me, our breath intermingling. "I know you, Zoe. And I know you tend to overreact—"

I shoved at his chest. "Hey! I do not!"

"But you also think things over after you've had a chance to calm down."

"I am calm," I hissed.

"You, Zoe, are a lot of things right now, but calm is not one of them."

Gritting my teeth, I barely managed to keep my tone even. "You couldn't be more wrong."

Xander shuffled the tiniest bit closer, his voice dropping an octave. "You think I don't know you. Probably because hardly anyone does. But I do. I know you better than you know yourself sometimes."

My heart quadrupled in speed. "What are you talking about? Lots of people know me."

He shook his head ever so slightly. "No, they don't. You're the whatever-happened-to girl."

"What?"

"You know, like 'Whatever happened to, Zoe?' That's what people always say about you."

"I still don't have a clue what you're talking about. I write under a pen name but lots of people know what happened to me."

He shook his head again. "No, I'm talking about knowing the real you. Hardly anyone ever did, and that hasn't changed. You flitted around, dancing between different social groups, popular by definition since everyone liked you, but no one ever got past your walls. You only let people in so far before you'd move on. You'd disappear off their radars after a while and no one would know what happened to you. It wasn't that they didn't care either, it was simply by your design. You left everyone behind."

I blinked at him, my mind racing. It was true I had a difficult time opening up to people, only letting them know the surface me. Part of it was because I was an introvert, another because I was shyer than I liked to admit, but mostly it was because I was afraid of rejection, I supposed. I never felt like I truly fit in anywhere, therefore I felt no one would genuinely like me and all my weird innards. But, if no one ever got to know the real me then I could never actually be rejected. It was a protection mechanism. I was well aware of this particular flaw, but I had no idea anyone, especially Xander, had ever noticed.

"People don't wonder what happened to me."

The corners of Xander's mouth curled. "Au contraire. I get asked all the time about you because of my connection to Adam." He reached up to snag a piece of my hair, slowly twirling it around his finger.

My breath hitched for some bizarre reason.

"You had tons of acquaintances, but how many real friends did you have? Even now? How many do you have?"

My stomach dropped into my feet. He wasn't right about the last part, was he? "You're wrong," I croaked. "You're just trying to throw me off-kilter, so I'll be easier to manipulate into doing what you want. People with low self-esteem are more pliant since they want to please."

Xander's brows knitted together. "How is it possible that someone like you could ever feel bad about themselves?"

My breath whooshed out of me. "What?" I wasn't sure what was happening anymore, or what I felt about anything. His plan to throw me off balance was one hundred percent working.

My hair slipped from his grasp as he ran the pad of his finger along the side of my jaw. "You heard me. How is it possible that someone like you could ever feel bad about themselves?"

"Yes, I heard what you said, but what does it mean?"

His pupils ate up the dark brown of his eyes, his lids dropping low. "It means that you hide in plain sight, Zoe. But I see you. I see who you really are, and that you are about as close to perfect as humanly possible."

I sucked in a shaky breath, my chest constricting to imprison anything I might have responded with. I wasn't sure what was happening between us. If it was almost anyone else on the planet, I would say we were having a moment, one laced with sexual tension, something I couldn't quite fathom. Sure, there was that one time on New Year's, the same year as the infamous shower incident, when he followed me into the pantry and kissed me. The encounter was brief and sizzling, neither of us speaking of it again. Because of that, I was convinced he

just wanted to see if he could, the cocky bastard, although
…

No. This was Xander, my little brother's best friend.
He'd outgrown his childish infatuation with me a long
time ago. The past was the past. I had to be misreading the
situation due to my brain currently being fried by Fantasy
Life.

Xander shifted his hand, his thumb making small
circles along my cheek as his long fingers stretched into
my hair. "I think—"

"Yes," I murmured.

"I think I fucked up." Yanking his hand away from me,
he spun in the opposite direction.

His reaction was like a bucket of ice water dumped
over my head. I gulped in huge lungfuls of air, my entire
body quaking with adrenaline mixed with anxiety. The
urge to cry crept up along my spine, flushing my skin, and
then pushing its way first into my throat, tightening my
esophagus before moving to my eyes, causing a burning
sensation.

However, before a single tear could spill, I found
myself being dragged through another door, a scream
prepped on my lips, but swallowed by the speed and
momentum of which I was forced to move.

Colors blurred, and the sensation of falling morphed
into oblivion once again.

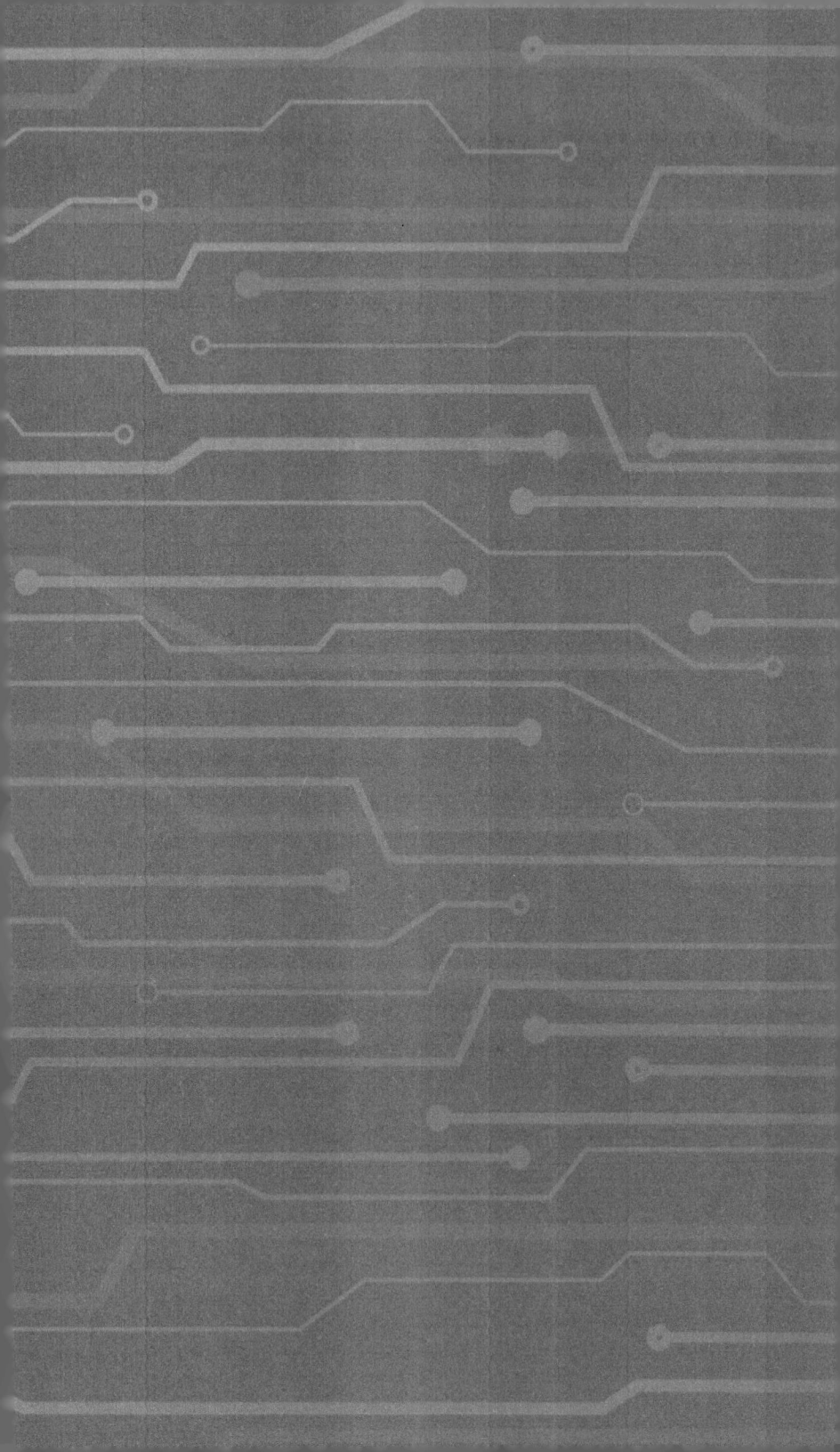

Chapter 13

Agitated, Xander ran his hands through his already disheveled hair, pacing back and forth across my living room, his gaze darting around warily. "They're not excuses, Zoe. It's the plain truth. I can't help it if you don't like what I have to say."

I tried to stay seated, to stay calm, but the moment felt pivotal somehow and I couldn't let things go on the way they were. "No. Wait. You don't understand. You have it all wrong."

"I think I have it exactly right." He tugged at his hair. "I thought ... I thought you and me—" He raised his hands and backed away slowly. "It doesn't matter what I thought. I was wrong."

My heart twisted and broke, dropping into my stomach to stir up dread. "If you won't listen to me, then all you have to say is a bunch of bullshit excuses. It's not the truth at all. You don't even know what the truth is."

Still backing away slowly, Xander's lips formed a sad

facsimile to his usual smile. "I want to believe you. More than anything. But I have to stop lying to myself."

"Please ... just, please. You need to listen. I just need time. That's all. You don't understand what he's like. He ... I'm afraid of what he'll do. He could try to take everything from me and succeed. I need to be in a better position." My throat closed up, choking off my ill-delivered ramble. Maybe I wouldn't be able to explain the situation even if given the chance, but I had to try.

"You're never going to leave him. I can see that now. And I don't even understand why."

"Yes, I am! I just need time! Please! Why won't you listen to me?" I knew he was technically hearing my words, but they weren't reaching him, not really. And I didn't know how I could get through to him. What was someone supposed to do when the truth wasn't good enough?

Xander turned away from me, head hanging as he braced his arms against the mantel of my fireplace. "I couldn't see the truth before because I didn't want to. I thought our story was going to be one for the ages like—" He shook his head harshly. "I was a fool. Your fool. But I won't be anymore."

Ripped away from the scene before me, my vision blurred and my head spun, dizziness quickly giving way to nausea. I clutched at my head, groaning.

"Zoe."

"Make it stop. You need to make it stop."

"It's okay. It'll settle in a second."

Bit by bit, piece by piece my current world slowed to a stop, leaving me with the urge to kiss the ground. It was then I realized I was curled up on said ground amidst a bed of multicolored flowers.

Xander hovered over me, concern etched into every line on his face. "Better?"

Confusion nettled, my brain filled with cotton candy. "Why did you drag me through another door the way you did and what the hell was the scene in my living room with you?"

His brow furrowed. "What scene in your living room?"

"Was it part of another trope?"

"Another trope?" he echoed, a frown tugging at his full lips.

"Yeah, maybe ... No. That doesn't make any sense. It felt more like reliving a memory, but—" I rubbed my temples, a headache blooming. "That doesn't make sense either. Unless Fantasy Life really is frying my brain." I gave a nervous chuckle, only partially joking.

"You need to further explain, but first we need to get a move on." He offered me his hand.

I stared at it a moment, a flash from the weird scene playing through my mind again. It felt like a memory, and it stirred up emotions that also didn't make any sense. I resisted the urge to throw myself into Xander's arms, the need to cling to him nearly overwhelming.

"Something's not right," I whispered, continuing to stare at Xander. "Why can't I remember coming to your office yet? And why do I ..." I clamped my mouth shut. I was not about to ask my little brother's best friend why I wanted nothing more than for him to hold me.

Xander leaned forward, gaze darting back and forth between my eyes. "And why do you *what exactly?*"

Grabbing his hand, I let him pull me to my feet. His skin was warm and inviting, the calluses on his fingertips comforting in a weird way. It made him more real, even though he was currently just a bunch of pixels existing in a realm of make-believe aka virtual reality. It made me wonder if his hands would feel the same in the real world, and if so, where had I gotten my information from? Questions, questions, and more questions layered on top of the others.

I sighed. "It doesn't matter. I mean, the part where I can't remember going to your office or signing the contract does, but I guess we'll deal with all of that once we get out of here." I glanced around as I spun in a small circle. "Why are we still in Fantasy Life and why did you drag me through another door against my will so abruptly?"

Xander grimaced, the expression overused in my presence lately. "Caz might have followed us."

My eyes widened to the point where I was a tad concerned they might pop out of my head. *Good thing none of this is real.* "Caz *might* have followed us? Explain. Now."

"Not much to explain since I don't have the answers yet. We were in that field, taking a breather, and without warning a door I didn't create appeared, Caz stepping through it a moment later. The rest you already know."

"You mean the out-of-control AI moved worlds? How

is that possible?" A chill ran up my spine. "And can he do it again?"

"Not sure. Which is why we need to get a move on now that you've adjusted."

"I don't want to get a move on, Xander, I want to get out of here, which I'm pretty sure I've already said a time or two."

He chuckled. "Yes, I think I may have heard you mention something like that once or twice."

I stamped my foot, hating the action, but loving the satisfaction of it. "This isn't funny. None of this is the tiniest bit amusing. This little test is over. I want to go home."

"You don't think that's funny?" He motioned at my feet, where shiny ruby slippers had appeared a la *The Wizard of Oz*.

Canting my head, I studied the glittery accessories from my vantage point. "Did you do that?"

He snorted. "Nope."

"Well, I certainly didn't."

"Yep, you did, even with the control limit we put on you. I guess you really want to go home." He sniggered, the action making him appear younger, and every bit the annoying, immature kid I once knew. "Thank God we did put that limit on you because who knows what kind of chaos you would have released inadvertently otherwise."

"Wouldn't have been worse than what we're already dealing with."

"I strongly disagree."

Wiggling my toes within the very uncomfortable and yet strangely pretty shoes, I couldn't help but grin. "Maybe these will work, and I can wish myself home without your help. After all, it is my brain."

Xander rolled his eyes. "Knock yourself out."

Closing my eyes, I did the Dorothy and tapped my heels together three times while saying the magic words, "There's no place like home. There's no place like home. There's no place like home."

Slitting my eyes open, I peeked through my eyelashes, huffing out a frustrated breath when I could still see Xander standing in front of me. I kicked at a patch of flowers. "Damn it."

"I wouldn't have let you try it if I thought it was going to work."

"Ah-ha!" I stabbed an accusatory finger in his direction. "I knew you didn't want me to leave!"

Xander rolled his eyes again. "I haven't been hiding that fact. Not even a little."

"But why?" I whined. "You keep giving me all these ridiculous, nonsensical excuses and none of them make any sense. Especially with a rogue AI on the loose. My brain could be in danger." I gingerly touched the top of my head and jutted out my lower lip.

"Your brain isn't in any danger."

"But we're in virtual reality in my brain."

"No, your brain is in virtual reality, or consciousness when you get down to it. Big difference. Which is part of the problem since you don't understand any of this. Your brain is firmly planted where it's always been, in your thick, stubborn skull and no one but you is in it." He smirked, mirth dancing within his eyes. "And I also witnessed first-hand the glazed-over expression on your face when I explained how all of this was going to work. You probably didn't hear a word I said about any of the technical stuff or programming."

"It wouldn't matter if I did since I can't remember going to your office in the first place. So there." I stuck my tongue out at him, quickly retracting it.

"Or it doesn't matter that you don't remember anything we talked about in the meeting since you didn't hear a word I said anyhow." His eyebrows climbed up his forehead in challenge. "Go ahead and try to deny it."

Squinting at him, I considered my options of a comeback. His point was valid, but I didn't have to let him know that I acknowledged it on any level. "Oooor, perhaps the answer is that your boring techy talk was irrelevant since your AIs have gone rogue, changing the rules of the game."

Xander sucked on his teeth. "One. One AI has gone rogue."

"One more than should be."

"All right, enough. We don't have time to do this anymore." He shook his head, cursing under his breath. "I don't know why I keep letting this happen with you. Every little thing doesn't have to turn into an argument between us."

"Are we arguing? I hadn't noticed."

"Of course not, since you probably think it's some kind of romance novel level banter."

His comment, although not out of left field, since hello, romance author, caused a lump to form in my throat. "Why would there be banter between us?" The question slipped from my mouth unbidden, like it escaped from a secret part of my brain with its own agenda, one that I wasn't privy to.

"I … what are you asking?" He pressed his lips into a thin line, back to studying me again.

I was beginning to feel like an amoeba under a microscope. Things had gotten bizarre between me and Xander. I could no longer deny it. Something had shifted, and even though I wasn't sure what, it was making things helluva awkward between us. I was fighting urges when it came to him that I couldn't explain, questioning things I wasn't sure I wanted the answers to, all while trapped in a twisted virtual reality where a rogue AI was apparently after us.

"You know," I dropped my gaze to my feet, "this whole thing is a disaster. All of it. If I was reading this novel, I'd say the author had lost the plot."

Xander shuffled closer to me, face a mask of neutrality. "What would you do if you were writing it then?"

I swallowed, the lump in my throat having transformed into a boulder. "Up the stakes." Sucking in a shallow breath, I continued, "And add some hot sex scenes."

The corners of Xander's mouth twitched. "Scenes? Plural, as in more than one?"

Cheeks heating, I shrugged. "Why should there be a limit on something good like sex scenes?"

"I don't know, too much of a good thing can be bad?"

"Are you sure you're a guy?"

"I'm not even going to answer that question. Instead, I'll ask one of my own: Are you sure you're a feminist? Because gender stereotyping me seems off brand."

Touché. Even I had things I needed to work on when it came to internalized issues. But I didn't want to admit it out loud. My internalized patriarchy needed to stay just that … internalized. At least until I could wipe it all from my psyche.

"Have you ever read any of my books?" Why I suddenly wanted to know … *needed* to know was beyond me. Both of my exes had been less than supportive once they got a gander at the content of my books. Apparently, romance novels, sprinkled with explicit sex to boot, were embarrassing when someone was your wife. I'd been cajoled, encouraged, and passively-aggressively threatened to write 'real books' as if what I was doing was pretend somehow. Xander's company was romance community adjacent with what they were doing … how did he really feel about the genre and what I did?

"Now is not the time, Zoe."

Grabbing onto Xander's arm, my fingers dug into lithe muscles. "Yes or no? Just tell me."

Chest heaving, he leaned closer, his lips nearly

touching the shell of my ear. "Yes. I've read every single one."

Every one? Every single one? That was surprising, to say the least. "And?"

His breath whispered along the side of my face, eliciting goosebumps. "And you're an excellent writer."

I wanted to press the subject, to demand that he tell me what his favorite parts were, the notion embarrassing and titillating simultaneously. I wasn't the type of author who enjoyed discussing my novels, preferring to lurk in the shadows hoping no one noticed me or asked any personal questions. Why I wanted to delve into my work with Xander was unexplainable. Suddenly his opinion on the matter of my life's work was important to me. *No, that can't be right.*

I scowled, forcing myself to step away from him. "Thank you for the compliment. It's very much appreciated." *Yep, there you go. You're not making an awkward situation more awkward at all. Way to go, Zoe.*

Sensing the shift in my mood, Xander cleared his throat and straightened to his full height. "Like I said, we need to get a move on."

"Here we go again."

"Zoe." He huffed out my name like it physically hurt him.

I knew I could be stubborn and a pain in the ass occasionally, but damn, him uttering those two syllables spoke volumes.

Good thing I'd always excelled at selective hearing and

avoidance. "Xander," I retorted, doing my best to mimic his tone.

"We're not leaving Fantasy Life. Not yet."

Because of where I was, and my lack of bodily functions, sometimes there was a bit of disconnect with the physical aspect of my current self. And yet, other moments, I was extremely aware of my avatar and how realistic it felt. Like now, when my anger seemingly boiled my blood, heating my entire system. "This is wrong, Xander, and you know it. Should I speak slower? Louder? What? What do I have to do to make you understand that you can't keep me in here?"

"I don't have a choice," he blurted, his dark eyes flashing with regret.

"Umm … what does that mean?" I was tired of asking that question, especially because I wasn't getting straight answers.

"I didn't—don't want to panic you." He tapped at the scar in his eyebrow as he regarded me with wariness.

I gulped. "I think you already know what's coming."

He nodded, color draining from his face. "Yeah, you're about to panic."

"Mmm hmm … yep. We're stuck, aren't we? It's because of my brain. It's sizzling like an egg on a griddle out there in the real world. It's like those old commercials, this is your brain on drugs, but instead, this is your brain on virtual reality." My pulse thundered in my ears, setting an erratic yet familiar pace. I had one foot on the path to panic attack city, which was a hop and a skip away from nervous breakdown town if I kept up at this rate.

Xander pulled me into his arms, enveloping me in his warmth and scent. Fisting his shirt, I latched onto him as I squeezed my eyes shut. "I don't want to die in here."

"This is exactly why I didn't tell you. I didn't want to set you off."

"You think I'm weak and I can't handle anything." The only thing worse than a panic attack was having one in front of someone who thought I could simply not have one if my will was stronger, or that I was a fragile creature who couldn't handle everyday life.

"I never said that. But you have anxiety and panic attacks, and I know the kinds of things that trigger you. I merely wanted to avoid having you feel this way. And by the way," he stroked a hand down my back, "I'm not saying that you're dying. I never said that or anything close to it."

"But we can't leave," I squeaked out between chattering teeth.

"We can't leave—"

I gasped.

"Now. We can't leave now. I didn't say we were trapped or stuck. The emergency exit is ... missing."

I grunted into his shirt, wanting to know more but terrified to ask. Instead, I concentrated on not hyperventilating, which of course, only made it worse. I'd learned some grounding techniques from my therapist but attempting to ground oneself in virtual reality was an impossible task.

"We simply have to continue through the tropes. When we reach the end of the program we will be automatically ejected since things will shut down."

Breathe in two, out three, in two, out three. Deep breaths. In two, out three ... "But what if it doesn't? Then what?"

"At some point, my colleagues will pull us out. We are being monitored in case something like this were to happen. But since all of my and your vitals are normal, they have no idea what's going on in here."

"Pretty sure my heart rate and blood pressure spiked just now, and numerous times before, in fact." *Deep breaths, in two, out three, in two, out three. There is nothing wrong with you. You are having a flight reaction to something you find fearful. But you are safe. You are safe. You are totally safe. Your heart is not going to explode. You are not having a heart attack. You are not having a stroke. In two, out three, in two, out three ...*

Fuck, what if I am having a heart attack? My arms and legs tingled, tightness spreading throughout my chest. *No one's coming because whoever is supposed to be watching us left on a coffee break and I'm going to need emergency medical help at the worst possible time. Yep, this is how I'm going to die.*

Xander stroked his warm hand up and down my back rhythmically. I leaned into him, wanting to escape my own body somehow, even though technically my body was lying somewhere else at the moment and I wasn't actually in Xander's arms at all. *I'm pioneering a VR mental breakdown. I'll be in the history and medical books. A cautionary tale for future generations. Don't freak out like Zoe Woods and give yourself an aneurism.*

"Listen to me. Listen to what I'm saying. Your vitals haven't reached concerning levels, or we wouldn't still be here. They probably think you're ... never mind. You're fine. We're fine."

He was doing it again. Hiding things from me. "Never mind wha—" It suddenly dawned on me. "Oh my God! They think I'm up in here having the time of my life getting down and dirty with the AI, don't they?"

A chuckle rumbled in his chest, barely audible except for the fact my ear was pressed into him. "Maybe."

"It's not funny, Xander!" I shoved at him, stumbling away enough to deliver him a scathing glare. I was not a fan of the way he was biting his lips to contain his laughter. "I'm in the middle of a panic attack, and you're laughing at me!"

He shrugged, nonplussed. "You seem to be over it now. Guess getting mad at me helps. Gives you a place to focus all the extra adrenaline and energy."

Huh. He was right. That was the quickest I'd ever either halted or come out of a panic attack before. It was unheard of for me. Not that Xander had known to distract me from my own worst enemy—me, and my out-of-control, overanalyzing brain. He'd merely helped by accident. *Wonder what my therapist will think about this method? Ha!*

I crossed my arms over my chest. "I'm not going to

thank you since it's your fault the panic attack started to begin with."

"My fault? That's not fair."

"What's not fair is you keeping pertinent information from me."

He pursed his lips, visage pinching slightly. He then gave me a single nod. "You're right. I apologize for keeping things from you. Although, in my defense—"

I raised my eyebrows.

"Fine. I won't try to defend myself. The reason doesn't matter. I will do better in the future."

Wow, that was a surprisingly mature response. Was it possible I was the problem? Could it be me not letting Xander redefine himself now that he'd grown and changed and was no longer a teenager. *Well, shit. I need to think about this.*

"Can we get going now? If you want to get out of here anytime soon, we're going to have to speed through the tropes."

"Do I have to interact with the AIs in all of them?"

"I don't think so, but I have no idea how any of this is going to work now."

My heart set off at a gallop again. "When did you know something was wrong? In other words, how long have you been lying to me?"

"Caz was the giveaway. Even getting us out of that world took some doing."

Things were finally clicking into place. "It's nice to know the truth even if it is a bit horrifying."

Xander regarded me with bemusement. "Complicated, yes. Horrifying, no."

"Well, shit," I grumbled. "You just jinxed us. Horrifying here we come."

A large, orange door appeared in front of us, and I reluctantly shuffled through it after Xander.

Virtual reality bites ... big time.

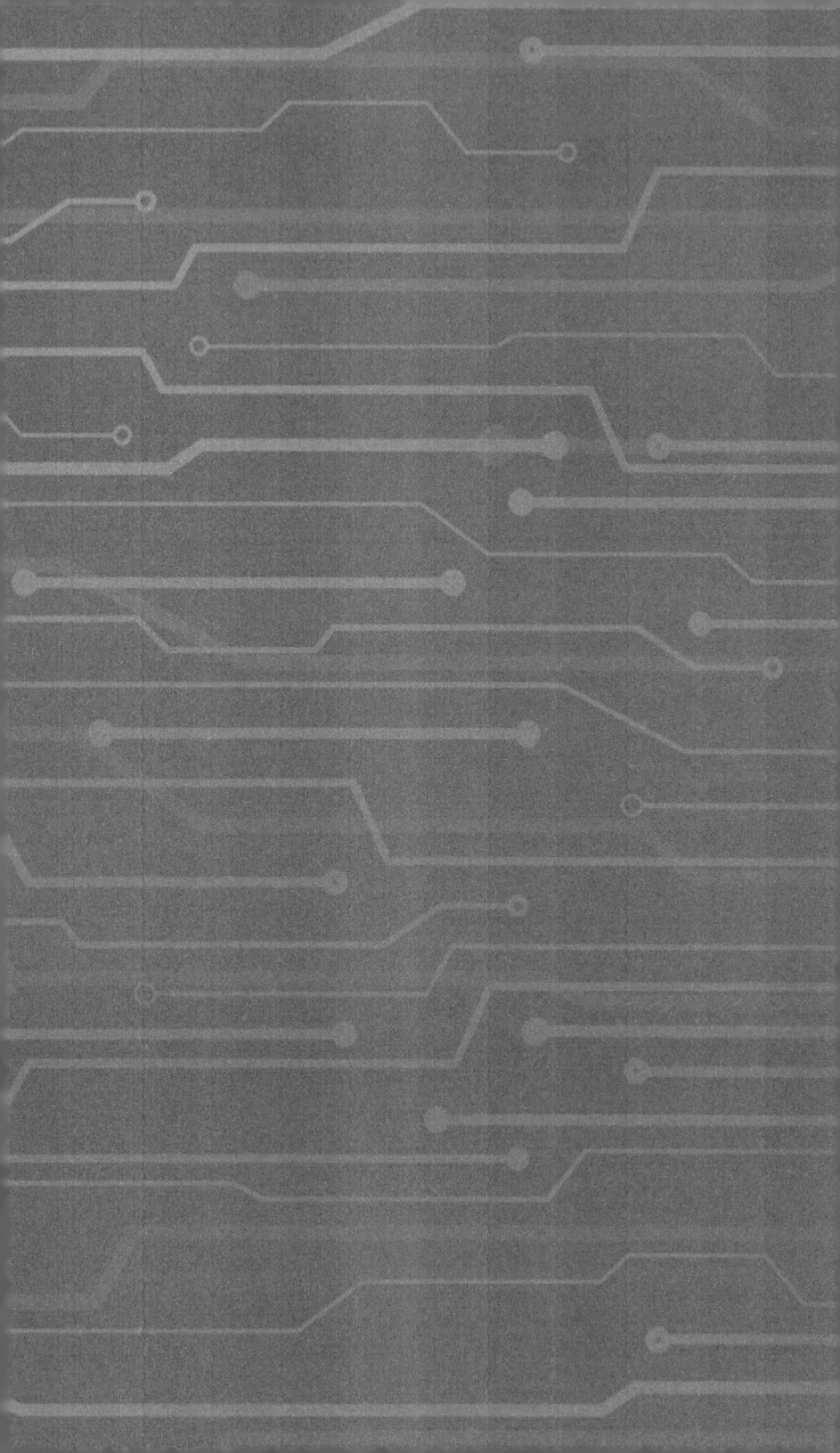

Chapter 14

M y hands went straight to the bulge in my lower abdomen, and I screamed, the sound reverberating in my head. "No, no, no, no, no."

Wide-eyed, Xander yanked me around toward him. "What's wrong?"

I motioned to the basketball-sized mound in my middle, as if he could miss it. "This is unacceptable. This is beyond fucked up. This is not something anyone would want to have in virtual reality. Who the hell let this happen?"

He scratched his head, bewildered. "I thought you wanted to have children of your own one day?"

"Yes! Of my own! Not pretend children that don't exist! This is …" I rubbed my belly, unable to look away. "This is fucked up."

"It's a secret baby trope, I think."

"Someone got their notes wrong because the baby is not supposed to be a secret to the mother." Hysterical laughter bubbled up from my chest. "What's in here anyways? Seriously? How is this happening? How is any of this happening?"

"Okay, okay. I got this. I can fix this. Try not to think about it."

"H-How can I not think about it?" Staggering away from him, I knocked on my stomach, half expecting something to knock back.

Xander slid up behind me, placing his hands on my shoulders. "Concentrate on the truth. The real-world truth. Concentrate on the fact that this baby isn't real, and you want it to go away."

"Am I supposed to will away the fake baby and its accompanying bump or not think about it? Because I can't do both at once."

"Change of plans." He moved around to stand in front of me, hands linking with mine. "Look at me, Zoe."

Lifting my gaze, I met his dark eyes, seeing determination swirling within their depths. "Okay, I'm looking at you. Now what?"

"Umm ... I'm working on it."

I scrunched up my nose. "You don't have a plan, do you?"

"I'm not good with people, Zoe. You know this." His frustration was palpable. It was clear he wanted to help, to fix what he undoubtedly had a hand in, but he didn't know exactly how.

Something inside of me thawed as I studied him. His tousled hair, his earnest expression, the hard set of his jaw, all of it told me that he genuinely cared, and yet he kept falling short. He was a lifelong overachiever when it came to things like school, grades, career, etc. However, when it came to knowing how to not stick his foot in his mouth with me, or to not saying no to a disastrous romance trope that could scar someone for life, he needed some serious guidance. Inexplicably, I wanted to be that guidance.

Squeezing his hands gently, I forced myself to smile. "You may not be good with people, but you know it's a weakness of yours so it's half the battle."

A muscle jumped in his already tense jaw. "I never do anything right when it comes to you."

"I ... well, I have extremely high expectations."

"No. Don't do that even if you're just trying to make me feel better. Don't put any of this on you. We've gone over this. Your expectations are not high, society's are just low when it comes to how people should treat each other. Especially how men should treat women."

"Okay, fine. So you're not great with people. And things haven't been going well with me in here, but you can do better. Like I said, knowing is half the battle."

A smile cracked his serious visage. "Suddenly I feel like we're in an after-school special trope. It wouldn't surprise me if the little star streaked across the sky with the rainbow followed by the 'the more you know' caption."

Dropping one of his hands, I rubbed my belly—

"It's gone!" Relief caused my shoulders to sag. "Thank the heavens, it's friggin' gone!"

Xander grinned. "Note to self. No secret baby trope or any other that requires a fake pregnancy."

"That one needs an asterisk next to it, and to be triple underlined. I mean, seriously, how could anyone think that was a good idea?"

He shrugged, the tips of his ears flushing. "Since I will never carry a child myself, some of that gets lost in translation."

"I think it's a bit more than—"

"Please drop it. I already feel like a big enough idiot, and I also feel bad for traumatizing you."

"Yeah, fine, I can drop it especially because I never wish to think of it ever again." I smirked. "Unless it's to make fun of you for having such a horrendous idea."

"Yep, sounds about right."

"Out of curiosity—"

His head dropped to his chest. "Here we go."

"How was the rest of the trope supposed to play out? Was I going to give birth? Was there going to be a fake baby? Or was the father-to-be going to find me and … and what? Was I going to be having pregnant sex? Would the trope have come to a conclusion before I gave birth, making the need for a fake baby irrelevant? Or would—"

"Please stop." Xander laughed. "I didn't build all of Fantasy Life myself. Believe it or not, this bad idea wasn't all my doing. Yes, there was a group of programmers that designed the finer details of some of the tropes. I can't be a thousand different places at once, after all."

Ignoring him, I continued, "And why are we in the middle of nowhere?" I squinted into the distance, spotting a small, rustic-looking cabin. "Am I hiding out or something? This keeps getting better and better."

Xander grunted. "Well, we're going to have to let this one play out for a while before we can go to the next world."

"I thought you said we could speed through the tropes."

"There isn't an option to leave this one yet. I tried to pull up a door already and nothing."

I sucked in a sharp breath. "What if we're stuck and the baby daddy comes looking for me but now there's no baby?"

"I don't know." He tugged at his hair. "But it will all be fine in the end. That much I can promise you." Gripping my arms tight enough to cause a hint of pain, he forced my gaze back to his. "I will protect you this time, I swear."

Swaying toward him, I murmured, "This time?"

He pulled away, leaving me strangely bereft. "Never mind. You know what I mean."

Did I? Because I had the weirdest sensation that I was missing something extremely important in the subtext of our conversation. Perhaps, it was merely the oddity of continuing to be in virtual reality, and the way even that wasn't behaving normally at the moment, and yet … yet it was as if something I needed to know—something vital to my survival on some level—was just beyond my reach.

"Come on." Xander motioned for me to follow him as he began to trudge across the field toward the small cabin. "I don't like being out in the open here."

Oh, now that didn't sound good. "Because you think Caz is going to show up again?"

He sighed. "I don't *not* think he's going to show up again."

"And what's he going to do if he does find us?"

"How about we don't find out?"

"Yeah, I like that plan. It's the best one you've had so far."

WE STOOD JUST inside the tiny, rustic, and definitely not what I'd consider a charming, cabin.

Clicking my tongue, my gaze darted from the leaky roof where an actual bucket had been placed on the floor to catch any water, to the twin-sized bed tucked in the corner. "Do you have any women on that programming team of yours? Or did you do a survey of the most popular romance tropes without any further research?"

"I'm not sure who designed this cabin, but there has to be a good explanation for it." He strode across the creaky floor, peering in every nook and cranny as if he might find a secret portal to a nicer place.

"Yes." I nodded. "The explanation is that a man must

have done the programmer version of mansplaining in this particular romance trope. Was it supposed to be a secret baby or the 'oh, no, there's only one bed?' trope? Quite possibly they combined the two, although I'm not sure how any of that would work."

Flopping down on the twin bed in question, Xander stretched out, his hands behind his head and his feet hanging off the edge of the mattress. In his splayed position, I couldn't help but appreciate the long, lean muscles of his arms and legs, or the way his dark hair fell across his forehead, accenting his sharp cheekbones. If he was anyone else besides my brother's best friend, I would—

Would what, Zoe? Jump his bones? He is who he is and it's pointless to consider anything else. Now wipe the drool from your chin and move on.

"I can feel you staring at me," Xander said, his eyes closed. "You going to tell me why?"

I shrugged even though he couldn't see it. "Just wondering why you get the bed?"

A lazy grin spread across his face. "You could always fight me for it."

"Don't be ridiculous."

"You're right. How could you be expected to beat me without any spoons or remotes, or ashtrays, or metal water bottles, or shampoo bottles …" His voice trailed off as his mind went to a place I'd rather him burn from his mind. The list he'd begun and abruptly stopped was of things I'd either threatened him with or actually thrown at him at some point in our shared past. The shampoo bottle was linked to a larger incident, one that had scarred me for life and undoubtedly been a highlight of his adolescence.

Stalking over to the bed, I kicked it, relieved to find tennis shoes back on my feet again instead of the ruby slippers. "You better not be thinking about what I think you're thinking about."

Face a picture of innocence, Xander remained silent.

I kicked the bed again. "Alexander Dai Tashiro. I know you heard me. Open your eyes right now and stop thinking about that ... that incident."

He chuckled, long and low, the sound caressing things on my insides. "The incident you are referring to is mine to remember as I please."

I kicked the bed repeatedly. "No, it's not."

Xander's dark eyes popped open, mischievous intent glinting. "I'm sorry, are you the thought police now?"

"Stop thinking about me in the shower!"

"That was a grand day for fifteen-year-old me, so no, I will not wipe it from my memory. I will reflect upon it with glee, even if Adam gave me a bloody lip for my minor transgression."

"You walked in on me on purpose."

"I was a fifteen-year-old boy, living in the nineties, and clueless about women and consent. At least the part of consent where sneaking a peek was that bad. I was innocent and naïve back then. Unaware of—"

"Unaware of how perverted you are. Yeah, I get it."

"I was in love, and you left the door unlocked."

"In lust, not in love. I was—am your best friend's older sister."

Xander's heated gaze slipped over me. "Two years back when I was fifteen and you were seventeen was a big deal. Now, not so much."

Unbidden, a barrage of images swept through my mind. Bits and pieces of what seemed like memories in their formation but couldn't possibly be anything but delusions brought on by suggestive talk.

Xander's lips trailing down the side of my neck, my head thrown back as I moaned.

His face buried between my thighs.

Our naked limbs entwined, bodies slick with sweat.

My head on his shoulder as his long fingers traced circles along my spine.

Gasping, I staggered back, bumping into an old rocking chair.

In a flash, Xander was by my side, gripping my elbow to keep me from ending up on my ass yet again. His touch sizzled on my bare skin, and I turned wild eyes toward his. "What was that? How did you do that?"

"What are you talking about? I didn't do anything." He smiled sheepishly. "Except maybe try to antagonize you about the shower incident. I won't deny trying to do that."

Yanking my arm away, I stumbled my way onto the bed. "It was ... I saw—" I tapped my forehead. "Never mind." We were in virtual reality, and he'd planted suggestive thoughts by bringing up the fact that we were adults now. The barrage of naughty images, us in sexual situations, was because of that and my out of control and recently deprived libido.

"Move over." Xander bumped me with his hip, scooting his large body into the bed. "I need to figure out what our next step is."

"And clearly it's of the utmost importance that you do it in this bed."

"I only vacated my prime position to keep you from falling. Not exactly sure why since you wouldn't have gotten hurt, but habits like that die hard. Now," he bumped me again, this time with his shoulder as he pushed farther into the bed, "move over. I'm bigger than you and need more room."

His warmth and presence were heady. The craving to curl into his side was sudden and unwelcome. "Just keep your hands to yourself," I grumbled, hating how a part of me, the stupid and prone to impulsiveness part, wanted the exact opposite.

"You don't have to worry. I can be a gentleman."

I grunted. "That statement on the heels of us reminiscing about my traumatic shower experience caused by your perverted roaming gaze."

"Hey, now. All joking aside, I had no idea you were in there. Adam and I just got to your house, the shower wasn't running, and yeah, the door was unlocked. What was I supposed to do? Not look? I mean, a was a fifteen-year-old boy who had been fantasizing about the very same girl who was standing blissfully naked in front of me."

I sniggered. "Blissfully?"

"You heard me. Blissfully." He raised his finger to make another point. "And let me remind you that I did my best not to stare when you found yourself suddenly naked in the Fantasy Life orientation."

"Did your best? Please. You saw everything."

He quirked an eyebrow. "I saw a decent amount, yeah. But if it makes you feel any better," he cleared his throat, "you are every bit as beautiful now as you were then. Even more so because, well, um, you're a woman now."

My insides warmed pleasantly, the glow of his twisted compliment disconcerting. His shy, awkwardness charming. When had Xander's praise started to mean something to me? When did his attraction to me shift from annoying to flattering? *Apparently, sometime within the last five minutes.* I peeked at him from under the fan of my lashes, my gaze darting along his face to settle on his full, supple lips.

I kept trying to remind myself of his relationship to Adam, as if that categorized him as off limits somehow, plus factor in that he was two years younger than me. But Xander was right. Two years meant nothing when I was forty and he was thirty-eight. And would Adam really care? Only if I chased off his best friend the way I seemed to eventually chase off all men I was interested in.

Wait. What? Did I just admit to myself that I'm interested in Xander? Alexander Dai Tashiro? The same dorky kid who followed me around for years? The same perverted teen who gawked at me naked when I was fresh out of the shower, and kissed me against the snack shelf in the pantry on New Year's?

"Okay, I'm feeling a little … I don't know, like I shouldn't have said any of what I just did."

"Oh." I swallowed to combat my suddenly dry throat. "No, not at all. I mean, it's fine. Don't worry about it."

We fell into silence, the energy between us humming. I was afraid to move, worried that my body would betray me somehow. Or worse yet, what if I was ultimately rejected by Xander? He thought he wanted me, but in many ways, I was an unattainable fantasy, one where the reality would fall short.

"I have underestimated the one-bed romance trope," Xander muttered.

Biting my lower lip, I stifled a laugh. This whole thing was utterly ridiculous. All of it from the start to wherever it would inevitably end up. A romance author trapped in virtual reality with romance tropes, also with quite possibly her real-live romance trope worked into the mix. The "oh, no, there's only one bed," meets "but he's my brother's best friend" … and let's not forget the "I'm older than him," and the "We grew up together".

Xander leaned up to perch on one elbow, his expression bemused. "Is my discomfort amusing?"

I shook my head, my chest shaking with my barely contained laughter. "No," I choked out. "That's not it at all."

His nostrils flared as annoyance flitted across his

features. "Then what?"

"It's hard to explain."

Leaning closer, he pinned my arms over my head. "Try me."

My breath caught in my throat. Suddenly there was no doubt. Xander was all man. A man my body yearned for, consequences be damned. The real question was whether or not it went beyond the physical.

Normally, aside from fiction-born fantasies, I required more than the mere physical to develop lust for someone. I could appreciate beauty wherever I found it when it came to the body, but getting to the point where I actually wanted to interact was another issue. It was the reason I imagined connections that weren't there, like with my exes, so that I could feel emotionally strong enough to move the relationship to the next level. Unfortunately, I assigned qualities to people that only existed in my mind. Bad boy with a heart of gold? Not outside of romance novels. Hot guy with violent tendencies who used those to make you feel safe? Not in this universe.

But I knew Xander. His strengths, his flaws, all the pieces of himself he would hide away from someone if he could. Just as he knew mine. He'd seen me at my worst, and if he still wanted me, well, then, maybe … just maybe …

Xander's gaze locked with mine, his grip on my wrists tightening, annoyance melting away as lust burned through his dark eyes, heating them up. "Zoe, I—" His Adam's apple bobbed in his throat. "This can't—"

Lifting my head, I slammed my lips into his. Electricity zipped between us, and I groaned when his tongue swept into my mouth to take over the kiss.

An image of Jared, ex-husband number two, standing on the front porch of my house, appeared in my mind's eye, jolting me away from the present.

"What are you doing?" I heard myself say.

"I wouldn't have believed it if I hadn't seen it with my own eyes." Jared took a step toward me, a vein in his forehead bulging, and a sneer tugging at his mouth. He brandished his phone, waving a blurry picture at me that was obviously supposed to mean something.

"What are you talking about?"

"You got something to tell me, Zoe?"

"No. I don't owe you any kind of explanation anymore."

"You were fucking around on me when we were still married."

I opened my mouth to deny it but didn't see the point anymore. "What I did wasn't right. I know that. But our marriage was already on the rocks."

"You going to move him in here now? Marry him, too? Make him husband number three until you get bored with him just like you did with me?"

"That's not what happened." My chest tightened. "Plus, he and I ... we're not together anymore."

Jared laughed, the sound menacing. "He was smarter than me then. Spotted you for the whore you are before he got more involved. Good for him."

My stomach twisted. "I won't deny he's smarter than you.

Although that's a pretty low bar. But none of it is your business. Nothing about me is anymore."

"You never had a problem with my intelligence before." He took another few steps toward me, but I refused to be cowed and stood my ground.

"That's because I saw what I wanted to see, not who you really are. You're the one who played me. I was nothing more than a prop to you. I was meant to stand next to you and look pretty—to make you look better at meetings and events. But then I embarrassed you with my work. Work that you knew about before we got married. You never wanted me. You wanted what you thought you could mold me into."

"You're right about one thing. You made me a laughingstock. First with your stupid books ... books that are nothing more than porn. Books that hurt people, raise their expectations for relationships to unrealistic levels," he snarled. "Which should have told me what you were really about. What you expected of me and what you'd do when I couldn't live up to your fictional characters." He took another step closer. "You cheated on me. People know. My family, my friends, they know."

"Oh, I'm sorry. Did I hurt your fragile ego in front of your adoring public? Do they wonder why I slept with someone else when you claimed to keep me satisfied? We both know you never could. You were shit in bed—" Stop it, Zoe. Just because he insulted you, something he's done a thousand times before, doesn't mean you should do the same in turn. Don't poke the bear.

And yet, I couldn't keep my mouth shut or the acid that poured forth from it. "You couldn't keep me happy because you were selfish and never cared about anything but your own damn pleasure. I had to find a skilled lover. Someone who knew how to give me what I needed—"

Before I even realized he'd moved, his fist collided with the side of my head. I gasped, staggering back.

Why did I provoke him? Why? I knew better. I friggin' knew better. His volatile temper was quick to ignite, one of the reasons it took so long to leave him. I'd been afraid of how he would punish me if I didn't do things just right—of how he could ruin my life and destroy everything I worked so hard to get. But I'd snapped, and I couldn't hold any of it in anymore. Or maybe I thought I was safe now that we were divorced since the physical violence had been limited to my possessions, and he'd never struck me before.

"You fucking bitch." His fist connected with my cheekbone, pain exploding behind my eye. "No one outside of fiction could ever live up to your expectations." Another punch smashed into my middle. I curled into a ball, hands over my head. "You're the one who cheated. You're the villain of this story. Not me. Not fucking me."

"Zoe!" Xander shook me, and I blinked his face back into focus.

My hand flitted to my forehead. "I don't feel right." My head pounded, dizziness and nausea assaulting.

He wrapped his arms around me, pulling me snuggly into his chest. "It's going to be okay, Zoe. Everything is going to be okay. I promise."

I let him hold me, even though I knew he couldn't keep the promise he'd just made.

Chapter 15

"**D**o you want to talk about it?" Xander spoke softly as if he'd spook me otherwise. Quite possibly he was right.

"I don't know what I saw just now. Or why it happened when it did." One moment I'd been lost in a kiss with Xander, and the next I was trapped in a nightmare with Jared.

"Fantasy Life isn't perfect." He chuckled darkly. "As you well know. There's a reason why we still need to do extensive testing." He sifted his fingers through my hair. "Especially with people like you who seem to be neurodivergent when it comes to virtual reality."

"Is that a polite way of telling me my brain is broken?"

Xander pulled back from me just enough so he could tilt my chin up to meet his gaze. "You listen to me, Zoe Marie Woods. There is nothing broken about you. You think outside of the box, which is something I've always lov—" he cleared his throat, "liked about you."

"Something's not right, Xander. I can feel it."

One side of his mouth hitched up. "That's your paranoia again. Whatever you saw, even if you don't want to talk about it, was normal. Or maybe I should say it wasn't abnormal."

I lifted my eyebrows.

"Okay, it may not be typical for this kind of experience, but your brain is fine." A grin stretched the span of his face. "Or as fine as it's ever been."

If he was teasing me, then I was confident that he wasn't worried. No worry translated to my brain being fine. "Shut up, asshat."

Silence, thick and heavy, abruptly settled over us as we stared at each other, breath intermingling. I could tell by the questions swirling in his eyes that he was thinking about the same thing I was … the kiss. The mind-blowing lip lock we'd been ensnared in when my brain had decided to take me on an unpleasant detour.

His fingers trailed up my neck, entangling in my hair. I gripped his shoulders, my heart skipping a beat before setting off at a breakneck pace.

What is this between us? And do I want to explore it in VR where technically none of this is real? Do I want to explore it at all? How much of it exists only in my mind? Literally?

Quite possibly I'd drummed up a connection that wasn't there between Xander and myself because of where we were. The circumstances were unusual, to say the least.

Or perhaps I was in denial about … everything. Maybe confused? Scared?

"Zoe," Xander murmured. "I can see your thoughts spiraling out of control."

There was no use denying it. "Yeah, a bit."

My skin tingled, calling out for him to touch me. I couldn't help but wonder about how fast all of this was happening. Abrupt even. If I was writing it into one of my novels, I would put the brakes on, knowing my readers would consider the turnabout in my emotions too sudden and unrealistic. Or weird. I'd gone from thinking of Xander as nothing more than my brother's annoying best friend to having uncontrollable sexual urges directed at him.

Okay, so maybe that wasn't one hundred percent true. I'd always thought Xander was cute, and that kiss when we were teenagers had felt like something even then. So was it strange, or was there something wrong with me in the way I hastened into relationships and romantic entanglements? Maybe I developed an attraction to Xander because he was the only viable option at the moment, and I was just that desperate and pathetic. There was a distinct possibility that I was attempting to write my own exciting ending to an extremely boring story.

"Zoe," Xander murmured again. "Talk to me."

But I didn't want to talk. And I didn't want to think for that matter either. Not about my motivations, where I was, or the problems facing and surrounding us, like the rogue AI. I simply wanted to exist in the moment with no worries or cares. To do what my heart screamed for me to do even if it ended as badly as all those types of decisions had before. Because that's who I was. I was the woman who trusted in the promise of love no matter how many times I got knocked down. I would always get up, and I would always try again. I was in love with love, and one day I'd find my own HEA, as long as I refused to give up.

Hooking my leg around Xander, I pulled him fully on top of me just as I slammed my lips into his. The motion ignited the fuse between us, sweeping me away in an explosion of lust. Teeth, lips, and tongues clashed. Hands roamed as fuzzy images of us naked and entwined many times over skittered across my brain, all of them resembling memories.

"I should have expected this," a vaguely familiar voice snarled.

Xander was ripped from me and thrown across the room. Gasping, I scuttled into the corner of the wall by the headboard, feet tucked up underneath me. Caz stood near the entrance of the cabin, visage dark with rage.

Xander jumped to his feet, transforming instantly into his fae costume. "You don't belong here."

Caz sneered. "You don't belong here with her either." He raised his hand, palm up, lifting Xander into the air again with the motion.

Fighting what could only be considered Caz's magic under the current circumstances, Xander flailed, his eyes dark with determination. "She's not yours."

"And I suppose you think to make her yours then? Is

this what it's been about since the beginning?" Caz glided into the cabin, his feet not touching the ground.

"I don't know what your plan is anymore, Xander, but I think it's about time you tell him the truth!"

"The truth?" Xander bit out, waving his arms in an attempt to counteract whatever power Caz had over him. "He would never believe the truth."

Caz's head whipped in my direction, his gaze softening for an instant as he regarded me. The moment passed so quickly I wasn't sure if I imagined it or not. "Mattius has you spelled. But I will free you so we can be together the way it is meant to be."

I fought the urge to roll my eyes. *I swear, I'll never write another book where the hero acts the fool like this again. It is not sexy or attractive when faced with it even in a real-life adjacent situation like VR.* "Caz, I'm not spelled in any way. We are not meant to be together. You just think that because you're programmed to."

He waved me off with a snort. "One who is spelled never knows when they are."

"Told you," Xander snapped, inching his way toward the ground, finally. For someone who was supposed to have control over Fantasy Life programming, he did not appear to have things in hand.

Scooting off the bed, I made my way slowly toward Caz, his gaze tracking my every move. If not for the fact that I knew he was AI, and I hadn't been having an extremely hot make-out session with Xander when Caz burst onto the scene, I might have stopped to appreciate the piece of artwork he truly was. Whoever had created the fae warrior's design had gotten it all the way right.

"Are you kidding me right now, Zoe? Are you seriously ogling him with me right here, hanging ten in the air?"

I sputtered on a laugh, the sound borderline deranged. "What can I say, except that your programmers got some things right in here."

Caz threw me a smug look. "She can't help but be attracted to me."

"There isn't a straight female alive that wouldn't be attracted to you." I continued staring, taking in all of his perfection. "I take that back, I think any human being would be attracted to you, male, female, gay, straight, nonbinary ... you are quite the specimen."

"You are not the first to say so."

"Well, there's no doubt that your confidence is well placed. Although the arrogance would get old quickly, I think." I glanced at Xander, who was fixated on me with his mouth hanging open. "I've written more than a few characters like him, and although fun to write, I knew in the back of my mind that living with someone so full of themselves would not be endearing in reality."

I tapped my chin, considering. "Although, no one said I would have to listen to him speak to fuck him." Slapping my hand over my mouth, I guffawed. Yep, I said that out loud. I was being the worst version of myself for some unknown reason, treating Caz like he was an object and not a living, sentient ... something.

"Zoe, this isn't funny anymore," Xander grated,

renewing his fight against Caz's unseen power.

He was right. None of this was funny, and once again I'd lost my way. *Seriously, what is wrong with me?* I put romance, even the imagined connection between me and Xander, ahead of everything else. Dangle a potential relationship in front of me, however fleeting, and I forget everything else. I wanted out of Fantasy Life, but instead, I'd been waylaid by Xander's lips, perfectly content to roll around in the minuscule bed with him in virtual reality. Sure, he'd claimed we were trapped, and he needed time to think, but then he'd been more than happy to grope me until Caz caught up with us.

I crossed my arms over my chest and tapped my foot. "Is this all part of the game?"

"What are you talking about?" Xander choked out, his face flushed from exertion, no closer to escaping though.

"None of it makes sense. You should have more power than Caz since—"

The fae in question scoffed. "None have more power than me." He gave me major side-eye, as if my comment, the one I didn't even get to finish, had been a huge insult.

"In here, I might as well be like them," Xander huffed out.

I grunted. If I looked at it that way, as if while in virtual reality we had the same physical limitations as the AI, then that made sense. Although ... "You should be more like Neo, I'm thinking. Which means this whole thing is a farce meant to keep me in here, isn't it?" And to think I'd swapped spit with him.

"Stop comparing Fantasy Life to the Matrix for fuck's sake! They're nothing alike!"

"The man doth protest too much, methinks." Throwing my head back, I laughed. I'd fallen for it. Who in their right mind would believe they were trapped in virtual reality with a rogue AI that just so happened to be their fantasy character preference? It was a trope within a trope or a game within a game. I wasn't sure which, but in the end, it didn't matter.

"Zoe, this isn't a trick," Xander hissed, snagging my gaze. His eyes darted behind Caz, to me, and back again a few times. He then mouthed the word 'run'.

All the hairs on my body rose in unison, followed by a full-body chill. Perhaps there was a chance I wanted it to be fake. Should I chance it? And what would happen if Caz locked me away in fae world? Would my consciousness be trapped there forever, essentially leaving my body to wither in reality?

And what about Xander? He didn't seem concerned about his own safety, therefore it stood to reason that I shouldn't be either. *Right?* Plus, when the creator of something sci-fi slash techy related tells you to run, it made sense to listen to them.

I stabbed a finger in the air at him. "There will be hell to pay if you're lying to me again."

"Zoe, please," he gritted out, his expression pinched as if he was in actual physical pain.

And what do I know, maybe he is? That thought twisted my stomach, causing nausea to roil my gut.

Indecision warred, my heart thrashing against my ribcage.

Caz twisted his wrist, rotating Xander until he hung upside down, his hair falling to touch the ground.

"Zoe, you need to trust me."

Something in his voice, or possibly his tone, convinced me. Spinning on my heels, I sprinted out the door of the cabin. Caz roared out English obscenities mixed with a language I didn't understand. Later I would need to ponder the awe-inspiring fact that the AI fae warrior invented a language.

Just outside, hanging wide open in the green meadow, was a burnt sienna wooden door. It was how Caz had transported himself to us, and it was going to be how I escaped.

Running as fast as my legs would carry me, I mustered every last bit of latent athletic ability, or in actuality, I informed my brain that it needed to get me to that door, and it had all the power since currently my consciousness was all that technically existed in VR.

Diving through the door, I kicked it shut when I was on the other side, the entire thing exploding into pixels before disappearing. I lay on my back, staring up at the blue sky, chest heaving as I struggled to catch my breath.

"Really, brain, you can accept that I don't need food, water, or to even pee, but you can't let me have more than moderate endurance physically?" Maybe I shouldn't have criticized Xander for not going all Neo in Fantasy Life when I couldn't sprint a few hundred feet without gasping for air.

I waited for my heart rate to slow, and for my lungs to act reasonably before lurching to my feet. Scanning my surroundings, I heaved a huge sigh. "Oh, come on! More woods? How about a city or something? Whoever's listening or monitoring me now ... I want to point out that some very good romance tropes don't take place in the middle of nowhere."

No answer was forthcoming, not that I expected one. Or maybe I did. I couldn't help but wonder how Xander was getting along with Caz since I made my escape. I had no doubt that both of them would be popping up again soon, so I only had one choice.

"Welp, here I go," I said out loud again, still hoping Xander would appear to make a snarky comment or to tease me about how ridiculous I was being. "I'm about to start this journey all on my own. Hope a big, bad wolf doesn't get me on the way to grandma's house." I chuckled nervously, trudging slowly across the silent field.

"What's your plan, Zoe?" I continued muttering to myself. "Keep going until you find trouble?"

A loud crash sounded off to my right in a cluster of trees. Adrenaline surging through my veins, I took off at a sprint, my lungs already burning again.

I so don't want to discover what the trope of this world is. Just find another door, and then another, and keep jumping until you come to the end of this virtual hellscape. It's as good a plan as any under the circumstances.

Chapter 16

My book-boyfriend crack had always been antiheroes, bad boys with hearts of gold, and sometimes even villains. There was something particularly intriguing about a deliciously handsome villain who would burn the world to the ground to save the heroine. He not only put her first but only cared about her, anyone else be damned. There was also something swoon-worthy about meaning so much to someone, that if you ceased to exist their universe would crumble. It was incredibly heady to think that someone would live and die for you, and above all else, that you could count on them to be there for you no matter what. Unconditional love, bordering on obsession. It was the stuff that kept romance book lovers like myself up late at night reading, and also, in my case, writing. But ...

To be someone's obsession in real life was another story. It wasn't sexy or comfort-inducing. It didn't leave you feeling cherished above all others, because the truth of it was, the type of man who wanted to own a human being was not the kind of man who you'd want to be owned by.

And I think I'm getting to the crux of my writer's block. Is it possible that by perpetuating these fantasies I'm setting women up for failure? Have I set myself up for failure? I don't need butterflies and danger, I need ... I need ... Xander.

His name whispered through my consciousness, halting me in my tracks. A cool wind blew, goosebumps erupting along my flesh, my hair floating like a cloud around my face. Tucking what I could behind my ears, I grumbled under my breath, "Yeah, now I know my brain is getting fried by Fantasy Life. Xander? Seriously?" And yet, even considering him as a viable option, one for more than just a romp between the sheets, opened a cavernous yearning within my heart. "What is going on with me?"

You haven't set yourself up for failure. You, Zoe Woods, are well aware of the difference between fantasy and reality. I paused to glance around the current virtual reality landscape. *Okay, at least when it comes to books and movies. Escapism in the form of romance and fantasy gives hope to people. And hope is the most important thing to hang onto when things get difficult in life. My readers are smart, they know the difference. They know the part of my romances to be coveted isn't the dark, villainous character, but the undying love aspect. If they raise their standards a bit because of the men in my books, realistic or not, and no longer accept being treated like shit, then that's a good thing.*

I stopped walking again. Wait. Why was I doubting myself? My motivations? It was like there was a computer virus in my brain corrupting my files. I had a conversation with Xander not too long ago explaining my beliefs on the matter, and part of the conversation rolled back through my mind.

"I don't know. Maybe real men aren't good enough for you because your expectations are set too high."

"Oh, no, you didn't. You did not just imply that because I'm a romance author and into romance in general, that I set unrealistic standards for the men in my life."

"I didn't exactly imply. But what I mean is that I simply think—"

"Stop thinking, Xander. I'm serious. That's some misogynist shit right there. Sure, most couples in romance novels are exceptionally attractive, because it's fantasy, and why not? But that's not the point, and it's not why people flock to them in droves. Let me ask you this: Is it wrong to ask to be desired fully and completely? Is it wrong to ask to be treated with respect? Is it wrong to want to feel as if my man loves me above all else, like I'm the most important thing in his world? I just want to feel wanted, loved, and to be treated like the queen all women deserve to be treated like. And yeah, it's about exploring our sexuality, too. But spoiler alert, we always get ours in the end in romance. It's about being the focus of love and desire, being cherished."

Could I have a corrupted file, so to speak, when it came to my previous feelings? Was it possible that something happened, something I couldn't quite put my finger on, to make me doubt myself? If that was the case, then my writer's block could have taken root because of cognitive dissonance. Things weren't jiving properly between my muse and the rest of me.

"You fucking bitch. No one outside of fiction could ever live up to your expectations. You're the one who cheated. You're the villain of this story. Not me. Not fucking me."

Jared's voice echoed through the trees, his words causing me to curl into myself. Shaking my head from the onslaught of vitriol, I continued trudging through the forest. Confused about the words and the partially remembered scene from before, I wasn't sure if I wanted answers anymore. I had no recollection of that fight happening with Jared, although it did seem on brand for the end of our relationship. It couldn't be a memory, though, because I didn't cheat on him. I didn't—

Pain spiked through my skull, and I staggered into a tree, leaning on it for support.

Once again, I got a flash of Xander standing in my living room, clothes and hair rumpled, his expression stricken. *"They're not excuses, Zoe. It's the plain truth. I can't help it if you don't like what I have to say."*

"No. Wait. You don't understand. You have it all wrong."

"I think I have it exactly right." He tugged at his hair. *"I thought ... I thought you and me—"* He raised his hands and backed away slowly. *"It doesn't matter what I thought. I was wrong."*

I clutched at my temples, groaning. "Why do I keep

seeing things that didn't happen? What am I trying to tell myself?"

"Do you often talk to yourself while wandering the woods lost and alone?" a deep voice grumbled with a hint of amusement.

Whirling around, I stumbled, catching myself before I fell on my ass yet again. *Note to self: Never again mock the heroine who keeps falling. Gravity is hard to deal with when also dealing with stress.*

"It's probably the only reason why you're still alive. Even the creatures of these woods aren't stupid enough to mess with an insane human woman."

Closing my eyes briefly, I inhaled and exhaled several times, failing to center myself. From the glimpse I'd gotten, my visitor was tall, dark, handsome, and massively stacked with muscle. He dwarfed even Lachlan, who I thought was built like Conan the Barbarian. If that was true, then this new guy was built like ... I don't know, Conan the Barbarian 4.0.

Opening my eyes, I back peddled a few steps, hoping to put some space between us. "Aren't you a creature of these woods, since here you are?"

He chuckled, the sound dark, menacing, and yes, also pleasing. *Ach! Beautiful men everywhere and me not able to fully appreciate any of them.* The romance aspect of Fantasy Life had turned into a means of torture, instead of a fun vacation for my brain ... and lady parts.

"It's all my fault." Xander's voice rang out through the clearing, a phantom touch running down my right cheek.

Trailing the path the invisible hand had just taken, I inhaled sharply as Xander's unique and undefinable scent lingered, swirling around me.

"Where are you?" I whispered. "What's happening?"

"Human," the star of whatever trope I was currently in rumbled. "You smell delicious."

Those words snapped me away from whatever weirdness was going on. *Oh, shit.* I knew what that meant. I'd written enough paranormal romances with werewolves, dragons, demons, and other males of that ilk to know exactly where the 'you smell delicious' thing was going.

I raised my hands in the air, backing away slowly. "I'm not your mate. The scent you're smelling that you think marks me as such is a lie. You ... you have a sinus infection or something." Okay, wow, I just went there. It was just that I didn't have time to deal with another AI that was intent on claiming me the way Caz now was. The fun and games were over, and my only goal was to get the hell out of Fantasy Life.

"Mate? Yes. I want you naked and underneath me now, human." His green eyes flashed bright, as if illuminated by flashlights, his pupils blown wide.

I shook my head. "No, it's not going to happen. I swear, I'm not your mate, and if you wait, I promise you your actual mate will eventually show up." And she would be whoever was the next person to test out these tropes, hopefully after all the bugs were worked out. But it definitely wouldn't be me. Once out of Fantasy Life there was no way I would ever voluntarily jump back in.

"The fact that you know what a mate is, and yet are denying it, means you sense what is between us, too." Moving forward with liquid grace, the man approached me slowly as not to scare me off.

"Look here, whoever and whatever you are, no means no. And to be clear, I'm saying no."

He smirked. "Soon you'll be begging me to fuck you."

I sighed. Yes, I wrote stuff like this—fated mates, etc.— but currently, I was a bit disgusted. Sure, I'd still write it in the future, but facing down a pushy male of undetermined species was annoying. I didn't want to get down and dirty with the sexy AI man.

You didn't seem to have a problem with it when it came to Caz or even Lachlan. What changed? My mind reeled as I pondered the situation. I had a moral quandary when it came to hooking up with Lachlan and then Caz, causing me to pendulum back and forth on how I wanted to handle the tropes with them. And yet I'd all but thrown myself at Caz when I first met him. What had changed indeed?

Xander's face flashed in front of me, his dark eyes filled with some unknown emotion. *"Thirsty much?"* he grumbled.

At the time, when he'd made the comment, I had myself wrapped around Caz while I enthusiastically approved of the idea of having sex with him. I'd relentlessly harassed the fae warrior with innuendos and repeatedly propositioned him.

Then there was the whole fade to grey sex scene with Lachlan. I replayed part of the conversation between me and Xander after the fact.

"Zoe, come on. I didn't do it on purpose. Yes, it's a setting option within Fantasy Life. After all, not everyone has the same kink level, but I didn't do this to you."

"Then why did you wish me good luck in that sarcastic way? You knew this was going to happen, and you were taunting me when I didn't even know it at the time."

"Obviously your subconscious was not fully on board with the whole sex with Lachlan thing."

"Mmm hmmm ... I call bullshit."

I slapped myself in the forehead. "Wow, Zoe, you really are an idiot, aren't you?"

I had feelings for Xander. I was well aware from an outside perspective I was as obtuse as the Jane Austen character Emma when she finally realized she had a thing for Mr. Knightly. Or maybe not quite as bad as her ... Xander wasn't my best friend after all. And I had at least admitted to my lustful leanings toward Xander, letting my lips and other body parts lead the charge for a few moments back at the cabin. However, lust and having legit feelings for someone were two completely different things. If I'd gone through with it and had sex with Caz, I wouldn't have started caring about his dreams and ambitions, his thoughts and emotions. The connection would have been physical only. It could have been an exception to me needing to have a bond to engage in intimacy since Caz wasn't a live human. This thing with Xander, whatever it was, it was about more.

Holy shit. I have feelings for Xander. How did that happen? I mean, seriously, how did that happen? I could shrug it off and blame it on his glow-up, because damn, the man was sizzling hot now. Or even the fact that we were in VR and things were just plain weird. But it was more than that, it was him. I wanted *him* because of all the things that made him the unique person he was, even the annoying parts, which suddenly didn't seem all that annoying. Again, I wasn't sure how it developed. It's not like we'd spent a whole lot of time together in Fantasy Life cultivating something deep between us, which meant ...

I shook my head, images of Xander and me, the two of us together in a myriad of scenes, smiling and laughing, played across my mind. Not from our shared past, but more recently, as if—

Pain surged through my temples, and I cried out, slumping forward.

An inhuman roar vibrated my teeth, and dark spots danced in front of my vision.

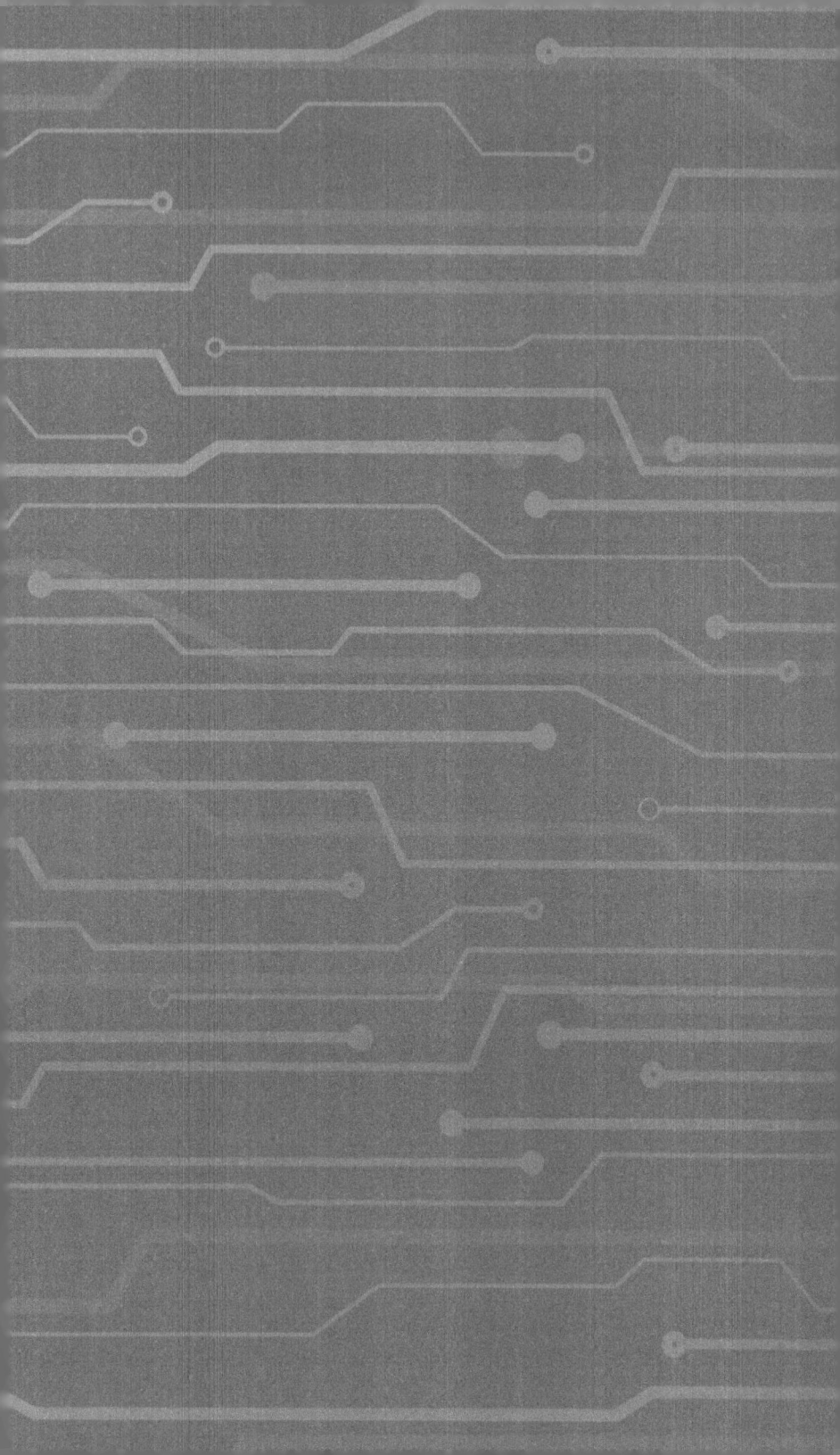

Chapter 17

"We shouldn't." My voice came out breathless and low, my protest more of an invitation than anything else.

"We should." Xander's dark eyes glittered with intent. "He doesn't treat you right. You don't want to be with him anymore. You want to be with me." Caging me against the wall, he leaned forward, his lips skimming up my neck.

Clutching at the back of his dress shirt, I shuddered, my nerve endings seemingly exposed and sizzling from the contact. "But he's my husband, and if we start our relationship like this, with me cheating, it will tarnish what we could have."

"No, no it won't." He pushed his face into my hair, his body trembling as he inhaled. "This is us. It's different because it's us."

I pushed at him weakly, my fingers instantly declaring their dissent and curling reflexively to clutch at him again. My body was waging a battle with my mind. And my mind was losing. "How could you ever trust me if you knew I cheated on my husband? Someone I took vows with? I want to do this right with you."

Xander's hand slid down to settle on my lower back, the warmth burning through my clothes. "I've been in love with you almost my entire life, Zoe. I've been waiting for what feels like an eternity for you to catch up. And finally, here we are. The rest doesn't matter, and it never will." His voice broke low and then cracked, belying the soft smile on his lips.

Despite the situation, I couldn't help but laugh. "You weren't in love with me back in the day, you were in lust."

"For teenage boys, lust might as well be love," he murmured against my skin.

My heart quadrupled in time, my pulse pounding in my middle, serving to remind me of our precarious position. We were in his office at Fantasy Life, Inc. like we'd spent so many nights before for weeks, working on the preliminary notes for the romance tropes he eventually wanted me to be the first to test when they were ready. It had started perfectly innocent, me more than happy to help, with the added bonus of spending as much time away from home as possible, my latest relationship on life support with me ready to pull the plug.

Shoving at him with more force, I said, "This isn't

right. I don't … what's between us is you thinking you're finally getting the girl of your dreams from your teenage fantasies. And for me … well, apparently, I'm a serial monogamist. You just happened to be at the right place and time as my marriage was falling apart."

I hated that part of myself, and how it made me wonder if I even knew what real love was. Did I want Xander for himself, who he was as a person, or merely what he represented to me … a new possibility, a fresh chance at love?

Stilling, Xander pulled away from me, staring into my eyes from inches away. He tucked my hair behind my ears, leaving his hands to cup my cheeks when he was done. "You're overthinking this. Because of course you are." One side of his mouth curled up in amusement. "You wouldn't be you if you didn't." He bit his lower lip, considering what to say next. "I've seen you at your worst, Zoe, and you can be pretty bad, especially when you're throwing heavy objects at my head."

I smiled.

"And it makes you smile to picture doing that. You are violent, and bratty sometimes, and high maintenance, and — Fuck, none of that matters because you're also the best person I know. I want to be the one who maintains you, Zoe. I want to be the one who listens to your rants and calms you down when you're having another one of your panic attacks over something I can't even make sense about. I just want you. None of it has to make sense. Real love hardly ever does."

He cleared his throat, glancing away. "Plus, you know, you're the kind of beautiful that people write sonnets about, and I've been dreaming about fucking you since I hit puberty."

I slapped at his arm. "Hey! Way to ruin the moment!"

He turned back to me, quirking an eyebrow in question. "Physical attraction matters, too. Don't deny that it's what first caught your attention when I showed up here in Raleigh again."

"That's what I'm worried about, that maybe the physical attraction is all that's between us." I'd somehow gotten stuck in his quicksand, and every second I was near him, I sank deeper and deeper. Eventually, I would suffocate. The problem was, I wasn't sure I cared.

"It's not. You would have bludgeoned me over the head at some point already if that's all that was between us. Probably as revenge for some slight you haven't let go of from years ago." He leaned into me, his lips brushing against the shell of my ear. "You love me, too. Stop questioning it. Love is unexplainable. Don't you write about that kind of thing all the time?"

"Yes," I whispered, "I do. But what is love, Xander? What is it really? And how do either one of us know if what we're feeling is real?"

All amusement washed from his expression, his grip tightening on me. "Love isn't a feeling, it's an action. It's unconditional, selfless action. What's between us is more than what I feel when I'm around you. I would do anything for you, Zoe. Anything."

"But would I do the same?"

He smirked. "We'll find out when I ask you to do butt stuff."

His levity was so out of left field that it took me a moment to process. Blinking, I returned his smirk. "Guess that's a no then. Because I'm not going there with you or anyone else."

His mouth spread into a wide grin, showcasing his dimple. "I fuckin' love you, Zoe, and you love me. Admit it. You know the truth in here." He tapped my chest lightly. "You won't find the answer here." This time, he tapped my forehead.

"But—"

"Zoe," he growled. "Admit it."

My gaze darted over his face, drinking in every line from the proud slope of his brow to the soft curve of his lips. "If love isn't a feeling, then why are you telling me to use my heart and not my head?"

"I don't know, I read that somewhere and it made sense at the time. But now the only thing that makes sense is being with you." And he was back to skimming his lips up my neck.

I groaned. "I'm sorry, I can't. Not now anyways."

He backed away slowly, hair hanging across his forehead, eyes blazing with a mixture of sadness and lust. "Okay, yeah, I get it. I'm crossing the line if I keep pushing." He nodded to himself. "I do listen to you when you talk about consent and … I'll wait. I'll wait until you know what you want. Or rather, until you admit what you want."

I chewed on the inside of my cheek. "It is the kind of thing I would write about."

Tilting his head, he regarded me with skepticism. "I don't think people enjoy reading about the heroine denying her love of the dashing, amazing, practically perfect in every way hero."

"Well, someone certainly has a high opinion of themselves." I rolled my eyes demonstratively. "I'm talking about the pair who have known each other almost their entire lives, one in love with the other, the other wanting to punch that one in the face most of the time."

He narrowed his eyes at me, mirth dancing within their depths.

Ignoring his reaction, I continued, "And then when they meet again when they're older, they finally connect, like fate or a second chance type of romance. I don't know. But what's between us ... don't I get to have my own HEA in real life? Shouldn't I stop being my own worst enemy and accept things for what they are?"

My throat tightened, and my eyes burned. Xander saw me as more than a sexual conquest or a trophy to collect and show off. I told myself otherwise, quite possibly to push him away, but I knew the truth of what was developing between us. And it absolutely terrified me. Because what would happen if I finally got the kind of relationship I'd always yearned for, and I lost it? Losing what I had with my exes was nothing, a bump in the road on the way to happiness, but if I screwed things up with

Xander, maybe the only person in the entire world who actually knew me ... I couldn't even contemplate what would happen.

"Now I'm confused. It sounds like you're trying to talk me into sex right now when you're the one who just told me to back off."

Spinning, I leaned my forehead against the wall and hit it with my fists. "I don't know. I don't know anything anymore. Especially not what's right or wrong. It's just—" I wanted Xander, there was no denying that even to myself anymore. I'd fed myself lies because I needed them. But even if our connection was the thing I'd been searching for, was acting on it another bad choice in a string of bad choices?

Xander hovered behind me, his voice low. "We could never be wrong, know that."

For someone who craved a soul-bonding connection, I wanted to accept all the things Xander was saying. That we were put in each other's lives again because fate had deemed us ready. He'd shown up when I could finally see him as he truly was—a sexy, smart, kindhearted, caring man. A man who loved me and would give me all the things I'd hungered for in past relationships but was left starving.

I wanted to open up to someone, to give them my all without feeling like they would crush my heart if I truly showed it to them. The truth was, even though I'd been married twice, I was more vulnerable with Xander than with either of my husbands. If he eventually rejected me, then it was no longer about me choosing the wrong people to be in relationships with, it would say something I wasn't sure I could face about myself.

Turning slowly, I peeked up at Xander shyly. He remained where he was, his breathing shallow, his jaw clenched. I could tell he wanted to touch me, but true to his word he was keeping himself in check, giving me what I claimed I wanted ... space.

That was what ultimately undid me. He was willing to do whatever I asked, to let me lead the way even if he thought I was leading us down the wrong path. "Xander."

He inhaled sharply, waiting.

"I want you to fuck me like I'm your everything. Show me that this isn't a mistake. Show me what—"

His mouth stole the rest, swallowing down my moan as his tongue slid in to dominate mine. Pressed fully into the wall by his large body, I gave in to my carnal urges, writhing against him in renewed invitation.

"You are my everything," he murmured, abruptly dropping to his knees. He shoved my skirt up and tore away my underwear in one smooth move. His gaze met mine as leaned forward to suck on my clit.

Holy fuck.

Grasping his shoulders, I threw my head back, my thighs trembling as they struggled to keep me upright. Xander lifted my right leg, settling it over his shoulder, opening me up wider and giving me the support I needed. Threading my hands in his silky locks, I gripped his hair tightly.

Shifting a bit, he slid one hand under my ass, kneading possessively as he lashed my core with his tongue. He was relentless, only slowing when he sensed I was close so he could draw things out.

I panted out incoherent words and sentences, wanting it to last forever, but of course, I also was impatient to come.

When he added two fingers into the mix, I squeezed my eyes shut, and bucked against him as I finally fell over the edge. My mind was blissfully blank, while my body begged for more of his ministrations.

Xander redoubled his efforts, quickly rolling me into a second orgasm, this one almost too intense, my flesh beyond sensitive. By the time he delivered me a third, I was convinced he was a sex god, and I was his newest acolyte, devoted to him eternally.

With my mind still swirling around ridiculous notions of daily worship, Xander rose quickly, spun me around to press my face into the wall, tipped my ass up, and slammed into me from behind.

I screamed, dragging my nails down the rough stone. He wound a swath of hair around his fist, yanking just the right amount to border between pleasure and pain.

He nipped at my earlobe. "Tasting you, being inside of you ..." He swiveled his hips. "It's even better than I imagined."

Reaching behind me, I dug my fingers into his ass, pulling him tight against me. "Stop talking."

He chuckled. "As you wish."

He pulled out and slammed back in, building a blistering pace, the rhythm pulsing throughout my entire body. The rest of the world fell away, every molecule in my being focused solely on Xander and the way he was moving against me, within me, around me ...

Dropping my hair, Xander let my face fall against the cool, rough wall, and he swept his arm around to pinch my clit.

My body spasmed, wave after wave of pleasure undulating through me. Dimly, I was aware of him grunting as his own release pulsed, and him slumping against me with his head on my shoulder.

My heart thudding in my ears, and our harsh breathing, was all I could hear.

Xander turned his head slowly, leaning in to place a soft kiss on my neck. I shuddered.

I was afraid to break the silence, a small part of me worried that even though my world had just been rocked, that I'd been a disappointment. After all, he'd built me up in his mind for years, and no one can live up to fiction ... I should know.

He pulled away from me hesitantly, and I squeezed my eyes shut, frozen in place. His clothes rustled, followed by the sound of his belt being buckled. A moment later, he tugged at my skirt, covering me up.

"Zoe," he murmured. "Talk to me. You're kind of freaking me out."

Sputtering on a laugh, I turned in his direction, my gaze unable to meet his. "I just ... I need to know ... I'm not sure ..." For the life of me, I couldn't seem to form a complete sentence. Dipping to retrieve my torn underwear, I hastily shoved them into the waistband of my skirt since the stupid thing didn't have pockets.

"You regret it." His words fell from his mouth like a bomb, detonating inside of my chest.

"No!" I staggered forward. "I'm just worried ... that maybe you do."

His eyes widened, shock playing across his features. "What?"

Gathering courage, I lifted my chin. "I guess I'm worried that you built things up too much in your mind on how it would be with me and now ..."

"Now what?" He dragged his hands through his hair.

"Now you might be disappointed and not want me anymore."

He exhaled a long sigh, his shoulders sagging. "Come here."

I remained where I was, fidgeting with my clothes.

Frowning, he reached for me. "Come here, Zoe."

"Just tell me whatever it is from there. I don't need you to comfort me. I can handle it." Even though my insides were twisting themselves into one giant knot. I should have known better. I was just as guilty as building Xander up in my head over the last few weeks. He'd had years to do the same with me. Of course we were destined to fall short of each other's expectations. Even though ... my expectations were emotional and his were sexual, I was sure. And he hadn't fallen short ... yet.

"Fine. If you won't come to me," he grated, closing the scant distance between us. He drew me into his arms, resting his chin on the top of my head. "I don't know what to say to make you feel better, except I love you, Zoe. What just happened between us was beyond anything I could have imagined, and it was nothing more than a glorified quickie. I can't begin to fathom how much better it's going to get."

I wound my arms around this waist, pressing my face against his chest, a smile tugging at my lips. His world has been rocked as well. Warmth settled in, leaving me to float in the afterglow of his confession.

His breath skated along the top of my head. "Zoe, come home with me tonight. Let me worship you until the sun comes up. Maybe then you'll stop feeling insecure about what's happening between us."

"I wish I could. But I have to go—"

"Home to him," he snarled. "Yeah, I know."

"Xander," I chastised. "I can't just leave him without any kind of explanation."

"Why not? Leave him tonight. I can't stand the thought of letting you go back to him after what just happened."

"I owe him an explanation, Xander. You know I do."

His fingers dug into my back. "You don't owe him anything."

"Then maybe I owe it to myself to not completely go against my moral code." The concept was laughable since I'd just cheated on my husband, but I had to try to limit the damage going forward. I was the one who had to look myself in the mirror every day, and self-loathing was not something I could hide under a good concealer and foundation.

"Please," he rasped, voice breaking low. "I can't let you walk away. I need you. I need to have all of you."

"I love you, too," I whispered. "How's that? I finally admitted it."

"And you don't love him."

"You know I don't. I'm not sure I ever did. I think I loved who I thought he was, and that person doesn't exist."

"Leave him tonight. Come with me," Xander persisted as he continued to hold me tightly. "Never look back. We can run away together. At least for a while. Take a long vacation. You can send him a postcard."

I snorted. "Yeah, that would go over well. 'Hey, Jared, hello from Cabo, or wherever. Sorry I disappeared without any explanation. Just wanted to let you know I'm alive and well. P.s. I want a divorce. Cheers, Zoe.'"

"Maybe a letter would be more tactful."

"An in-person explanation needs to happen, Xander. And I probably should contact my lawyer first. I don't want this to get ugly."

"If you won't come back with me, don't go home just yet. Stay with me for a little while longer."

Tilting my head back, I stared up at him. His eyes ensnared mine, pulling me into their murky depths, where all his insecurities were laid bare to me. I wanted to soothe and assure him the way he'd done for me. Make him understand that he was worth more than another warm body meant to replace soon-to-be ex-husband number two. To let him know that what just happened between us had ripped me wide open, forcing me to see the truth—that he had somehow become my everything, too. "I'll stay. But not too late."

Rising onto my tiptoes, I pressed my lips sweetly against his. He groaned, deepening the kiss almost instantly.

I don't think I'll ever get enough of him. How is it possible that I feel this way about Xander of all people? And after all this time? All the years I spent searching, and there he was waiting ...

He lifted me onto his desk, and I wrapped my legs around his waist, losing myself in him completely. For the moment, I didn't want to think, I just wanted to feel.

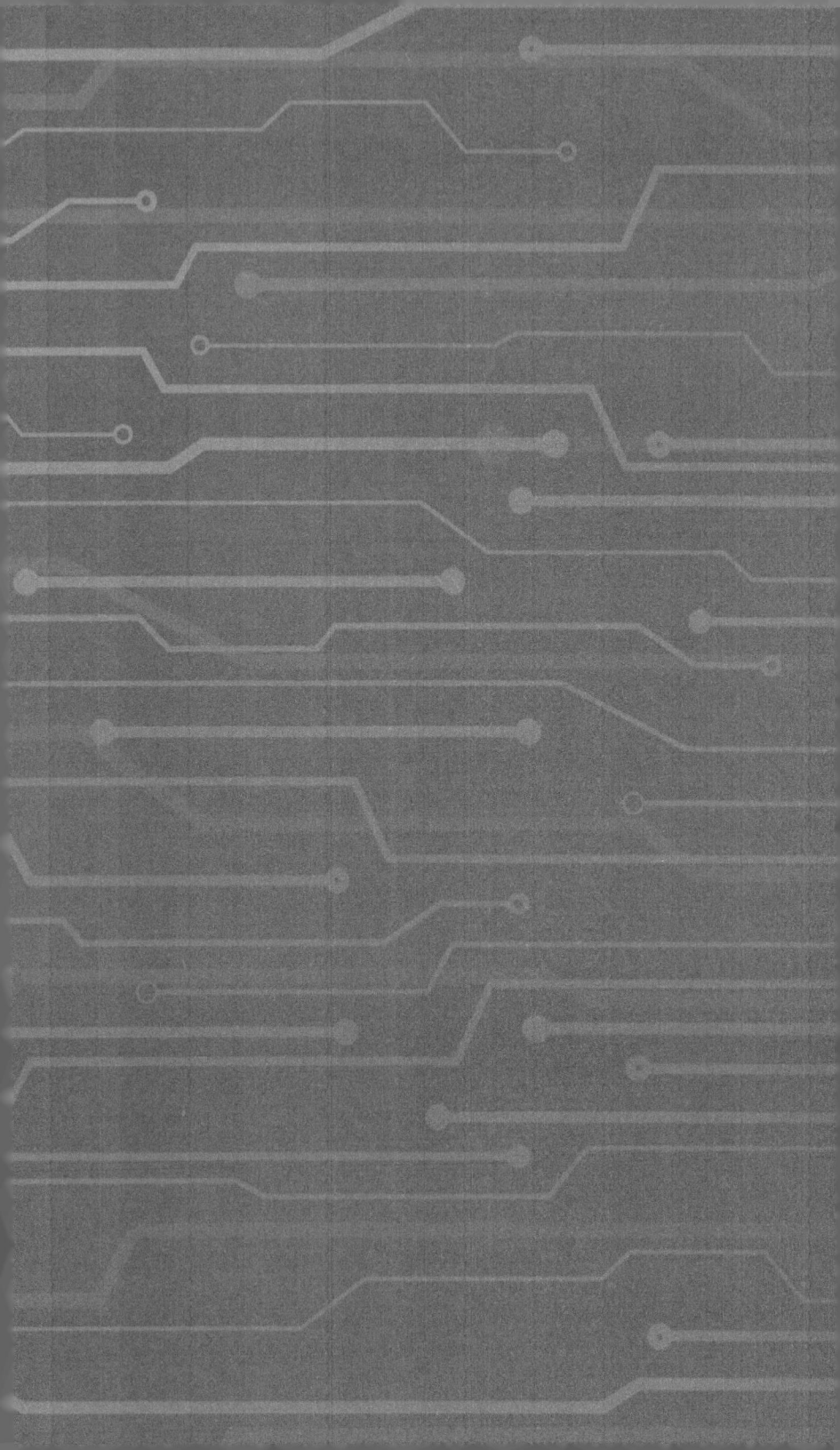

Chapter 18

Present

My thoughts were muddled, confusion intermingling with a strange clarity. Xander and I had an affair, or something akin to one, because the timeline was off. At least what I remembered so far. Either the memory of our first time together was wrong, or the ones about when Xander returned to Raleigh were. Because I clearly remember Xander making his grand reappearance in my life the night of Adam's high school reunion, which was after my divorce from Jared. That would mean I didn't cheat on Jared, although what was just revealed to me told a different story. None of it made sense, the bits and pieces of what I remembered an incomplete and mismatched puzzle.

I have to be wrong about the details of the memory with

Xander ... I just have to be. My brain is getting fried in here, that's what it is. I've always judged and abhorred cheaters. I wouldn't do such a thing. I couldn't. Cheating is unforgivable, no matter the circumstances.

"Human," a deep voice rumbled, calling me forth from my inner turmoil. "I know you're awake."

I opened my eyes, spotting the AI I had begrudgingly interacted with before I'd been thrust into my extremely realistic sexcapade memory with Xander. My body trembled at the mere thought of it, clenching with desire.

Get a hold of yourself, Zoe ... seriously. This is why your life is a mess, because you're a grown woman who is still led around by her hormones and teenage notions of romance.

Pushing myself onto my elbows, I sighed heavily. Mr. Tall, Dark, and Growly was yet another perfect specimen created by the Fantasy Life programmers. It was a shame I couldn't appreciate him, especially because my body seemed to only want Xander now.

Truth was, I had no idea what was going on. I was positive about the facts I knew, but then again, they didn't quite fit together. Maybe I couldn't trust myself. I was a thousand percent an unreliable narrator of my own story, which was an added insult to injury since I hated those types of MCs in the books I read. *Ugh. Focus. You need to focus.*

All that considered, I was brought full circle back to my plan of getting the hell out of Fantasy Life to get my brain sorted. I would focus on that and that alone for the time being. It was truly the best, and quite possibly the only, option I had.

"Look, whoever you are—"

"Cole," he interjected. "My name is Cole."

I arched my eyebrows. "Someone was really feeling the names starting with C when they were doing these tropes."

"What is your name, human?"

Oh, no. He'd already entered the getting to know me part of his programmed infatuation. First, he'd scented me and decided I was his fated mate. Then, he decided he didn't want to spook me so he would attempt to get to know me and be gentler than before, especially since there was the added concern about whether or not I was injured.

"My name isn't important."

He growled in frustration. "Yes, the name of my mat— your name is very important to me."

I didn't have the time or patience to deal with another AI slowing me down. I needed to figure out a way to get him to help me move through this trope as quickly as possible ... without having sex with him.

"You are my everything," Xander's phantom voice zipped through my brain on repeat.

Damn him. He had some serious explaining to do. And I didn't know what to think about how he'd been treating me since I'd stepped into Fantasy Life either. It was not like a man in love or even one who'd fallen out of love. He was acting as if no sexual or romantic relationship had ever existed between us before our steamy make-out session at the cabin.

An idea sparked. "Cole." I placed my hand lightly on his arm, watching with satisfaction as he shuddered. "I need your help."

He covered my hand with his. "All you need to do is ask. But first, tell me your name."

"Fine, fine. My name is Zoe. And without your help, I'm going to die."

"No!" he roared. "I will not let that happen. Tell me what I need to do."

Swallowing a smile, I nodded. The big galoot was reacting exactly the way I expected. "I need to find a door."

His long, jet-black hair fell into his face as he angled his head down to stare at me intently. "What kind of door? I am going to hazard a guess that you need a specific one."

At least none of the AIs were programmed to be himbos because that would be an entirely different level of annoyance. "You would be correct with that guess."

He nodded resolutely, nostrils flaring as he inhaled deeply, no doubt taking in my scent. Which made me idly wonder what exactly he was smelling. Would he smell the same thing with every person who was meant to be his temporary mate? For me, the aromas of VR seemed realistic, except for the fact that sometimes I got a random whiff of something out of place, or I went long swaths of time not noticing any scents at all. I wasn't sure if I simply didn't notice, or a piece of tech needed adjusting.

Why am I thinking about this now? You just had some life-altering memories and now you want to ponder the minute details of Fantasy Life? Although, it wasn't bizarre for me to do such a thing. I excelled at avoidance and denial. It was why I could appreciate escapism in the form of fiction books the way I did. Long before I became an author myself, I'd exchanged my problems for those of the characters in the novels I read. It was simpler that way, and a lot more enjoyable.

Cole was staring at me with what could only be considered bated breath, his large form focused on every little move I made.

I shifted to prepare to stand, but Cole lifted me onto my feet before I could protest, tucking me protectively into his side. Sucking in a breath, I coughed in surprise when I made the instant realization that I did indeed smell him, and his personal scent happened to be the same as Xander's.

Great. I slid my eyes shut. *My brain is definitely doing this to me. I'm sure the programmers didn't make all the men in Fantasy Life smell like Xander. Apparently, I'm obsessed with him now ... even though I don't know what's between us.*

"Okay, hands off." Ducking under Cole's arm, I did a weird shimmy dance to avoid being snagged by him again.

He scowled at me. "Keeping you close will enable me to protect you best."

This was going from zero to sixty fast. There was a good chance I would need to rethink some of my fated mates insta-love romance plotlines in the future because facing it in VR, not even real life, was a bit much. Then again, fantasy is fantasy. And there was nothing like pushing aside the inconveniences of reality to focus on how we wish the world would be.

"You can protect me just fine from where you are," I said sternly, using the tone of an elementary school teacher.

Still scowling, Cole inched closer, reminding me of a huge puppy needing to have contact with its owner at all times. "What are you?"

"I'm not human. But don't be afraid. I will never hurt you, only those who seek to do so."

"Duh. Obviously, you're not human. But what are you?" My nose scrunched up as I considered. He was in the woods, but since I'd already come across the fae world trope I could scratch that one off the list. Definitely a shifter. He was all growly like one ought to be. Which probably also pointed at him being a predator. Werewolf perhaps? Mountain lion shifter? Bear? Hmmm ... "Please just tell me what you are. Consider it a dying wish."

"I'm not going to let you die," he snarled, eyes lighting up like flashlights.

"Then tell me what you are so we get can a move on finding the door that will save my life." It shouldn't have mattered under the circumstances, but the curiosity was overwhelming, especially since it would be my last chance to be close to any kind of shifter, even if he wasn't technically real.

He lifted his head with pride. "I am dragon."

My mouth fell open and I sputtered like a fish out of water for a couple of seconds before regaining a small amount of composure. "A dragon? Well …"

Could he shift? *Oh my God, will I get to see a dragon outside of CGI?* Excitement surged through my veins. How cool would it be to feel a realistic version of a dragon? To run my hands over his scales? To see him take to the sky? Would he be able to carry me? I had so many questions, regret that I wouldn't get to play in Fantasy Life dropping like a brick in my stomach. *I want to play with the dragon, damn it.*

Although, the way Cole's eyes burned with lust let me know how he wanted to play was very different from how I wanted to play. If I asked him for a ride, he would be happy to comply, but his definition would vary vastly from mine in that respect as well.

"We need to find that door."

"Describe it to me," he commanded.

"Um, okay, this is where it gets a bit complicated. I don't actually know what it looks like or where it's going to show up, just that it will … I hope."

Fear instantly replaced the lust in his gaze, his eyes flashing brighter. "How much time do we have?"

That was a good question. I didn't want to send him into a complete panic, but I also didn't want him to dilly-dally. "I-I'm not sure." It was best to stick to as much of the truth as possible.

"Where does this door lead and how will it save your life?"

Why does he have to ask so many questions? I'd changed my previous opinion, it wouldn't be a bad time to run into a himbo that was easy to steer. "The door leads to, um, a world that has the cure for me." Again, not exactly a lie, therefore it would be a snap to remember it later if need be.

"And how did you find out about this world that contains the cure? And what is it that ails you?"

Seriously ... so many friggin' questions. He's worse than me. "A spell was cast on me. That's all I can say without repercussions."

"What kind of creature placed this spell on you?"

I pinched the bridge of my nose. "A fae," I blurted, hoping that in this current trope fae existed, in theory at least. Because if Cole asked—

"What is a fae?"

Tugging at my hair, I contained the urge to scream. No wonder mothers want to jump off bridges when their kids get to the age where they can't stop asking questions. Through gritted teeth, I said, "It's a magical creature who resembles a human, although they're prettier."

Unbidden, an image of Xander in his fae get-up, dark eyes glittering, and long hair blowing in the breeze, skittered across my brain. "Much prettier," I whispered. If Xander dressed up like he had as Mattius back in the real world, I would be begging for him to fuck—

"Please. I need you now. Please, Xander."

He stared down at me, gaze luminous. "Tell me exactly what you want, and maybe I'll give it to you."

"I want you to fuck me. Please, Xander, please fuck me."

Gasping, I covered my mouth. Apparently, at some point, I begged Xander to do just that. My body flushed at the illusive image. It flustered me on so many levels. For things to have been that way between us, for me to beg him to fuck me, I would have had to be helluva comfortable about the things happening between us, and then to have him respond the way he did ...

What is happening to me? All of this escalated extremely quickly. And I still don't know the full scope of things with Xander or why I couldn't remember any of it until recently. Why is there a big, black hole in my brain? And why am I suddenly so calm about all of it? Normally, I'd be having a massive panic attack.

A low growl escaped from Cole. "I do not like you speaking of other creatures as being pretty."

"Sure, big guy." I forced a smile, my thoughts still swirling around Xander and the holes in my memory. "You're pretty, too."

Cole's upper lip curled into a snarl. "I don't want to be patronized either."

"I can't help that fae are beautiful. Do you want me to lie?" I did not have the bandwidth to deal with Cole at the moment.

Touchy males weren't fun. Watching what I said was not something I wanted to ever need to do in my private life. Especially around someone I should be able to trust my true self with. I wasn't talking about caring about not hurting their feelings or other kinds of relationship considerations, nothing like that. It was more of the: 'If you ask the question, then expect an honest answer. If you don't want to know, then keep your mouth shut and I'll keep mine shut as well.'

Ugh, whatever. Cole would soon be in stasis, hopefully, like a good little AI, and none of this would matter.

"Now they're beautiful rather than pretty?"

I threw my hands up in the air. "You're going to argue with me about what I consider fae to be appearance-wise when the clock is ticking on my life?"

He reared back as if I'd slapped him. "Point taken. I have one further question."

"Of course you do." I waved him on. "Well, go ahead, what is it?"

"Will this fae creature be coming after you?"

"He will try, but I'm not sure he's able."

Cole nodded once curtly. "Do not fear. Dragons are impervious to magics aside from dragon magic."

I wasn't sure that if two tropes clashed that the rules of either would remain true in such a way, but hopefully we wouldn't need to find out. All things considered, having Cole as my guide and protector wasn't a bad deal. Although Xander—

Nope. I refuse to think about him anymore until I can get out of here and get some real answers. I won't worry about where he is or what happened to him with Caz.

"Okay, now that all of that's settled, we should get going."

"What is your strategy for finding this door?"

I shrugged.

"Do you plan to wander about hoping to stumble upon it?"

I shrugged again.

"We must come up with a better plan than that. As you said, the clock is ticking on your life, and I could not bear it if … if you—" His jaw muscles rippled, and his eyes lit up again. "I can't even utter the words out loud."

"I don't know how to find the door, just that I need to." I hated admitting, even to an AI, or myself for that matter, that I was completely out of my element when I should have some kind of kickass strategy. After all, how many fantasy-type books had I read? More than I could count. Even though the doors between tropes were not technically part of the tropes themselves, it would stand to reason that they followed the general rules of a fantasy romance in the sense that the program would know when the storyline had reached its goal.

Freezing, I ran over those words in my mind again. *"When the storyline reached its goal."* My stomach twisted at the realization. I knew what the answer was, but I didn't want to see it. It was ridiculously obvious. I was in a romance trope, and what do all romances require to be considered a true romance in the genre? A HEA of course. Yep, to get the next door to appear without the help of Xander or Caz, I was going to have to reach some sort of happily-ever-after situation … with Cole.

I rubbed my temples. "No, no, no, no, no. Just when I

come to a final decision about will I or won't I with the AIs, this happens."

Cole shuffled closer to me. "What are you speaking of? What has happened now? And what is an AI?"

Staring up at Cole, I let my gaze roam over his perfect features. He was beautiful in his own rugged way, there was no doubt about it, but since I'd received the flashes of Xander and me together, I couldn't seem to get my lady-wood up for anyone but him. It was laughable, all of it. I accused Xander of sabotaging the potential sexy times with the AIs, and now that he was out of the way, and I could do whatever I wanted with Cole, the desire was gone.

"Damn you, Xander."

"Zoe." Cole was now touching me, his large hands on my arms. "Tell me what I need to do to save you."

"I don't need saving as it turns out. I know how to find the door."

His grip on me tightened. "What is it? Tell me."

"The problem is, I don't like what I'm going to have to do."

"A few moments of unpleasantness or even pain will be worth it to save your life."

A laugh bubbled up, exploding from my esophagus. "This whole thing is a cruel joke, it has to be." Did I end the affair with Xander, and he was using virtual reality to get his revenge on me? Was there the potential for emotional torture more than him harassing me in a relatively good-natured way? Was he playing me? Or maybe it was all a test of some sort?

Cole shook me lightly, forcing my gaze up to meet his. "I'm not sure where your mind keeps goings. Perhaps it's a side effect from whatever spell placed on you. Regardless, Zoe, you must tell me what we need to do to save your life."

I didn't like having my hand forced one way or the other when it came to making choices of even the most irrelevant in nature, so I especially didn't care for the fact that the choice for sex with Cole was being taken out of my hands ... if I wanted to jump out of this trope.

Or maybe not.

You always have a choice. You just have to be willing to accept the consequences of the possible outcome of said choice. For instance, if someone puts a gun to your head and demands for you to do something you find morally reprehensible, then you can refuse. Most likely you will die, but in the end, you still were able to make your choice. The only time options are truly taken away from you is when you let them be. I would not let them be. My situation was not life or death, or anything so dramatic. I was uncomfortable. I found being in Fantasy Life under the current circumstances unpleasant. But I could deal, make the best of things until I was pulled out. I wasn't truly trapped. Which meant all I had to do is wait.

I could wait.

I *would* wait.

Chapter 19

B ored, bored, bored, bored … bored. If I had a laptop, or a typewriter, or even a pen and a durable leaf, I would be writing to entertain myself. My first book was born of boredom when I broke my leg and wasn't able to leave the hospital for a week. I'd written the first part of the novel in a notebook from the gift shop. Not that anything I could produce at the moment would do me any good. It wasn't like I could download to print straight from my brain. Even still, my patience was wearing thin. Who would have thought spending so much time with a sexy dragon would be completely … boring.

Yep, my word for the day, or however long it's been, is boring.

Drumming my nails across my thigh while I sat cross-legged under a tree, I stared at Cole as he busied himself gathering wood for a fire. He was hyper-focused on my comfort, something that mattered little since we were in VR, but it wasn't like I could explain that to him.

With a satisfied grunt, Cole completed his fire pit, the flames crackling as they roared to life. He didn't even use any dragon power to start the blaze, just a run-of-the-mill method of dry leaves and two stones. I wasn't sure it would work in the real world or if it was simply more fiction, but I couldn't care less.

"Cole," I drawled out his name.

He stood abruptly, rushing to drop down beside me. "Yes, *mo chroi*."

Mo chroi in Gaelic translated to my heart, and Cole had quickly started using that term of endearment for me, which was ... annoying. "I'm not your heart," I snapped. "We've been over this, Cole. You don't even know me, so you can't possibly love me in any way."

"I can't explain the ways of a dragon to a human," he grumbled, gaze flitting over my features hungrily. He practically hummed with the need to 'claim me' as he'd previously put it. But there would be none of that today.

"Oh, I understand exactly how dragons work." I raised my eyebrows. "You see, you want, you take."

After all, I had a sneaky feeling I had something to do with the creation of this particular trope. My memory of Xander and I having sex in his office had started with mention of us working on notes for the romance aspects of Fantasy Life. And Cole had my type of hero written all over him. One of my longest-running series was a paranormal romance involving dragons just like the one currently staring at me. I hadn't invented dragons, or even romance involving dragon shifters, but I'd put my own spin on it and their lore … Cole was one of mine, I was almost positive.

I wonder why I wasn't involved in all of the tropes? Because I know I had nothing to do with that pregnancy debacle. Maybe they sourced multiple authors and mistakenly used a horror author on that one. Hmmm …

"I have not taken you … yet." Cole's gaze sparked with light as he leaned closer to sniff at me. "I'm giving you time to come to terms with things because of you being human."

I let my head flop back, and it thunked against the tree. "I'm not going to come to terms with any of this. I'm not your mate."

"Agree to disagree," he growled.

"And you need to back off. Seriously, I just wanted to ask you a question and you sped over here like your pants were on fire the second I said your name."

He vibrated with tension. If this had been a few tropes ago I might have felt sorry for him. As it currently was, I was over Fantasy Life completely. I didn't want to think about what interacting or not interacting with the AIs meant, or if their feelings were truly human-like, and what any of it meant. I had to turn my brain off completely otherwise thoughts of Xander and the pieces of memory that I'd seen would drive me insane.

"You said before that you knew how to find the door,

but then you never fully explained." Cole reached out to touch my cheek.

I slapped it away. "No touching. We've been over this."

How did things come to this? The old saying *be careful what you wish for* came to mind. I used to wish for the characters in the novels I read, and the ones I created, to come to life. To be real. I think every booklover at some point has had a crush on a fictional character. It wasn't limited to romance fiction, but it did seem to occur more often in that genre. Fantasy Life was not only my chance to find my writer's mojo, but to interact with the types of romance heroes that didn't exist outside of make-believe. Yet, when it all came down to it, the few that I'd been exposed to turned out to be less than … less than Xander.

Aaaah! I tugged at my hair. *Do not think about him.* One VR make-out session, a few hot as fuck memories, and I was sprung on Xander Tashiro. I was alone with a prime specimen of a dragon shifter, one who would endlessly worship my body, and I wanted nothing to do with anyone sexually other than Xander.

But why? If I didn't remember loving someone, could my heart still feel it? Or was it just another instance of me overromanticizing a connection between me and someone else? Maybe I was simply in love with being in love. It wasn't the first time I'd considered that as an option of why my relationships seemed to always go horribly wrong. I wanted that fate-created connection more than anything else in the world.

What if you actually have that with Xander? It's not impossible. Think about it.

Psshht ... yeah, right. The most unrealistic hero in any trope was a billionaire with any kind of moral compass. And although not a billionaire yet, Xander was well on his way, his crowning achievement to be the further development of Fantasy Life and the AIs within.

Stop. Think about something else.

"Have you ever been in love before?" Cole asked, the question surprising me.

I blinked up at him, trying to figure out if I'd missed something while I was mentally elsewhere. Had I mumbled parts of my internal dialogue out loud? "Umm ... what?"

He clenched and unclenched his jaw, grating out, "I wish to know if you've ever been in love before. Be truthful. I have a point, and the past is the past."

Yeah, he said the past was the past, but I'd written characters like him. He wanted to mean it, but his possessiveness and jealousy would make it nearly impossible to handle the mere mention of me with another male. "We shouldn't talk about this."

A low growl rumbled in the back of his throat. "Just answer the question."

Turning my gaze to the fire, I stared into the flames, the whole setup in the woods reminding me of my short time with Caz and Xander in the fae world. Maybe the programmers were reusing some of the background designs where they could. Quite possibly the cityscapes were more complicated because more characters would need to be involved. Even so—

"Zoe," Cole said sharply. "Please, answer the question. Have you ever been in love?"

I glanced at him, before turning my gaze back to the fire. Sighing, I said, "Honestly, I don't know. I'm not sure I know what love truly is. A feeling? A way you express your emotions? How does anyone know when they are in love or if they're in love with being in love? There are too many variables. So, yeah, I don't know."

Did I love either of my ex-husbands? I thought I had at one point or another in the relationships, otherwise I wouldn't have married them. In hindsight, I had my doubts. There were lines I wouldn't cross, things I wouldn't do, and my pride always came first. It was the same in every relationship I'd ever been in. I ended things before anyone could leave me. I didn't mourn the end of the relationship either. I made excuses, such as they couldn't possibly be the one, so I owed it to myself to keep looking. Therefore, I simply picked up and moved on. Would it be that easy if I'd truly loved any of the men I'd welcomed so willingly into my life? Even if they weren't *the one* I was meant for above all others?

Or perhaps I was ultimately afraid of the very thing I was searching for. Because if I found my soul mate, then what happened if they were ripped from my life by way of a tragedy? Would I be broken beyond repair?

Cole cleared his throat as he leaned forward to stoke the fire. "I've never been in love. Even now, the pull I feel for you, the bond I wish to deepen, I know it's not love, although I know that eventually it would grow into such a thing if given the chance."

"Hmmm … has a dragon ever fallen in love with someone other than his mate?"

"Was it love at all if the dragon can walk away from it?"

Scooting away from the tree, I moved closer to the fire. I wasn't cold, but I sought the comfort the flames represented. "Since I'm not sure I know what love is, I can't answer that for you."

"It's good that you don't love anyone now. It will make things easier for us." Cole smiled to himself. "I would have felt guilty if I took you away from someone you loved since you are human."

I quirked an eyebrow. "But you would have anyways."

"Of course."

"Ah, then there seems to be a problem." I couldn't help myself. I should have kept my mouth shut, but having some kind of conflict would do wonders for my boredom.

"Problem?" Cole turned toward me, his lips twitching down. "What kind of problem, aside from you not telling me what I need to do to end the curse?"

"I might love someone. I'm just not sure if I do or not. I can't stop thinking about him, even now." My heart fluttered rapidly as my nerves ratcheted up. I'd needed to say that to Cole, not merely to stir up trouble, but because it was true. There was more than a chance that I loved Xander. And that absolutely scared the shit out of me.

"This whole time? This whole time you've been with

me, demanding for me not to touch you or be near you, because … because you're thinking of this other male?"

Gulping, I turned my attention back to the flames. "Pretty much."

"And where is this male who you might love?"

"I'm not sure."

"He abandoned you, left you for dead? No wonder you don't know if you love him or not. You will forget him soon enough." Cole relaxed, seemingly placated with his own rationale.

"You are my everything." Xander's words echoed through my skull.

"I don't think I could ever forget him."

"You will."

"That's the thing, I think I did, for a time, but the pieces of him—of us—they're coming back to me."

Cole laughed. "You forgot him? Please. This male is nothing to you."

Irrational anger heated my blood. "He isn't nothing. He's … he's something. I just don't know what because I'm missing some of my memory."

That got Cole's attention. "Is it part of the curse? Will you lose more of your memory?"

"You know what, we're done talking about this. I need—"

"What do you need, Zoe?" Caz's familiar voice wafted across the clearing, his tone mocking.

Jumping to my feet, I spun to face him. But before I could do anything else, Cole shoved me behind his massive frame. I peeked around him, my gaze searching for Xander.

"Where is he? What did you do with Xan— Mattius?"

Ignoring my question, Caz focused his attention on Cole. "And who is this? He seems quite intense." He chuckled. "He is no match for me though."

"Why don't you give me a shot?" Cole snarled.

Caz flicked his dark hair over his shoulder. "What are you? Not fae. Not human. Perhaps you are something entirely new to me."

"Where is Mattius?" I demanded again. I knew Xander wasn't injured in real life, but what if he was trapped in his avatar and temporarily unable to get out? What if he was experiencing pain of some sort brought on by whatever kind of punishment or torture Caz had dealt him before the fae warrior had tracked me down again?

Caz's eyes regarded me coldly. "Here I am, the future high king of the fae realm, debasing myself by chasing after a human, and all she wants to know is where Mattius is. You should reconsider your actions."

I clicked my tongue once. "Is you being a high king supposed to impress me? Because it doesn't."

"This is the fae who cursed you," Cole growled. "If I kill him, will it reverse it?"

I didn't want to find out how much longer I'd be stuck in Fantasy Life if Caz got ahold of me again, especially since Xander seemed to be temporarily out of commission. Maybe Cole would come in handy after all. "It wouldn't hurt to kill him, that's for sure."

"You think this creature can kill me?" Caz sneered. "Not likely."

Pushing around Cole, I met Caz's gaze and shrugged. "Then let's find out, shall we?"

I shoved at the mountain that was Cole. "Go on, get him." He turned to me, stunned, not expecting me to encourage such violence. "Yes, you heard me. Go kill the fae bastard who won't leave me alone."

A sound of approval hummed in the back of Caz's throat. "So violent. I think I might like it."

"Whatever," I huffed out. Now I had two AIs who were programmed to think of me as their fated mate in one place. If the circumstances were different, I would have been fanning myself or requesting a threesome, probably both. *And by different circumstances, I mean a few hours ago.* I giggled, because, well, why not?

Surprisingly, Cole hadn't budged from his protective stance in front of me, despite my encouraging him to take out Caz.

"What's the holdup?" I demanded. "Go wipe that smug smile off of his arrogant fae face."

"Are you sure you want me to kill him?" Cole asked hesitantly. "How do you know his death will end the curse and not fix it in place?"

A legitimate question if I'd been telling the truth. But since Cole believed I knew what I was talking about when it came to the curse, then why was he hesitating long enough to question my directive on the matter? "It's cool. His death will fix the curse problem." I shoved at him again. "So go ahead, start the maiming and killing."

Whether or not Cole could do any permanent damage to Caz when they were both AIs remained to be seen, but hopefully, dragon trumped fae and Caz would run home with his tail tucked between his legs.

"I'm not sure it's a good idea to kill him when you don't know how it will affect the curse. It might be a better plan to capture him."

"Are you serious right now? He needs to die for what he did to me—your mate. Why is he not already torn limb from limb?"

"Mate?" Caz scoffed. "Does this ridiculous creature believe you to be his mate when you belong to me?"

Cole's muscles tensed as a low growl reverberated through the clearing. "Zoe is mine—my mate. She will never belong to you."

Caz inclined his head, all arrogance in repose. "As if she could be the mate of an oaf like you. She will be royalty, a queen. What could you offer her? A forest? A cave?"

Back to my word of the day: boring. Because instead of fighting, these two idiots were going to bore me to death with their insults of each other, and proclamations of their ownership of me. I needed to get the ball rolling into something … something other than what was currently going on.

I tapped my foot rapidly against the ground. "Umm … I'm human, remember? A crazy human who you didn't even want to touch when we first met. In what world will I be queen?"

Caz's ice eyes met mine with challenge. "In my world, my word is the law. You will be my queen."

"She belongs with me," Cole growled.

Throwing my hands in the air, I let my head fall back, screaming in exasperation. "Oh my God! I don't belong with either of you!"

They both turned their gazes to me as I shuffled away from Cole slowly, while also putting distance between me and Caz. "I want you to leave me alone. Both of you. Do you hear me, Caz? Leave me alone. I don't want to be with you in any way, shape, or form, so go back to doing whatever it is you were doing before you came across me in the woods—"

"You mean when you clung to me, begging for me to fuck you? You knew then what you refuse to accept now. That the attraction between us—"

"No. Just no. I was a different person then." With fewer memories, and therefore no idea of what I was doing. Or, well, okay, I still had no idea what I was doing, but at least I'd figured out what I didn't want to be doing. It was a step in the right direction.

"You do seem different. But the spell placed upon you can explain that."

"You admit openly that you placed a spell on her?" Cole demanded. "And you still claim she's meant for you?"

"I didn't place the spell on her, idiot. Mattius did."

Gritting my teeth, I strung together a few choice swear

words. I would get nowhere with these two. When I wanted to talk things out, I was presented violence and coercion. When I asked for violence, I got a physical standoff with playground-level insults thrown about. Why Cole and Caz were unwilling to make a move against each other was beyond me. Unless ... unless it had something to do with their programming.

Hmmm ... I'll add it to the list of things to think about later.

Whirling around, I dashed into the woods, away from the sexy dragon and hot fae who were driving me insane.

I thought I could wait things out—be patient until I was pulled from Fantasy Life. As it turned out, my patience level was barely above zero. I could fake it for a bit, fool myself for a while, but eventually, I needed to do something ... anything to feel like I was making progress toward my goal. And currently, my goal was to get the hell out of virtual reality.

"Zoe!" Cole's roar of outrage intermingled with Caz's. Guess neither one of them expected me to make a run for it. Which was kind of surprising since I'd already run from Caz more than once, and I'd attempted to do the same to Cole when I first met him.

Crashing through the underbrush, I was grateful that finally I seemed to have some sort of stamina granted to me in VR. Normally, I would be heaving my guts out in the bushes by this point. Or I would have needed to stop for a pee break or two. Either way, running from Cole and Caz would have been pointless, and—

Cole appeared in front of me, popping in from thin air.

Shit. I should have known. Dragons can shift through space.
Caz appeared a moment later, directly at Cole's side. *And
so can fae. Double shit. Are they working together now or
something?*

Caz waved his hand, hurtling Cole into a tree. *Guess
that answers that question.*

Spinning, I sprinted back in the direction I came from.
I didn't bother to check if Cole was injured or not,
because, in the end, he wouldn't be.

"Zoe," Caz called after me. "This is pointless. You're
only going to tire yourself out."

"Joke's on you because I won't get tired." But he was
right about the pointless thing. I couldn't get away from
either of them on foot, and currently it was my only
means of travel.

"Zoe." Caz popped into existence in front of me again,
and I reared back, kicking up dirt and pine needles. He
grabbed my wrists, yanking me against him. "I have
grown weary of this game."

My heart threatened to burst from my ribcage. "Let
me go."

Cole appeared behind Caz, his flashlight eyes casting
dark shadows across his features. "You heard my mate. Let
her go." Raising his arms, water circled his biceps, moving
down to shoot off his hands.

Not faltering for even a second, Caz flung me over his
shoulder as we rose into the air on a huge gust of wind.
"Water? You seek to use water against me? I have control
of all the elements."

A dragon and a fae fighting over me …

Once it would have been a dream come true. Even though not real, it would be the type of imagery to conjure for the rest of my life any time I needed to flick the bean. And I could have sex with them here and now if I wanted. The pervert part of me still wanted. *But … but Xander? How do I know the memories of us are legit? What if I'm wasting this golden, once-in-a-lifetime opportunity under the pretenses of loyalty when I don't need to?*

My heart fisted, and my stomach knotted. *Goddamn it. The heart wants what it wants. And mine wants stupid, asshat Xander. I will murder him in cold blood if he did something to alter my brain for temporary funsies. But even he wouldn't take things that far, right? It would be helpful if I could talk to him, like now, before I make a huge mistake.*

"Xander!" I hissed. "Xander! Your friggin' company made all of this! There is no way Caz beat you at literally your own game!"

"Fight me!" Cole bellowed.

"Why would I bother when I have what I want?" Caz responded, nonplussed.

With a swat to my ass, my world blurred before going dark.

Chapter 20

"**Y**ou can't stay here, Xander."

He shifted underneath me, his warm body still entangled with mine. Muttering something incoherent, he wrapped his arms around me, drifting off again.

I swatted at his chest. "Xander. Do not fall asleep. You can't stay here tonight."

He groaned. "Why not? He's not here."

"Because what if someone sees you leave in the morning and tells Jared?"

"Good."

I pinched his nipple. "Not good. Not good at all. We're not divorced yet. He still lives here."

Xander rubbed at his nipple. "No need to get violent." He kissed the top of my head. "Come stay at my place then. I don't like being here anyhow, not when his things are everywhere."

"That's not a good idea either and you know it."

I couldn't see his face from where I was, but I could feel his

271

frown by way of his mood darkening. "I don't want us to be a secret anymore. I can't even tell my best friend about us the way things are."

"How about we never tell him?" I joked, trying to lighten the atmosphere again.

"He'll be happy for us."

"It's just weird is all."

"He knew about my ... crush on you when we—"

"Were kids and he thought you didn't stand a chance. Yeah, he probably made fun of you for liking his sister."

Xander chuckled, bouncing my head up and down on his chest slightly. "As I recall, the word gross was used on more than one occasion."

"That's what I thought. But what happened when you saw me naked? Hmmm? He punched you. How do you think he's going to react when he finds out—"

"I've been fucking his sister? Eh. He'll just have to deal with it."

I sighed. "This is complicated, Xander, and we need to tread carefully ... with everybody."

"It's not as complicated as you're making it out to be. I love you, and you love me." Suddenly I was on my back, with him looming over me. "And I'd like to express that sentiment again right now."

"Xander," I chastised, even though my body instantly responded, crying out for his touch.

Pushing my legs apart, he slid down to bury his face between my thighs, his wicked tongue stealing my breath, and any other arguments I might have had seconds ago.

"Oh, fuck. You're ... you're too good at this," I choked out on a moan.

He paused, and I could feel his smile against my heated flesh as he redoubled his efforts. Writhing under his ministrations, I closed my eyes, losing myself completely.

Maybe he's right. Maybe it's not that complicated after all.

JOLTING UP, I came to instant awareness, the memory of Xander and me together fresh in my mind, along with the fact that I'd blacked out again.

Scrubbing a hand down my face, I was not startled to find myself in a room completely saturated with opulence. It was exactly what I'd expect when provided with accommodations by fae royalty who thought himself destined to be with me. Everything was covered in either gold or jewels, glinting softly in the dim lights dancing around the gigantic room. As for me, I was splayed out in the center of the biggest bed I'd ever seen, golden bedding cushioning me in a heavenly cloud.

"Guess the fae won," I muttered. I was convinced the dragon would have given more resistance if not for my presence in Caz's arms. Cole was probably worried about injuring me if he—

As if any of it matters or is real. How quickly I lose myself in fantasy.

While considering what my next move would be, I

rolled several times to get to the edge of the bed. "Hello? Anyone there?" I couldn't imagine Caz leaving me alone for an extended period of time. Now that I was awake, I expected him at any moment. Although, I was still holding out hope for Xander to make an appearance. Goosebumps erupted along my skin, the latest memory of us together titillating.

"Xander? Where are you?" Could his brain have been damaged by whatever Caz did to him? Was he out in the real world unconscious and injured, unable to get to me? If that was the case, wouldn't one of his colleagues have pulled me out of Fantasy Life by now, not wanting to risk me getting hurt as well? Most likely, Xander was fine, so why wasn't he coming for me like before?

The double doors to the room swung open, their heavy wood hitting the wall as Caz swaggered in, dressed head to toe in black with silver embroidery to match his skin. I paid little mind to his clothes though, his otherworldly beauty keeping me riveted to his strong, yet feminine features. He was the embodiment of perfection in contrasts by design, and I was not unaffected by it, even now.

He smirked, his glacier gaze melting. "Like what you see?"

His words echoed Xander's from only a short time ago when I'd first gotten a gander at him in his fae getup. It was enough to bring me back to my senses from my libidinous reverie. "I told you I didn't want to go with you." I swept my arms wide. "And yet here I am. Has the whole consent thing not reached you here in this world yet? No means no. And leave me alone means leave me alone. I could make you a helpful list or key if you want. You could hang it on your wall and check it anytime you were unsure."

I didn't know why I was bothering to engage him in any kind of conversation since he was a slave to his programming. Modern feminist sensibilities sometimes took a backseat in the romance genre, which was okay since it was all a fantasy. Unfortunately, the realism of Fantasy Life changed that for me, causing me to dislike some of my favorite tropes when coming face-to-face with them. They no longer existed in the safe space of my imagination, which is the only place they belonged as far as I was concerned.

"I have a better idea of how you can keep that smart mouth of yours busy."

"Ugh. No. Just no."

"Come." Caz motioned for me to follow him. "First we dine, then we can revisit the—" He froze where he was midsentence.

"What the—"

Xander appeared in the center of the room, a dark suit draped over his lean frame. "Zoe, you need to listen to me, we don't have much time."

Rushing him, I launched myself into his arms. "I'm so glad to see you. I mean glad isn't even the right word. I remembered things. I know about us. I know—"

His arms wound around me, holding me snug against

his chest, his chin resting on the top of my head. "Please, listen. We only have a few minutes and I need to tell you some things. It's important."

"Why do we only have a few minutes? What's going on?"

"You'll be waking up soon. I was notified that the process has begun and that I needed to prepare you so it won't be as jarring."

Ice pumped through my veins. "What are you talking about? Who notified you and what do you mean *as* jarring?"

"Things won't be what you expect them to be when you wake up. But it'll be okay."

"What?" He said it was important, and I was doing my best to pay attention, to keep my pending anxiety at bay, but when he kept using words and phrases like *jarring, not what you expect*, and *it'll be okay*, it signaled that something was wrong.

"I'm not supposed to care. I was programmed not to. It's the entire reason I was created and why I'm here and he's not. He wanted to give you this, to make you happy, at least for a little while. He didn't want you to remember any of the negative stuff or anything that might upset you. It's why your moods were tweaked at times."

He laughed, the sound absent of humor. "I can't even begin to imagine how bad things would have gotten if that weren't the case. And yeah, it worked better the longer you were in here even though you continued to fight it the entire time."

He pulled away from me, dark eyes glistening. "But he made me, put all of his memories and thoughts about you in here." He tapped his temple. "And I fell in love, just like him. Or maybe that's not right at all. Maybe it's because you're so much a part of him that the love couldn't be erased, and it took me some time to find it within myself. Hell, I can't ... he can't ... we can't even look in the mirror without thinking of you." He pressed one long finger against the scar in his eyebrow I'd given him. "No matter the reason, in the end, I love you because he loves you."

"What are you talking about?" I didn't want to accept what this confession could mean. It was impossible, even for a virtual reality as realistic as Fantasy Life.

"You need to let me finish, Zoe, because I won't be able to answer all your questions. There isn't time. Remember what I'm telling you when you wake up and fit the pieces together. Make it work. I have faith in you."

My arms and legs trembled, and I gnawed at the insides of my cheeks to keep my teeth from chattering. "Okay," I managed.

"He loves you. He loves you more than I can begin to fathom. Because I know he loves you more than I do, and what I feel for you— I willingly risked my life for you. I could have been destroyed in here, erased from existence by Caz. But I didn't care. All I wanted to do was to protect you and make you happy."

"If he can destroy you, then how are you able to control him now?" I motioned to the statue-like Caz, still frozen in the same position.

"Don't you get it? I'm not in control. I never have been. Not the way I made you think. Not the way you wanted me to be. The only reason I'm not like him right now is because I am meant to transition you out of here, like I said, make things less jarring. But I'm spending that time trying to explain things to you—trying to impart the most important information to you before it's too late."

My mind was reeling, none of pretty much anything making a whole lot of sense. But I would listen, because, well, I shouted at enough characters in books and movies to do just that at a pivotal point in the plot. Of course, they never did. It ratcheted up the tension and stakes. I refused to make the same mistakes now that it was happening to me. "Tell me then. Quickly."

"Remember … remember that he loves you." He snorted. "See, you went and turned me into a romantic. I wasn't meant to be this. I'm more like him than I was ever programmed to be. Which is why I sometimes forgot that I wasn't him. Or quite possibly I wanted to be him so I could have the remote chance of being with you in the end. But if I can't be with you, then I want you to be with him." He blinked rapidly, his eyes glistening. "I know he can make you happy."

He glanced away briefly before continuing, "I was created to make you feel comfortable, to have his memories to draw on to make me seem like I was him, b-but … never quite … and not be—" He rifled his hands through his hair. "Fuck. How will I survive here without you? These poor saps," he flicked his hand in Caz's direction, "they'll be fine. But me …" A brittle smile formed on his lips. "I'll be begging to be deleted in no time."

My throat closed up, and I convulsively swallowed. Somehow, I managed to croak out, "How? How are you AI, too? And how can you love me? How is any of this possible?"

"Because Alexander Dai Tashiro is brilliant, and he loves you. And like I already said, I love you because he loves you, plain and simple. No matter what he says or what he does, don't forget that. Okay? Never. A man doesn't do what he did for you and then walk away, at least not willingly."

"Walk away?"

"Forget I said that part. Forget everything else I said except the part where he loves you." Xander, or the AI formally known as Xander, closed the scant distance between us, cupping my cheeks. "I love you, Zoe Woods. You are my everything. That's how I know you're his everything. What I'm experiencing … my emotions are just a piece of him, an echo of something unfathomable to me." He pressed his lips to my forehead once, then stepped away from me again.

My eyes burned as I blinked back tears. "I don't know what to say." I smiled, laughing sharply. "You were messing up the tropes so I wouldn't have sex with the other AIs."

He grinned. "Ironic, isn't it? I was placed in here

because Xander didn't think he would be able to handle seeing you with the AIs. Turns out I couldn't either."

"I-I'm sorry." The Xander standing in front of me was AI, and I never would have known. I'd been so worried about whether or not I was hurting the AIs I interacted with in the romance tropes, but I'd been hurting this one all along, and I had no clue how I would ultimately harm him. "So sorry. I'll tell him to erase your memories or programming or whatever that involves me. I'll tell him to give you—"

"No. I don't want to lose you in that way, too. There is no version of a Xander without Zoe. We're— you two are meant to be. There is no other explanation for how I've been altered in your presence. It shouldn't have been possible. But it happened. So please don't take that experience from me."

"What will happen to you after I leave? Will you go into a stasis like the other AIs?" An image of Xander leaning in a corner somewhere, unmoving, like a broken robot, flashed across my mind.

"No," I said before he had a chance to answer. "This isn't right. Any of this. You and the rest of the AIs deserve better than what Fantasy Life is offering you. I couldn't make up my mind before about where I stood about a lot of this, but now I know—now I know that this whole romance trope thing isn't romance at all. It goes against everything I stand for. And I won't let Xander continue on with this program, and I won't let him delete any of you either. He'll just have to figure out something else for all of you. Something else that involves choice and autonomy and—"

AI Xander's lips crashed down on mine, stealing the rest of my rant. But just as quickly as he'd initiated the intimate contact, he pulled away, delivering me a bittersweet smile. "Our first and last kiss with you knowing what I really am."

Everything pixelized and washed to white, fading to nothingness.

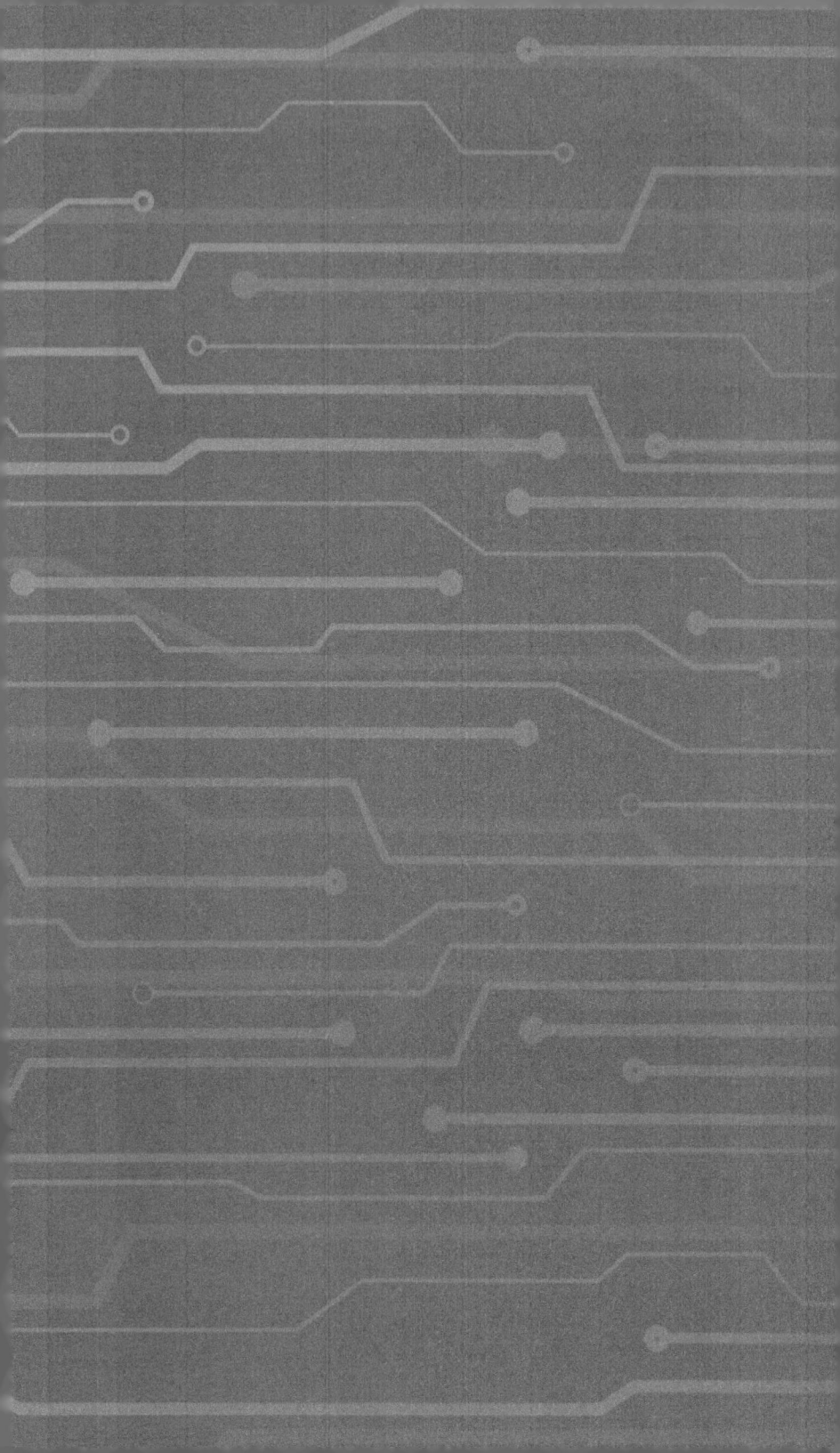

Chapter 21

Steady beeping filled my ears, joined by a low whirl, and the staccato rhythm of my heart. "She should be aware soon. Her vitals have normalized," a feminine voice I didn't recognize stated calmly.

"How will she be? Will she know us?" my mom asked, tension riding her tone.

"With these kinds of injuries, there's no way of knowing. I can tell you that her scans are healthy and normal, the swelling down. Although, in this case, with Fantasy Life involved, and the feedback from their technology, you shouldn't worry. It really is quite amazing." There was a smile evident in her voice.

My entire body was heavy, my eyelids weighing what seemed like fifty pounds each. Struggling to open them, I whimpered. My throat was raw and scratchy, and yet I wasn't thirsty.

"Zoe, my baby," my mom said, her voice cracking. "Can you hear me?"

My tongue was thick in my mouth. "Wh-What happened?" My eyelids fluttered, revealing my mom, my brother, and Tina crowded into a larger-than-expected hospital room. The wall to my right was entirely glass, saturating the area with bright light. Surrounding me were about a half dozen machines, clicking, beeping, and whirling.

"What do you remember?" my mom asked.

"I-I—" My gaze slid along my family, warmth filling my chest, and yet ... "Where's Xander?" The words spilled from my mouth before I had a chance to consider them.

Adam's lips curled in over his teeth, essentially disappearing, and my mom turned to whisper something to him. He nodded once curtly in acknowledgment of whatever she'd told him, his expression remaining tense. "He's not here."

Images played across my brain, spreading out to fill in the pieces I'd so desperately needed while inside of Fantasy Life, although there were things still missing. I wasn't divorced when Xander came to town for the reunion, or when I started working on the Fantasy Life project with him. Or when our affair had begun. The timeline was altered for me in virtual reality in an attempt to help me avoid some of the unpleasant stuff, like I'd been told.

After several months of us sneaking around, Xander had walked away, unable to accept the fact that I needed to break the divorce to Jared carefully, his temper volatile. I'd ultimately let Xander end our relationship without much protest, thinking that I needed to get things in order before we could share any kind of life. I truly believed that Xander and I would end up together.

And then …

"Jared, he came to my house … H-He had pictures of me and Xander. He knew about the affair. We fought. He hit me …" My hands trembled as I reached up to feel along my face and scalp. He'd more than hit me. He'd beaten me until I'd lost consciousness.

My mom snatched my hand away, holding it within hers. "Honey, don't. You still need time to heal. You'll be fine though, I promise."

Nausea roiled my gut. "Am I scarred? Disfigured? And why isn't Xander here?"

It was obvious that my family didn't want to discuss Xander, but I wasn't going to be persuaded. I remembered our time together, all of it. And how it ended. But that was the thing. It didn't truly end. It was merely a great love story on pause, or rather, we were still working our way toward our HEA. Because of that, and the use of Fantasy Life, and what AI Xander had shared with me before my abrupt ejection from virtual reality, I fully expected Xander to be close by.

Tears glistened in my mom's eyes. "No. You're not scarred or disfigured … you just need time to heal. They put you in a medically-induced coma to help with the brain swelling."

Wow. Jared must have beaten me within an inch of my life. That knowledge left me numb. "Okay. That's good. My brain seems okay now though." I was alive, with no permanent damage. "How long have I been in Fantasy Life? And I guess, more importantly, why was I in there?"

"It's the least that bastard could do after the trouble he caused. All of this is his fault," Adam blurted. "To make your medically-induced coma pleasant for you—to make sure you didn't spend the entire time having nightmares or reliving trauma or some shit like that ... yeah, it's the least he could do."

Confusion nettled. "How? What does—"

It dawned on me. Adam was blaming Xander because of the affair. He thought Jared wouldn't have attacked me otherwise. And quite possibly that was true, but it didn't mean any of it was Xander's fault. That would be like blaming the rape victim. The only one responsible for Jared's actions was Jared himself. "No. You listen to me right now, Adam Woods. What happened is not Xander's fault in any way, shape, or form. I love him."

"You love him?" Adam grated. "Let me repeat ... All of this is his fault."

"Hey. Don't yell at her. Especially now," Tina said firmly, having been pretty much mute up until then. Which wasn't completely surprising. She was probably trying to keep my stupid brother under control.

Adam waved his hands wildly at me, his face flushing. "She just came out of a coma and she's about to do the same brand of stupid that put her there in the first place."

Anger of my own surged, filling me with energy. "Xander is your best friend. How can you talk about him that way?"

"Ha! Some fucking best friend. He seduces my sister while she's still married and then leaves her to deal with the fallout. You could have died. Do you understand that? Xander almost got you killed. He almost got you killed because of some adolescent obsession with you he could never get over."

My fingers fumbled along the table next to my bed, closing over something hard. Without looking to see what it was, I flung it at Adam's head. He ducked at the last second, the empty plastic cup sailing out into the hallway. "You don't get to pass judgment on a relationship you know nothing about. When did you form all of your one-sided opinions? Huh? When I in a coma, literally?" I reached for something else to throw at him, but my mom grabbed my hand.

"Honey, don't get yourself worked up again. The doctor should be here soon, but—"

"No. Adam needs to hear this and he needs to listen and absorb what I'm telling him."

Adam glared, arms crossed over his chest. "I don't want to hear it if it has anything to do with that asshole, Xander."

"I love him!" I screamed, my throat crying out in protest. "The rest is none of your fucking business!"

Tina stood, placing her hand on Adam's arm. "Come on, let's go get a snack. We can call my mom to check on the twins while we're at it."

Once my brother and sister-in-law were gone, I flopped back on the bed, my entire body announcing it was ready for a nap.

"Honey." My mom scooted her chair closer to the bed, leaning over to prop her chin against the bedrail.

I couldn't help but laugh. "Mom, that can't be comfortable."

Smiling, she straightened. "It made you laugh." She was like that, always doing something odd and out of place to lighten the mood.

I sighed. "I don't understand why Adam is blaming Xander."

"Although it took some doing, Jared is in jail for what he did. The whole thing was caught on your neighbor's doorbell camera. And despite that it wouldn't have done much good if not for that friend of your uncle's who knows some very powerful people." She sighed. "But it was anticlimactic for Adam, I suppose, and he wants to punish someone. Plus, I think his feelings are hurt because the two of you kept things from him."

"Like I was going to tell him," I muttered. "And Xander did want to tell Adam. Xander wanted to tell everyone. He was all in, it was just the little problem of me—"

"Still being married. Yes, that tends to get in the way of starting a new relationship sometimes."

I studied my mom, her green eyes relaxed. "And you? Because I'm going to be fine, you're okay with everything else? I cheated, Mom. I did a thing I never thought I would." I blew out a long breath. "I love, Xander. And I want to be with him. But I'd be lying if I didn't say there is guilt, even now. I behaved selfishly, and cowardly … and saying it was for love doesn't make any of it right even if I wish it did."

She turned, staring toward the window. "I don't like how you handled things with Jared, and with Xander for that matter. But after your father's death it's hard not to think about how short life is." She shook her head. "I believe you've suffered enough. We all make mistakes in life, it's unavoidable. The important part is how we clean up the messes we make."

Grinding my teeth together, I kept my thoughts about my father to myself. My parents had been together for forty-seven years. And although my mom loved to wax poetic about their love, their relationship had been nothing short of tumultuous. He was dead though, so I'd let her cling to her own fantasies if it helped her in any small way.

I cleared my throat. "What about Xander? How do you feel about me saying I love him?" I knew I didn't have to remind her of how often I'd claimed the same about others before, me quick to anger when she'd expressed her doubts on the matter.

She met my gaze head on. "I believe you. I believe you for the first time ever. You love that boy, and I know he loves you." She tittered. "He's been in love with you since he was a teenager."

"What do you mean?"

She shook her head, grinning. "Age offers wisdom, that's all I'll say about that. Which brings me to your brother. Give Adam time. He'll get over it."

"And if he doesn't?"

My mom clicked her tongue. "You woke up from a coma asking where Xander is. You never even wanted to split a dessert with either of your ex-husbands. I think Adam is going to have to get used to the idea of you and Xander being together if you have anything to do with it."

"Why isn't Xander here? Why isn't he fighting to be by my side? Do you think I screwed things up beyond the point of repair? Maybe our love won't be enough."

"Well, honey, as you well know, people do stupid things when love is involved. Xander was so torn up about you that he may have let Adam get to him. Ultimately, he just needs some time, too."

I fiddled with the IV in my wrist. "Xander walked away before any of this happened. I mean, I thought we'd get back together after I settled some things, like my divorce for one, but I was in a coma and ... and he's not here."

"Men aren't that different from women in the way that they want to feel like they are loved above all else. They want to be number one in the eyes of the person they love. You only need to make Xander feel that to make him yours again. Not that he ever stopped being yours, even for a second. I'm guessing he only walked away when he did because you were still married, and he didn't feel like you loved him the way he loved you."

I opened my mouth to protest, but my mom patted my

leg. "Trust me on this. Now, get some rest, the doctor should be here soon. You can worry about all the rest when you get out of here."

I nodded, my mind already whirling around things I needed to do when I got out of the hospital. The truth of the matter was that in the real world, love is messy and can cross lines. People make mistakes, and we all have days when we aren't likable, and days when we are unlikable. Fiction is easier, predictable, and just that ... fiction. I wanted Xander, and if for some reason he decided whatever overture I ultimately made to win him back wasn't enough, well, the reality was, sometimes you lose.

I'd been in a coma, put there indirectly by ex-husband number two. While in said coma, I was immersed in Fantasy Life, a virtual reality company owned by the man I loved. That man was now M.I.A. because both he and my brother blamed him for my injuries. The entire thing was stranger than the fictional worlds I'd been trapped in.

I threw my head back, laughter escaping from my chest to release some intangible emotion, leaving me lighter, buoyant even. I'd been taking life too seriously. If Xander made me happy, if putting romance first made me happy, the rest was insignificant in comparison. And if Xander and I didn't end up together, then I'd cope, just like I always did. The new me would be all about accepting the old me, who as it turned out, wasn't so bad after all. Although, I still had some issues to work through with my therapist. Not so bad does not equal no room for improvement.

"Mom," I murmured, sleep pulling me down quickly. "I need my laptop."

If nothing else, at least I got my writer's mojo back because I knew exactly what my next book would be about, and it most definitely would have a happily-ever-after, even if I wasn't guaranteed one in my real life.

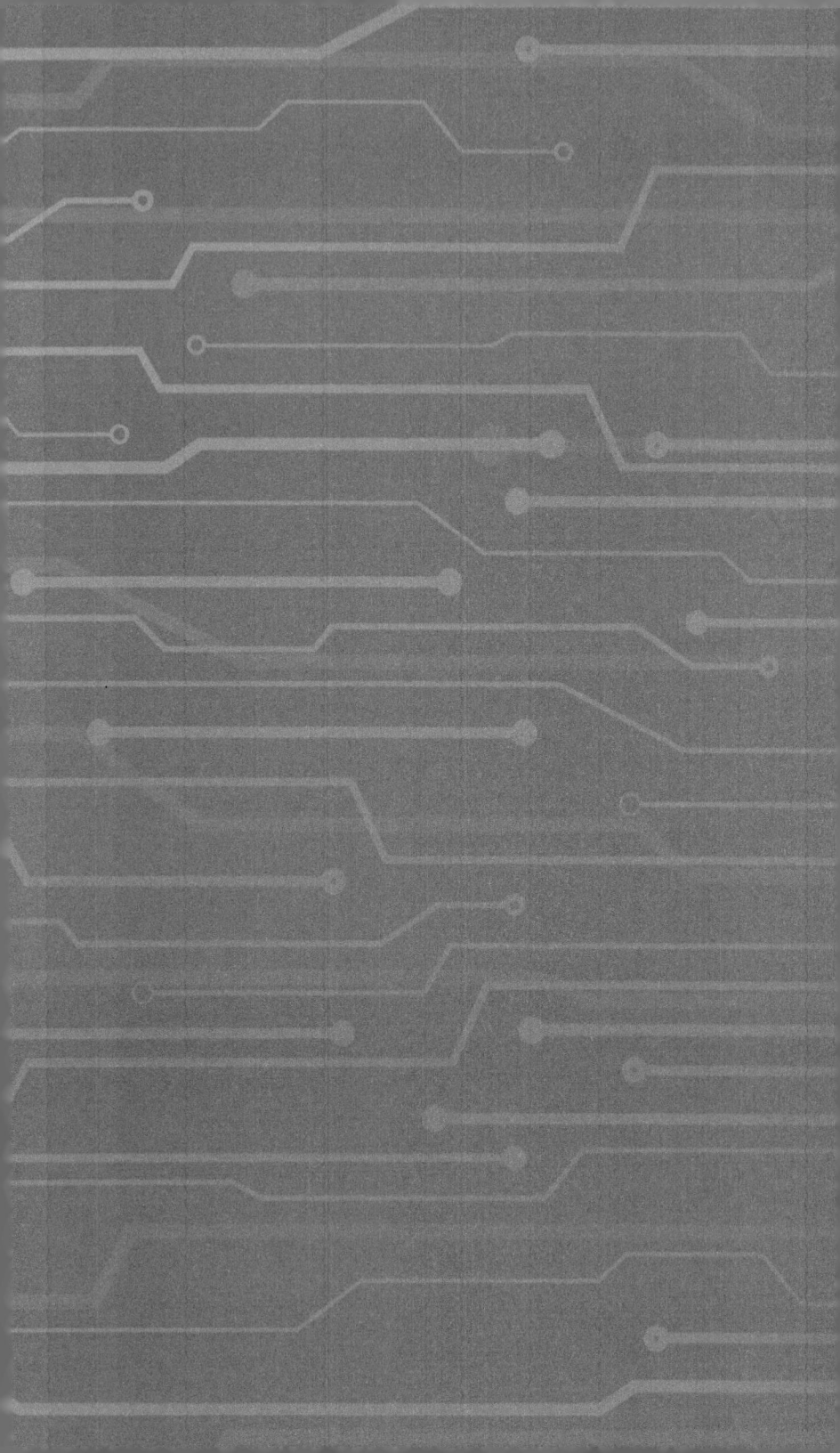

"**C**lara." *Mattius' deep baritone penetrated her concentration, and she whirled as the book she'd been reading slipped from her grasp, thudding against the floor.*

She blinked, the shock of his presence freezing her in place. "I thought ... I thought you were lost to me."

Mattius closed the distance between them, sweeping her into his arms.

"Are you sure?" Clara swayed within his embrace, her chin trembling.

Mattius swore under his breath as his grip on her tightened. "How can you ask me that? I've never been surer about anything in my life. You and me, us ... together forever. Nothing else matters. Nothing. You are my everything."

I paused, sucking in a breath before lifting my head to gaze out at the small group of people seated inside of the bookstore. I preferred intimate events such as the one today, public speaking of any kind sending me into an anxious tizzy.

Closing my book, I gave a nervous laugh. "Okay, that's it for now. I guess it's time for questions." Thankfully, my readers by and large seemed to understand that putting words together to form a book was not the same as having the spotlight on me in a public venue.

A woman, probably about my age, in her early forties, stepped to the microphone set up in the space between the two groupings of seats. She smiled good-naturedly and cleared her throat. "Is Fantasy Life as realistic as you portrayed in your book? Or did you take some creative liberties?"

I returned her smile. "I definitely took many, many creative liberties in this book, but I can say that the realism of Fantasy Life wasn't one of them. Let me tell you, people will be fighting for a chance to use the technology when it's available to the public."

"I could interact with a fae warrior, or a dragon shifter one day? Lord have mercy on my soul." She fanned herself for dramatics. "Can I get in line now?"

Grimacing, I said in a rush, "You're probably going to hate me for this, but thanks to me and my objections about the romance program aspect of Fantasy Life being morally wrong on so many levels ... well, that part of the program may never happen."

I'd been informed by an official letter from Xander's company that my complaints had been logged and shared, and the owner of the company trusted my opinions. Therefore, the romance trope portion of Fantasy Life, Inc. was shut down for the foreseeable future until a feasible solution could be arrived upon. Also, I shouldn't worry about the AIs because they wouldn't be deleted since the science of them was entirely too impressive to waste.

Gripping my book, I forced myself to continue, "I hope the romance tropes can be fixed and the program will one day be available, but, like I said, with the AIs involved …" I shook my head. "But you'll still be able to take advantage of the technology to go on death defying adventures without the, you know, death part, and all the rest of what Fantasy Life has been promoting, just no fae warriors or dragon shifters yet."

The woman eyed me with disappointment. "I guess I understand. The artificial intelligence does throw some shade on things, morally speaking. I hope Fantasy Life, Inc. finds a solution to the problem."

She made her way back to her seat as another woman took her place at the microphone. This one was probably in her seventies, I was guessing. She pushed her small, wire-framed glasses up her nose, while frowning at me. "You admit to cheating on your ex-husband while still being married to him, and yet you speak of having moral objections to the romance program of Fantasy Life. How do you reconcile those two things?"

I'd been dreading this potential type of question from the moment I made the information about my affair common knowledge. Sweat gathered on my upper lip, the temperature of the room seemingly dialed up by several hundred degrees. I let out a harsh breath, the burst of air hissing over the microphone, much to my chagrin.

Fidgeting for another few seconds, an eternity filled with anxiety, I finally gathered the willpower to respond. "I don't have an excuse for my actions. They were selfish and shortsighted. Everyone makes mistakes, and not waiting to move on with the man I love until I was divorced is not something I'm proud of. I tried to rationalize my actions by telling myself I'd never betrayed my heart and loving someone the way I did was undeniable, but that's the kind of flawed logic that people use to justify their actions when they know they're wrong. I was wrong. I regret the decision to cheat, even if I don't regret loving for the first time in my life with all of my heart. But just because I failed before, morally speaking, doesn't mean I can't do better moving forward. In fact, my failure made me push harder to see the right thing done with Fantasy Life."

The light glinted off the woman's glasses as she inclined her head, apparently satisfied with my answer, which was a relief since I already forgot what I'd word vomited because of my nerves. "I have one more question."

Nodding once, I sent a silent prayer to the heavens that it wouldn't be worse than the first one.

"This book was a departure from your usual subject matter in the sense that you took parts from what happened to you while you were in a coma. My question is: Did you get the guy in real life, or was your book the only thing that got a happily-ever-after?"

Well, surprise, surprise. I did not see that one coming. My cheeks heated as I considered what to say. "Oh, umm ..."

The truth was, Xander had disappeared, leaving me no way to contact him. I'd left him messages via email, and cell phone, and texted him nonstop. I'd harassed his employees, and tracked down his parents in Topsail Beach, North Carolina, where they'd retired. No one would tell me where he was. I had my doubts that they even could.

But I hadn't lost hope. Xander needed time to process things, I knew that better than anyone. My way of doing it had been to write my latest novel, *Virtual Reality Bites.* It was a confession of sorts, and a sixty-thousand-something word love letter. Within those pages, I told him how I felt, and I let him know that I didn't blame him for anything. I also let him know that there would be no one else. He was it for me. Before him, I didn't know what love was, so I jumped from relationship to relationship. I had no idea what I was doing, even if I thought I did.

Although, I still didn't have a clue since there was no blueprint for matters of the heart. Love was different for everyone, how they expressed it, how they felt it, and how they coped with it. With Xander ... well, I couldn't quite put into words how I knew my love for him was the real deal, but I did. Somehow, I just did. Quite possibly I'd always known and simply didn't want to accept it for various reasons, the number one being deep-seated fear.

"Umm …" I stammered, still not sure how to answer the woman's question. Getting personal in my book was one thing, talking about it in front of a group of strangers was something else entirely. "It's amazing how missing pieces of memory can change one's whole view on things such as personal convictions and attitude. Normally, I would have been crushed not to reconnect immediately with," I raised my hands to air quote, "'my guy'. But once I remembered everything hidden from me while in Fantasy Life, I found myself again, and I knew, just like with so many other things, I had to do better. Now, don't get me wrong, my love life will always be a priority to me, because it's just who I am, but this time around I wanted to get it all right. I focused on my book first, knowing I couldn't push things, knowing … I … well, I knew … *know* that working on myself was the only way I would be ready for the kind of relationship I wanted with my guy. Umm … or what I mean is …"

I'd lost it. The point I'd been trying to make, my confidence to continue speaking, all of it. And yet the word vomit was about to reach *Exorcist* levels at any moment. I wanted to express so much, like how I wanted to give hope to others with my books and give them a respite from their problems, and how I supported an inclusive romance community for everyone who wanted to be there no matter their race, sexual orientation, etc. But all of that, along with my thoughts of Xander, were a tangled mess inside of my head and I wasn't sure how to work any of it into the conversation.

You have a platform, don't let your nerves ruin the chance to throw some good into the world. Stop overthinking and only answer what's asked. There will be plenty of time to express yourself at many different events, but if you come off as a neurotic fool with your eagerness then no one will ever listen to you. Do it—you can do it. Just refocus and don't babble on for an eternity while not making one single coherent point. You can do it. Focus on one thing at a time.

But my vision blurred, and a high-pitched ringing had taken residence in my right ear. *Please don't have a panic attack in front of all of these people. Don't you dare, Zoe Woods.*

"I have a question, too," an achingly familiar voice called from the back of the room. "Why'd you skip over the parts about what happened to Clara after she left the hospital? Why go straight to the ending after that?"

Problem solved. Xander is officially the only thing on my mind now. Unable to look at him just yet, I kept my gaze riveted to the microphone inches from my face. "No one likes to read the boring stuff. Deep thoughts, personal growth, blabbity, blah, blah, blah. What happened during that chunk of time was implied."

"Well, I disagree with that choice. Some people might want to know everything about the character. Even the boring stuff, as you put it. Also, don't you think the ending was a bit, I don't know, cheesy?"

My throat burned, and I reached for my water bottle, hands trembling. "Maybe. But who doesn't love a good, sappy ending sometimes? Plus, I write genre romance.

Everyone knows it can't be considered romance without a HEA, or at least a HEA for now."

"One more question…"

"Yes?"

"I'm sorry I interrupted before. You didn't get around to answering that nice woman's question. Did you get the guy in real life? Because it seemed like he was a stubborn ass, who, you know, might take a while to figure his shit out."

"I don't know. Why don't you tell me? Did I get the guy?" I gripped the podium, wanting to go to him, ever hopeful, but irrationally terrified. This was the moment I'd been waiting for since I woke up from the coma. My reunion with Xander. All things pointed to him wanting to be with me, but what if … what if I was wrong? What if I was misreading something? Or what if he was merely giving me some good publicity because he was about to reject me privately? I'd laid my heart out there for the world to see, the ball was now in his court.

"I don't think you got the guy because you can't get something you never really lost."

Blinking rapidly, I swear I saw a brightly colored string appear, the red yarn connecting us, stretched taut at the moment, but remaining strong, never having frayed or broken, despite our temporary separation. It was the kind of bond I'd been searching for almost my entire life, and I'd nearly missed it out of my own stubbornness. Relief spilled over me as I sucked in a raspy breath.

I lifted my head, searching out his gaze, and when I found it …

To this day, I'll never know if he moved first or I did, but the next thing I knew we were in each other's arms while the crowd cheered.

"This is ridiculous," I muttered as I lifted onto my tiptoes to hide my face against Xander's neck. "Even I wouldn't write something this corny."

"The only ridiculous thing here is you." He tightened his arms around me. "But it's one of the reasons I love you."

"Don't piss me off, Xander. We're supposed to be having a moment." I grinned against his flesh, resisting the urge to nip him.

"You say piss off, I say challenge."

"Puh-leaze." I twisted my hands in his shirt. "And don't get me started on how you thought it was a good idea to disappear the way you did. Or tweak my memories while I was in Fantasy Life. Not to mention—" I expelled a long breath. We still had some things to work on, but they could wait. Preferably until after we got reacquainted with some naked time. "Umm … yeah, don't piss me off, because I love you, too, but I will be forced to hurt you regardless."

He pulled away from me, and my greedy gaze swept over his face, as his did the same to mine. "I missed you so much. I can't even begin to explain. And I'm sorry I left, I just—"

"Kiss me, Xander Tashiro. Kiss me now."

He smirked, his dimple popping out on his cheek, making him appear every bit the boy I used to know, and yet, still the man I loved. "I can do that."

And he did.

His lips scorched mine, burning the promise of his love into my soul, while also wiping away any lingering doubts. The past could stay in the past, he was my future.

Of course, since I'm the one writing our story, that's where I'm choosing to end the book. On the grand kiss, and the beginning of our happily-ever-after. Fade to grey. Cut. The end.

There's no point in discussing the reality of what came next. And how after the kiss, we had to awkwardly make our way out of the bookstore, while I nearly died from mortification, regretting the public display of affection. Like I told Xander before, no one needs to read about those kinds of boring details. Fantasy and reality can co-exist, as long as we know which one is which. And romance readers are pros at navigating both.

Whoops, that got away from me there. Where was I? Right.

Xander and I are still kissing, and ...

The end.

Acknowledgments

Once upon a time, there was a teenage girl who borrowed her mother's car to go "gallivanting". (Her mom's word, not hers.) Distracted by both her friends and the blaring music, the girl had to slam on the brakes to avoid rear-ending the car in front of her. That's when something shocking slid out from under the front passenger seat.

It was a book. (Clearly, that wasn't the shocking part.) This particular book had a glossy cover showcasing a muscular, shirtless man clutching a dainty woman in a flimsy gown to his chest. (The girl didn't even know a gown could be flimsy. But there it was in vivid shades of violet.) The woman had her back arched, neck exposed, as the man's mouth hovered inches from her flesh. (Totally scandalous!)

The girl and her friends didn't know what to make of the book and her mother's reading preferences. Much giggling filled the car as a closer inspection of said book was conducted. It was finally concluded that the situation was not to be understood, and the book was returned from whence it came, only to reveal that there were several more books of the same nature with similarly clad couples adorning the covers.

Perplexed, the girl decided to revisit the topic at a later date. You see, she'd always been an avid reader, consuming everything she could get her hands on, but this —this was new. A type of book she'd never come across before. Was it porn? Something only older adults needed or comprehended? She had questions—questions that demanded answers. Thus, the girl began her lifelong love affair with romance novels.

Yes, that girl was me. And I'd like to thank my mom for inadvertently introducing me to romance novels. I wouldn't be here writing this if it wasn't for her. Of course, it was probably only a matter of time before I discovered them on my own, but before social media, the path there would have been a tad more circuitous. (Oh, crap, I just time-stamped myself! Eeep!) So thanks, Mom! (Even though you still only read historical romance and refuse to branch out even after all these years. I mean, how about a paranormal romance here or there, or a sci-fi romance once in a while? No? Okay. *sigh* I guess it would be hypocritical of me to judge you for your choice of reads. As long as you like it, that's all that matters. *whispers* "Although I do have a cool fae romance you might like. It'll be here waiting for you if you want it."

Aaaalrighty then, after my mom I would like to thank …

My amazing Hubby! Words can't begin to explain how supportive and truly amazing he is. Hmmm … I think I already used the word amazing. But unlike in books, when honestly applied to someone, the word amazing means something, well, amazing. And my hubby is all of the things that word implies. Romance heroes are nothing compared to him.

Lindsay Tiry … what would I do without you? I hope I never have to find out. From cover design to interior graphics to logos, you do it all. Your talent is awe-inspiring, and I hope one day everyone else will be able to appreciate how you shine.

Melissa Ringsted … my illustrious editor. Without you, this book probably would have gone straight into the trash. Thank you for giving me the confidence to publish when I convinced myself that I was the worst writer in the history of writers, and for fixing all the words.

Ren, Kristin, Shona, Ruty … my O.G. chicas … I wouldn't be here without you. I'm beyond lucky to know all of you.

And last, but certainly not least, thank you to everyone who has taken the time to read this book. Hopefully, you enjoyed it, but even if you didn't, I still appreciate the fact that with so many options out there today, you even gave my book a fleeting chance.

About the Author

Ava Wixx escaped into books at a young age and decided to stay there. It was only a matter of time before she was driven to create her own fantasy worlds from fear of running out of places to explore. Reader, writer, dreamer … Ava only toils in reality when absolutely necessary. She lives in North Carolina with her husband, and spoiled mini-poodle.